William Richard Morfill

Slavonic literature

William Richard Morfill

Slavonic literature

ISBN/EAN: 9783337206000

Printed in Europe, USA, Canada, Australia, Japan

Cover: Foto ©Andreas Hilbeck / pixelio.de

More available books at **www.hansebooks.com**

The Dawn of European Literature.

SLAVONIC LITERATURE.

BY

W. R. MORFILL, M.A.

Slavianskie l' rouchi solioutsa v' Rousskom moré?
Ono l' izsaknet? Vot vopros.—POUSHKIN.

Shall the Slavonic streams flow into the Russian sea?
Or that be dried up? That is the question.

PUBLISHED UNDER THE DIRECTION OF
THE COMMITTEE OF GENERAL LITERATURE AND EDUCATION
APPOINTED BY THE SOCIETY FOR PROMOTING
CHRISTIAN KNOWLEDGE.

LONDON:
SOCIETY FOR PROMOTING CHRISTIAN KNOWLEDGE.
NORTHUMBERLAND AVENUE, CHARING CROSS, W.C. ;
43, QUEEN VICTORIA STREET, E.C.;
26, ST. GEORGE'S PLACE, HYDE PARK CORNER, S.W.
BRIGHTON: 135, NORTH STREET.
NEW YORK: E. & J. B. YOUNG & CO
1883.

PREFACE.

—◦◦—

THE object of this little book is to supply a want
in English literature. There· is nothing in our
language on the subject, except the work of Mrs.
Robinson (Talvj), published in 1850, at New York,
which is now out of date. Moreover, it hardly had
any circulation in England, and to the majority of
Englishmen, even philologists, is absolutely unknown.
It was never reprinted in this country. The materials
for my compilation have not been taken at second
hand, but in all cases from original authorities.
It may be as well to state this, as, with a few
remarkable exceptions which need not be here specified, most of the books published in this country on
the Slavs are mere adaptations from the French and
German. I have found the Russian work of MM.
Pïpin and Spasovich, "History of Slavonic Literatures" (Istoria Slavianskikh Literatour) of very great
help, and have used it extensively. Very valuable
also have been the articles in the " Archiv für
Slavische Philologie," edited by Professor Jagic, and
the " Journal " of the Bohemian Museum (Casopis
Ceského Musea)—a mine of Slavonic lore. Other

works consulted will be found mentioned in the foot-
notes. An attempt has been made to spell the proper
names of those Slavonic nations which use the Cyrillic
alphabet on a fixed and accurate plan. Generally they
are treated among us as a mere jargon and written at
random : thus, the same person will frequently be
found writing Gortchakoff and Woronzow, though
the termination is identical in both. The names of
those Slavonic peoples who use the Latin alphabet
have, of course, retained their original orthography,
just as no one would think of altering the spelling of
a French word to suit English pronunciation. Unfortunately, the printers in this country have not in
every case the requisite diacritical marks, but I have
still thought it better not to tamper with the words,
and have occasionally added a foot-note. It is to be
hoped that, in time, the gross misspellings of Slavonic
words will disappear from our maps.

My little book will have amply fulfilled its purpose,
if it serve as a humble guide to those who wish to
pursue further the study of these languages, so
interesting to the philologist, but, strange to say, so
ignored among us.

W. R. MORFILL.

OXFORD.

CONTENTS.

CHAPTER I.

CLASSIFICATION OF THE SLAVONIC RACES.

The Slavs in Greece—The Slavonic Languages—The
Bulgarian Language—The Serbs in Hungary—The
Lithuanians and Letts—The Ursprache of the Slavonic
People—Foreign elements in the Russian Language—
The stages of Palæoslavonic—The Revision of the
Church Books—The Cyrillic and Glagolitic Alphabets
—Had the Slavs any runes?   ...   . *Page* 1

CHAPTER II.

THE NOMENCLATURE OF THE SLAVONIC RACES.

The Russians—The Poles—The Bulgarians—The Serbs
and Bohemians — The Wends — The Croats—The
Scythians 26

CHAPTER III.

EARLY RUSSIAN LITERATURE.

The Bilini—The Bogatîri—Vladimir and his Drouzhina—
The Lay of the Boyar—Ivan the Terrible—The

Taking of Azov—The Lamentation of the Sinful
Soul—Latin and German Words in Old Slavonic
—Slavonic Mythology—The Ostromir Codex —Nestor
and the Chroniclers—The Old Russian Travellers
—Vladimir Monomakh—The Expedition of Igor—
The " Rousskaia . Pravda "—The Ordinance of the
Emperor Alexis—The Printing Press in Slavonic
Countries — The Domostroi — Sergius Koubasov —
Kotoshikhin—The Foreign Students in England—
Krizhanich—Simeon Polotzki ...   . *Page* 45

CHAPTER IV.

EARLY MALO-RUSSIAN AND WHITE RUSSIAN LITERATURE.

The Cossacks—The Discipline of the Sech—The Doumî
—The Haidamaks — Professor Bodenstedt on the
Poetry of the Cossacks—No Early Documents in the
Lithuanian Language 101

CHAPTER V.

EARLY BULGARIAN LITERATURE.

The Earliest Codices—The " Texte du Sacre "—The
Golden Age of Tzar Simeon—The Bogomiles—Customs of the Bulgarians—The Brothers Miladinov—
Auguste Dozon—Jovan Popov—The Janissary and
the Fair Dragana—The Ballad of Liben   114

CHAPTER VI.

THE EARLY LITERATURE OF THE SERBS, CROATS, AND SLOVENES.

Anonymus Presbyter Diocleus — Early Servian Codices —The Code of Stephen Doushan—Andrew Kacic-Miosic—The Servian Improvisatori—The Battle of Kosóvo—Paul Orlovich —Marko Kralevich—A Bosnian Idyl—The Dalmatian Poets—The Slovenish Language —The Frisingian Manuscripts—Primus Truber—Juri Dalmatin ... ... *Page* 145

CHAPTER VII.

THE WESTERN BRANCH : EARLY LITERATURE OF POLAND.

The Present State of the Polish Language—The Psalter of Queen Margaret—The Bible of Queen Sophia—Gallus and Kadlúbek—The Reign of Casimir III.—Jan Dlugosz—The Socini in Poland—Translations of the Bible—Jan Kochanowski—The Idyls of Szymonowicz —Peter Skarga—Stryjkowski 178

CHAPTER VIII.

THE EARLY LITERATURE OF BOHEMIA.

Influences during the Earliest Period of Bohemian Civilisation—The Judgment of Libusa — The Königinhof Manuscript—The Rose—The " Mater Verborum "—Premysl —The Satires on the Trades—Early Translations of the Bible—"The Weaver "—Thomas Stitny —Jan Hus—Poděbrad and the Pope—Bohemian Literature at the Renaissance — Quarrel between Ferdinand I. and the Citizens — Lomnicky—Wenceslaus Vratislav—The Slovaks 203

CHAPTER IX.

THE WENDS IN SAXONY AND PRUSSIA.

The Upper and Lower Lusatians—Michael and Abraham Frencel—The Present Condition of the Wends *Page* 240

CHAPTER X.

THE POLABES.

The Lutitzer and Bodrizer—The Labours of Christopher Henning—Johann Parum-Schultz — The Germanisation of the Baltic Slavs—Russian Proverbs—Polish Proverbs   247

EARLY SLAVONIC LITERATURE.

CHAPTER I.

THE SLAVONIC LANGUAGES.

BEFORE I treat of Early Slavonic Literature under the various heads into which I propose to divide it, my readers will, no doubt, be glad to have a list of the Slavonic peoples and their languages, as at present existing in Europe. To trace the early history of the Slavs would be out of place here, and the student must be referred to the useful book of the Rev. G. F. Maclear on "The Slavs," published by the Society for Promoting Christian Knowledge. The great source of our knowledge on the subject of their ethnology and early history is still the monumental work of Schafarik, originally published in Bohemian, but made more familiar to scholars by a German translation. I shall take my statistics from those lately furnished' in Russian by Boudilovich, as an accompaniment to his valuable ethnological map.[1]

---

[1] "Statisticheskia Tablitzï." St. Petersburg, 1875.

B

Eastern Division.

I. Russians.

(*a*) The Great Russians (Velikorousskie), occupying the governments round Moscow, and thence scattered in the north to Novgorod and Vologda, on the south to Kiev and Vorónezh, on the east to Penza, Simbirsk and Viatka, and on the west to the Baltic provinces. They amount to about 40,000,000.

(*b*) The Little-Russians (Malorossiane). These including the Rousines or Rousniaks in Galicia, the Boiki and Gouzouli, in Bukovina amount to 16,370,000.

(*c*) The White Russians, inhabiting the western governments, amounting to 4,000,000.

II. Bulgarians, including those in Russia, Austria, Roumania, the Principality, the temporary expedient called Eastern Roumelia, and those still left under the government of Turkey, 5,123,592.

III. The Serbo-Croats, including those of the Principality, the Black Mountain (Montenegro), the southern part of Austria and a few in the south of Russia, 5,940,539.

Under this head may also be classed the Slovenes, including those in the provinces of Styria, Carinthia, and Carniola, amounting to 1,287,000.

Western Division.

I. Poles, shared between Russia, Austria, and Prussia, 9,492,162 under which head may be included the small population of the Kashoubes, 111,416.

II. The Cechs and Moravians, 4,815,154, under

which head may also be included the Slovaks,
2,223,820.

III. The Lusatian Wends, Upper and Lower, partly
in Saxony and partly in Prussia. Of the Upper there
are 96,000, of the Lower 40,000.

It is acknowledged by all those who are conversant
with the subject, that the Slavs may be traced in many
other countries. Thus they have left their names
marked on all the north-eastern coast of Germany,
Rostock, Berlin, Potsdam, Zerbst, and many others
being of Slavonic origin; in fact, Pomerania and
Mecklenburg are thickly sprinkled with this nomenclature.[1] Traces of them may be found in Europe
as far west as Utrecht, which was originally called
Wiltaburg. I cannot, however, agree with Schafarik
when he connects our English Wiltshire with the
Slavonic tribe of the Wilzen—the derivation obviously
being from Wilton, the town on the river Wily.

The Slavonic population in Greece has formed the
subject of a keen dispute, and although Falmerayer
may have pushed his opinions too far, yet some of
them have never been overthrown, and the attempt
to explain away the ἐσθλαβώθη πᾶσα ἡ χωρὰ of the
Emperor Constantine Porphyrogenitus, by M. Sathas
and others, cannot be considered successful. The
whole of Greece, especially the Morea, abounds with
Slavonic names, which are now being gradually
replaced by others taken from classical times. The
Slavonic elements in the Neo-Greek language have

[1] See P. Kühnel, " Die Slavischen Ortsnamen in Mecklen-
burg-Strelitz." 1881.

formed the subject of a valuable dissertation by Miklosich. The views of Kollar that a large population of Slavonic origin may be found in Italy are merely the fantastic dreams of a man, who, although a good poet, has no claim to be considered a critic or an historian.

CLASSIFICATION OF LANGUAGES.

In my classification of the Slavonic languages I shall use the division given by Schleicher, which is modified from that of Dobrovsky, with some help from the table published in the " History of Slavonic Literature," by Pîpin and Spasovich.[1]

SOUTH EASTERN BRANCH.

RUSSIAN.

Dialects.

1. Great Russian ...
   - Moscow,
   - Novgorod, and the Northern,
   - Siberian,
   - Middle-Russian.

2. Little Russian ...
   - Eastern,
   - Western (sometimes called Red Russian),
   - Carpathian.

3. White Russian.

BULGARIAN.

1. Old Bulgarian (the ecclesiastical language).

2. Modern Bulgarian
   - (a) Upper Mœsian.
   - (b) Lower Mœsian.
   - (c) Macedonian.

---

[1] Vol. i., p. 19.

SERBO-CROATO-SLOVENISH.

1. Serbo-Croatian...
- (a) Southern, or Herzegovinian.
- (b) Syrmian.
- (c) Resavian,
- (d) Language of the Coast.

2. Slovenish ... ...
- (a) Dialects of Upper, Middle, and Lower Carniola.
- (b) Styrian.
- (c) Ugro-Slovenish.
- (a) Resanian.
- (e) Croato-Slovenish.

WESTERN BRANCH.

Dialects.

1. Polish... ...
- (a) Masovian.
- (b) Great Polish.
- (c) Silesian.
- (d) Kashoubish.

2. Bohemian ... ...
- (a) Cechian.[1]
- (b) Moravian.
- (c) Slovakish.

3. Lusatian Wendish
- (a) Upper Lusatian.
- (b) Lower Lusatian.

4. Polabish (now extinct).[2]

I will here add a few remarks upon the geographical extent of the various languages and dialects. For the complete understanding of these matters a good ethnological map is above all things necessary, such as that published at St. Petersburg by Mirkovich.

---

[1] In this word pronounce the c like ch in church.

[2] A good idea of the relation between the languages and dialects may be formed from Erben's book, "A Hundred Slavonic National Tales." Prague, 1865.

The Russian language is hemmed in on the west by Polish, Magyar, and Roumanian, on the south by Little Russian, and on the east by Finnish and Tatar dialects, and on the north by Lithuanian and Ugro-Finnish dialects including Esthonian.

The Siberian dialect is spoken by the colonists who have settled in that vast tract of Northern Asia, since it was discovered by Yermak in the time of Ivan the Terrible. There are other less important dialects than those specified, but it would be impossible to enumerate them in a small work like the present. They will be found discussed in the "Opît Oblastnago Velikorousskago Slovara" (Attempt at a Provincial Dictionary of the Great Russian Language); published at St. Petersburg in 1852. The Little Russian is spoken in all the southern governments of Russia. It is called Red Russian as current in Galicia and Bukovina. There is also a thin streak of Little Russian population in the kingdom of Hungary, north of the Carpathians. White Russian, one of the dialects most neglected by philologists, is spoken chiefly in the governments of Mohilev, Minsk, Vitepsk, and Grodno.

Bulgarian covers the ground originally occupied by the ancient Mœsia, Thrace, and Macedonia : it is bounded on the north by Rouman, from which it is separated by the Danube, on the west by Servian, south-west by Albanian, and south by Greek, which begins to prevail from a line drawn from Saloniki (the ancient Thessalonica) to Adrianople. Its area is dotted by small Turkish colonies, and here and there a considerable admixture of Greeks. The Balkans separate the territory of Bulgaria into two portions, which, as a result of the Berlin Congress, constitute the Principality of Bulgaria and the autonomous territory of East Roumelia, soon, let us hope, to be united like Moldavia and Wallachia, formerly so absurdly separated in consequence of a timid and ungenerous policy. The modern Bulgarian language shows Slavonic in a very corrupted form. A great many Turkish words have been incorporated, which can very easily be detected. The wonder is, that after so many years of oppression the language was not altogether stamped out. We get fearful pictures of the sufferings of this unfortunate people from the travellers of last century. Take the account given by Edward Clarke, for instance, who visited European Turkey at the close of that period. The modern Bulgarian has taken the Slavonic demonstrative pronoun for an article, which is placed at the end of words, as in Rouman, Albanian, and the Scandinavian languages. The cases are very defective, the genitive being supplied by a preposition, so that the language is in a very advanced stage from synthesis to analysis. There is also (as in modern Greek) no regular form of the infinitive, which is expressed by a periphrasis. Till recently, the appliances for learning Bulgarian were very meagre. In 1852, the brothers Tzankov published a grammar at Vienna, which was useful at the time, but laboured under considerable defects. Latin letters are employed, and the orthography is of the most confused nature. A dictionary (Bulgarian-French) has since been published by Bogorov, and there is a prospect of the language being scientifically treated, in proof of which I might appeal to some excellent papers which have appeared in the "Archiv," edited by Professor Jagic, already mentioned. Thus it is shown, that in the Bulgarian dialects the nouns are much more fully inflected, and traces are found of the nasals, which existed in Old Slavonic, but are almost lost in the modern forms with the exception of Polish and the Kashoubish dialect. The geographical extent of the territory over which Serbo-Croatian and its dialects, and Slovenish and its dialects, are spoken, has already been specified. The influx of Serbs into the kingdom of Hungary dates from a time posterior to the battle of Kosovo (15th June, 1389), in which they lost their independence, and of which I shall shortly speak more at length. The Turks made themselves masters of the right bank of the Danube, and the Serbs became tributary to them, their tzar changing his title into the more modest one of despot. Immediately an immigration began into the adjoining Christian countries. It is to this period that we must assign the Servian churches and monasteries on the left bank of the Danube. In 1481, the Serbian chieftain, Vouk Brankovich, brought 50,000 Serbs with him, who were established in the environs of Temesvar. In the time of the Emperor Leopold of Germany, about 35,000 or 40,000 families, or zadrougas, came. These zadrougas are not families in our sense of the word, consisting of a father, mother, and children, but communities of families, according to the patriarchal custom existing among the Slavs, and such as they have remained to the present day on the military frontiers.[1] The number of those who emigrated at that time would therefore amount to something like 400,000 or 500,000 persons. Others also came in 1738 and 1788. These Serbs have kept their religion and language. All attempts to Magyarise them have failed, and they are looked upon with a very jealous eye by the Hungarian Government. The only one of the Slovenish dialects which demands any special notice is the Rezanian. It may be said to have been discovered by Professor Baudoin de Courtenay. At all events, he was the first person who made any critical study of it. The Rezani are in Venetian territory and number 27,000 according to Boudilovich. They live in the north-eastern corner of the Italian frontier, in two valleys of the Julian Alps. The dialect, Ugro-Slovenish (marked *c*), although it has been but little employed in books, is interesting, because it shows some connexion with Slovakish, and is thus a link between the eastern and western branches of the Slavonic languages.

Of the remaining dialects only one seems to demand any special notice—viz., Kashoubish, spoken by about 200,000 persons (according to Hilferding: some, however, make the number much less) in the neighbourhood of Danzig. This dialect of Polish presents

---

[1] See "Revue des Deux Mondes," 1876, vol. iv., p. 832.

some very interesting variations. According to Dr. Cenova (" Die Kassubisch-Slovinishe Sprache," p. 79), the word Kashoub is a nickname, their proper appellation being Slovintzi. The derivation of the word has not been settled. Schafarik connects it with a word meaning a goat.

A few remarks may be here introduced on the Lithuanian and Lettish languages, which stand in close relationship to the Slavonic, and have been so politically mixed up with them. According to a recent calculation, there are 1,900,000 Lithuanians in Russia (including the Samogitians, or Zhmudes). There are also 1,100,000 Letts. The rest of the Lithuanians, numbering 146,312, are in Eastern Prussia, commencing not far from Königsberg, and extending along the shores of the Curisches Haff.[1] The language is now fast dying out, and in a few years will be extinct. Its literature is exceedingly scanty, consisting of a few songs, and some poems on rustic life and the seasons, composed by a native clergyman, named Donalitius, in the latter part of last century. These have been carefully edited by Rhesa, Schleicher, and Nesselmann. Schleicher and Kurschat, a native Lithuanian, have written excellent grammars, and thus, before the language becomes extinct as a living tongue, it will be preserved for philological purposes. There is also a Lithuanian society which labours to preserve the songs, the proverbs, and the folk-lore of this interesting people.

[1] See the excellent map prefixed to the Lithuanian grammar of Kurschat.

The Lettish language, spoken in the neighbourhood of Riga and Mittau, exhibits a more advanced stage of Lithuanian, and has incorporated Finnish elements. There is a collection of Lettish songs, with a Russian translation, published by Sprogis at Vilna in 1868. Some of the old Lithuanian and Lettish catechisms have been edited by Bezzenberger. Of the Old Prussian, a language very closely connected with Lithuanian, which died out in the sixteenth century, a few fragments have been preserved, viz., a translation of Luther's Catechism and a few vocabularies. Some of these were printed in the very curious work of Hartknoch, "Alt-und Neues Preussen," 1684, and a complete list of all the known words has been published in the "Thesaurus" of Nesselmann. They are of primary importance to the student of comparative philology. These languages, as I have previously said, bear, of all other members of the Indo-European family, the closest affinity to the Slavonic in their phonetics, grammatical construction, and roots. The Slavonic languages, however, far surpass them in the copiousness of the verb.

The Lithuanian national songs are, on the whole, colourless productions. They are chiefly interesting on account of the pagan allusions, which seem to show that they are of considerable antiquity. We must remember, however, that the Lithuanians were the last people in Europe to become Christianised; and probably, when Jagiello was baptised in 1386, and his people with him, in a summary fashion, the

influence of Christianity was but slight, for we find
them indulging in many heathen habits much later.
Thus Herberstein, in his travels in the sixteenth
century, tells us that he found them still worshipping
the lizard as their *lar familiaris*. As the Lithuanians,
as a people, have had no history, and, like the Finns,
have merely been receding in the historical period,
we do not find any tales of bold robbers or local
heroes, as in the Servian, Bulgarian, and Russian.[1]
The love-poems are pretty. Altogether, this Lithuanian people has had a curious fate ; their language
has never been anything more than a tongue of
peasants, and those who talk of the Lithuanian
principality must remember that the language of its
laws and court was White Russian.

In the past year, a collection of folk-songs and folk-
tales of the Lithuanians was published by Leskien and
Brugman. The valuable translations into German by
Brugman, appended to this work, will make it wel-
come to the many students of the growing science of
Comparative Mythology.

Having now enabled my readers to form, it is to
be hoped, a clear idea both of the geographical
extent of the Slavs and the classification of their
languages, I must say, before leaving this chapter, a
few words on the theories as to which of these languages most resembles the *Ursprache* of the Slavonic
people, as the Germans would term it. As this is a
work for general reading, I cannot go much into philo-

[1] In some of the later songs collected by Juszkewicz we have
allusions to Charles XII. of Sweden and Bonaparte.

logical detail. It will be enough to say that there are three main theories.

(1) That it was Old Bulgarian. This opinion has been held by Schleicher, Schafarik, J. Schmidt, Leskien, and other eminent scholars.

(2) That it was Old Slovenish, *i.e.*, a language spoken in the modern Styria, Carinthia, and the southern parts of Hungary, as previously shown. This opinion has been held by Miklosich and Kopitar. A great supporter at the present time is Professor Jagic. (See his "Specimina Linguæ Palæo-slovenicæ. 1882.)

(3) The opinion of Geitler, a professor at Agram, who finds that the Palæoslavonic is best represented by the Russian. This view, however, had been previously held by some Russian scholars. That the early stages of the languages show them much more resembling each other is evident to all students. We may truly say,—

> Facies non omnibus una
> Nec diversa tamen, qualem decet esse sororum.

Baron Vratislav, of Mitrovic, whose travels form such a pleasant monument of the Bohemian literature of the sixteenth century, tells us how easily he made himself understood by the Bulgarians. If we look at the old Polish we see how very different it is from the modern forms of the language,—as, for example, in the statute of Wislica belonging to the year 1449, among other words we get the form *cirekwe* (church), and not, as in modern Polish, *kosciol,* which

is derived from *castellum*.[1]   The tendency to develop
into dialectic variation caused by the low state of
civilisation soon began, and all the modern Slavonic
languages show signs of foreign influence.   With
regard to Russian we must, in the first place, remember that for upwards of two centuries (1237–
1462) the country groaned under the yoke of the
Tatars, and it is therefore only natural to expect that
we should find some traces of their dominion.   The
Asiatic garb worn in Muscovy till the days of Peter
the Great, the curious custom of the *pravezhe*, or
public flagellation of defaulting debtors, the seclusion
of women, and perhaps the use of the knout, may
be traced to the presence of these truculent invaders;
but when we turn to the actual Tatar words in the
language we find them very few.   Scherzl, in his
" Comparative Grammar of the Slavonic and other
kindred Languages," Kharkov, 1871, vol. i., p. 95,
writes as follows :—" In the purity of its vocabulary,
in its structure and syntax, the Russian language has
preserved the Slavonic type better than the other
members of the family.   The Tatar words which have
entered into it are limited to a small number, relating
to clothes, precious stones, and articles of every-day
use, such as *chemodan*, trunk ; *kinzhal*, dagger ; *bash-
mak*, a shoe ; *boulat*, steel, and others."   Little Russian
has incorporated a great many Polish words, as Bulgarian and Servian have Turkish.   Many of these,
however, in the renovation of the languages caused

[1] Cited by Koulish, "Essays on Southern Russia" ("Zapiski
o Youzhnoi Rousi"), St. Petersburg, 1857, vol. ii., p. 274.

by national independence are being expelled. Of the western branch, Polish has always been greatly under foreign influences. Many German words may be found in the language. During the whole of the seventeenth century the pedants and Jesuitic school-masters with which the country teemed were introducing Latin words with Polish terminations, and this mischievous practice was at its height in the days of Sobieski. In the eighteenth century the language suffered more than any other from the Gallomania then rampant throughout Europe. Slovenish, Cech and Lusatian-Wendish show also the influence of their German neighbours. On the other hand, German has borrowed some Slavonic words, as *stieglitz*, a goldfinch; *grenze*, frontier; and, according to some scholars, *pflug*, a plough.

The following few remarks on the characteristics of the Slavonic languages, considered as a family, may be interesting to the student. These languages are all in a highly inflected state, having terminations to mark the seven cases which they employ, and the genders. The only exception to this is the Bulgarian, which has lost its cases almost entirely; a few being kept in a provincial dialect here and there as we might expect, from the rule that the dialects of a language are truer to its spirit than the literary form. Bulgarian has also in its dialects preserved traces of the original nasals which existed in the Palæoslavonic, and are now only regularly found in Polish. But besides these remains in Bulgarian there are also a few in Slovenish, and even more in the words which Magyar has borrowed from Slovenish at an early stage. The article is altogether wanting in the Slavonic languages (as in Latin). Owing to German influence the demonstrative pronoun has been occasionally used for it in Slovenish and Lusatian-Wendish, but it has been rejected by purists. In these two last languages (the least cultivated of all the Slavonic family) the dual has been preserved both in the nouns and verbs. Perhaps the most characteristic feature of these Slavonic languages is the extraordinary development of the latter. Every verb undergoes a certain number of aspects, which will remind the classical students of the forms in *urio*, *sco*, *ito*, &c., but what is but a casual modification of a verb in other languages is developed into a system in Slavonic, and minute shades of meaning are thereby expressed which are sometimes very difficult to translate.

The history of the Palæoslavonic or Church Language, as it is often called, has been divided by the eminent scholar Vostokov, the editor of the Ostromir Codex, into three periods.

(1) From Cyril, or from the ninth century to the thirteenth century. This is the genuine ancient Slavonic, as appears from the manuscripts of that period.

(2) From the thirteenth to the sixteenth century. This is the middle age of the Slavonic, as altered gradually by Russian copyists, and full of Russisms.

(3) From the sixteenth century to the present time. This comprises the modern Slavonic of the Church-books printed in Russia and other countries, especially

after the so-called improvement of those writings. In the course of time, after passing through the hands of so many ignorant copyists, the sacred books had been corrupted, and in many places unintelligible. In a learned paper in one of the earlier volumes of the "Bohemian Magazine," frequently quoted in this work, Schafarik has given some curious and amusing examples of these perversions of the text. Absurd, however, as they were we shall find afterwards that men were willing to be burned alive in their defence. The sufferings of the Dissenters in Russia who adhered to the old forms, furnish some very gloomy pages in the annals of the country. We find such books as Yesipov's "People of the Old Time" (*Lioudi starago vieka*) full of terrible stories. There grew up a general feeling among the more intelligent of the necessity of a revision, and in the time of Basil, the father of Ivan the Terrible, Maximus, a learned Greek monk, was sent from Mount Athos to Moscow to correct the Church books according to the original Greek. But he seems afterwards to have fallen into disgrace, and the work was never accomplished, although repeatedly resumed, till the time of Nicon, in the reign of the Tzar Alexis, of whom I shall speak more at large in the chapter on Russian literature. The study of the Old Slavonic, or Church Language as it is styled, has been greatly facilitated by the admirable Comparative Grammar and Lexicon by Miklosich, and the "Handbuch der Altbulgarischen Sprache" by Leskien. There is also a good grammar by Schleicher.

C

A few words may here be added on the Cyrillic and Glagolitic alphabets. In what relation they stand to each other has always been a very difficult question. That one was moulded upon the other is evident, because the order of the letters is the same in both, and the difficulty of expressing the præiotised vowels is the same, perhaps the one great defect of these Slavonic systems of writings.

Among the various opinions held concerning these alphabets the following may be specified :—

(1) That the Cyrillian was invented by St. Cyril, and called after him; the chief part of the alphabet, as is evident, being derived from the Greek. The letters wanted to express sounds not existing in the Greek language, he took from Hebrew and Persian. The eminent Bohemian scholar Schafarik held that the Glagolitic alphabet was invented by Cyril and the Cyrillian by Methodius, although bearing the name of the former. His reasons for this opinion he has given in his work, " Ueber den Ursprung und die Heimath des Glagolitismus." For an account of the labours of these two Slavonic apostles, see Dr. Maclear's book previously cited. We must remember that Constantinople was a city frequented by the inhabitants of all nations, and Cyril and Methodius could easily have made acquaintance with some members of these nationalities there. Cyril also, as we are told by his biographers, travelled among the Khazars, who spoke Hebrew, and also lived for some time with the Caliphs of Bagdad.

The following account of the conversion of the Slavs is taken from the twentieth chapter of Nestor, and may, perhaps, prove interesting to my readers :— "When the Slavonians and their princes Rostislav, Svatopolk and Kotzel had been baptised, they sent to the Emperor Michael saying : 'Our land has been baptised, but we have no teacher to preach to us and instruct us and translate the sacred books for us. We do not understand the Greek and Latin languages ; one teaches us in one way and one in another, and therefore we do not understand the meaning of the writing and its force : therefore send us teachers who may translate the words of the books and their meaning.' When the Emperor Michael had heard this he called together all the philosophers and told them all the words of the Slavonic princes. And the philosophers said, 'There is a man in Thessalonica, by name Leo, whose sons are well acquainted with the Slavonic tongue ; he has two clever sons who are philosophers.' When the emperor heard this he sent to Thessalonica to Leo for them, saying, 'Send to us thy sons, Methodius and Constantine, quickly.' And Leo having heard this sent them quickly. And they came to the emperor and he said to them, 'Lo ! the Slavonic land has sent to me to ask for an instructor, who might translate the sacred writings for them, for this is what they desire.' And they allowed them-selves to be persuaded by the emperor, and he sent them to the Slavonic land, to Rostislav, Svatopolk and Kotzel. And when they arrived there they began to devise a Slavonic alphabet, and translated an

Apostol[1] and the Gospel.   And the Slavonians were
glad that they heard the great things of God in their
language.   And afterwards they translated a Psalter,
an Oktoich[2] and the other books.   And some began
to abuse the Slavonic books, saying, ' No other nations
must have a writing of their own except the Hebrews,
Greeks, and Latins, according to the writing of Pilate
which he wrote on the cross of the Lord.'   But when
the Roman Pope heard this he blamed those who
found fault with the Slavonic books, saying, ' Let
the word of the Scriptures be fulfilled, that all
languages should praise God'; and in another
place, ' All shall declare in divers tongues the greatness of God as the Holy Spirit shall give them to
utter."[3]

(2) The Glagolitic was credited with having been
invented by no less a person than St. Jerome.   A
more sober criticism, however, in modern times has
dissipated this belief.   Dobrovsky, the eminent Bohemian scholar, author of the " Institutiones Linguæ
Slavicæ veteris Dialecti," assigned them to the thirteenth century, and, at a later period of his life,
even the fourteenth.   Kopitar, in his edition of the
" Glagolitic Clozianus," endeavoured to raise the
antiquity of the alphabet to the tenth century.   But
we must remember that this is a mere conjecture,
since up to the present time no Glagolitic manuscript
has been found with a date, whereas we know by a

[1] See p. 36.   [2] A book of hymns.
[3] Bielowski's edition of "Nestor," p. 569, in Monumenta
Poloniæ Historica.

note subjoined that the Ostromir Codex, written in Cyrillic, was begun October 21, 1056, and finished May 13, 1057.

The Glagolitic question is intimately bound up with the introduction of the Roman ritual into the Southern Slavonic countries. The Slavonic liturgy was forbidden by the Roman Catholic councils of 925, 1059, and 1064, in Dalmatia, but the service in the Slavonic language was preserved notwithstanding. At last, by a bull of Pope Innocent IV., in 1248, the Slavonic service, with the use of the Glagolitic alphabet, was permitted. It is in this bull that we see the Dalmatian Slavs assigning the invention of their alphabet to St. Jerome : "quod in Slavonia est litera specialis, quam illius terræ clerici se habere a beato Hieronymo asserentes eam observant in divinis officiis celebrandis." After this time, the use of the Glagolitic spread along the coast of Croatia, and a great part of Dalmatia. But the employment of Latin in the religious services accompanied it. In the fourteenth century it had extended itself to the Slavonic monastery founded by Charles IV. at Prague for the Croatian Benedictines.[1] Here the Glagolitic breviary was used for a hundred years, when it was changed for the service-books of the Utraquists. In 1483 was published, apparently at Venice, a Glagolitic breviary, and in the middle of the sixteenth century some books appeared in it at Tübingen, as I shall afterwards show when speaking of Slovenish literature. Nor was the

[1] See p. 35.

Glagolitic entirely confined to sacred subjects. In this alphabet is written the Statute of Vinodol, so called from a district in Croatia, one of the most important monuments of South Slavonic law. This manuscript is now preserved in the public library at Agram. It has been printed *in extenso* in the valuable collection of Slavonic Laws, published by Jirecek at Prague in 1880. In the Glagolitic alphabet, according to some scholars, the chronicle of the priest of Dioclea, mentioned in a subsequent chapter, was written. A list of Glagolitic manuscripts is given in Schafarik's "Geschichte der Südslawischen Literatur," but it is not complete, as it does not include some which are to be found in the Bodleian Library. It is to be regretted that a Psalter of the year 1222, which was seen by Levacovic in the seventeenth century, has since disappeared. The manuscripts and printed books in this curious character are, for the most part, of a religious nature. There are, however, exceptions, as in the Glagolitic letters which passed between the commanders of the Austrian and Turkish frontiers, and are cited by Schafarik as still preserved in the Lyceal-Bibliothek of Laibach, the head-quarters of Slovenish philology. The Glagolitic writing is passing more and more out of use. It is not a little curious that in many manuscripts we find both Cyrillic and Glagolitic writing, as in the Psalter of Bologna of the twelfth century.

Besides these two alphabets there is another less known, the so-called *boukvitza* (Servian, alphabet), which prevailed almost exclusively in Bosnia. The basis of this was apparently the Cyrillian, but approaching more to a cursive hand with some new forms, and mixed to a certain extent with Glagolitic letters. This has also been considered by some writers as an invention of the clergy to draw the people from the use of the Cyrillic liturgy. There are many documents preserved in this boukvitza, which seems to have been more frequently employed for mundane purposes than the Glagolitic; thus even collections of songs have been written in it. Perhaps the most important document which has come down in it is the Statute of Poljica, a place near Spalatro in Dalmatia. The manuscript dates from the second half of the fifteenth century. It has been included in Jirecek's work previously mentioned.

As regards the relative antiquity of the alphabets, some have asserted the priority of the Glagolitic on account of its having incorporated some of the (supposed) Slavonic runes. The view that the Slavs had runes is based upon a passage in the writings of the Monk Khrabr, who tells us that they used to draw figures and make cuttings to express their ideas. But no Slavonic runes can be distinctly shown to have existed, although wild theories have been propounded on the subject by such writers as Wolanski, Kollar, and Cybulski. Schleicher, in his " Formenlehre der Kirchenslawischen Sprache," held the Glagolitic alphabet to be later than the Cyrillic. On the other hand, Kopitar has attempted to show, in his " Glagolita Clozianus," that older linguistic forms occur in the Glagolitic manuscripts than in the Cyrillic.

The admirable remarks of Professor Jagich ("Archiv," iv. 2, 316) seem to sum up the question very accurately. They may be briefly stated as follows :—

(1) The two alphabets are certainly connected.

(2) They are both as certainly derived from the Greek, the Cyrillic, as would appear from the Uncial, and the Glagolitic from the Cursive. Among the first persons to suggest the latter of these views appear to have been Professor Leskien and the Rev. Isaac Taylor.

(3) On the other hand, the alphabets must have been separated for a long time, as we see by their letters having different numerical values.

The Cyrillian alphabet is used at the present time by the Russians, the Serbs, with a few additional letters, and the Bulgarians. From 1436 to 1828 this alphabet was employed by the Roumans with certain modifications. In the latter year the learned John Eliade modified their shape and diminished their number. In 1847 the first Rouman newspaper was printed in Latin letters, since which the Cyrillian have given place to them. The Glagolitic alphabet has a much more limited range, being only employed by the Croats of Dalmatia in their religious books. There are two forms of these letters, the Bulgarian and the Croatian, the latter being bolder and more square in their appearance. The first Glagolitic book was a missal, printed in the year 1483.

Before leaving the subject of Slavonic writing it may be further remarked, that besides the allusion of the Monk Khrabr, already mentioned, we have the description given by Bishop Dittmar, of Merseburg, of the City Riedegost, and its temple :—" In this city is only a temple cleverly made of wood, supported on the horns of different kinds of animals. Various representations of gods and goddesses, wonderfully sculptured to all appearance, ornament the walls outside ; in the interior are figures of the gods, with their names engraved on them, terribly arrayed in helmets and breastplates, the chief of whom is called Zuarisci, and is honoured and worshipped before the rest by all nations."

Supposed Slavonic runes have been found on some objects, as the so-called idols of the Obotrites, which, however, have been proved to be forgeries, and some stone figures, but none of them have been successfully deciphered. The whole matter has been thoroughly sifted by Nehring and Jagic in the " Archiv für Slavische Philologie," and it may be as well to quote their opinion, incisively expressed, that up to the present time no genuine Slavonic runes have been found.

CHAPTER II.

THE NOMENCLATURE OF THE SLAVONIC RACES.

In this chapter I propose to discuss some of the chief explanations which have been attempted of the Slavonic territorial names.

(1) Russian.—This name was formerly derived from the Rhoxolani, but these have been shown by Schafarik to have been a Medish tribe, and to have had nothing to do with the Slavs. In the last century, the derivation was first suggested from the Finnish name of Sweden, Ruotsi, and Ruotsalainen, a Swede. We must remember that the empire of Russia was founded by three brothers, Rourik, Sineus, and Trouvor, who came from Scandinavia, and for a long time, as Professor Thomsen has shown, the Russians and Slavonians were considered to be different races. The names also admit of a Scandinavian explanation; thus Ingar becomes Igor, and Helga, Olga. The most celebrated passage relating to the difference between the original Russians and the Slavonians is the description of the waterfalls of the Dnieper by the Emperor Constantine Porphyrogenitus, where the names are given in two languages, Slavonic (Σκλαβινιστί) and Russian (Ρωσιστί). But in a few

---

[1] Thomsen, "The Origin of the Russian State," Oxford, 1877.

generations the Scandinavian origin of the settlers was forgotten. The grandson of Rourik, Sviatoslav, has a purely Slavonic name, and Nestor speaks of Slavonic and Russian as being identical. The Finnish name, Ruotsi, Professor Thomsen supposes to be itself a corruption of the first syllable of the Swedish word *rothsmenn*, or *rothskarlar*, rowers or seafarers. He considers the view that the word Russ has anything to do with the Hebrew *Rosh* mentioned in Ezekiel xxxviii. 2, 3, and xxxix. 1, untenable. In the old Slavonic writings, from the twelfth to the sixteenth century, we always find the country called Rous. The form Rossia was introduced by the Greek revisers of the Russian Church-books, and by the Byzantine writers.[1] It is clearly formed on a classical model. Of late years many attempts have been made by Ilovaïski, Gedeonov, Zabielin, and others, to upset the theory of the Scandinavian origin of the Russian empire, but they cannot be considered to have succeeded. The most important argument upon which those rely who reject the Scandinavian theory, is the number of geographical names in which the root *rus*, or *rous*, occurs, especially in Pomerania and the Isle of Rügen, in Lithuania, in White Russia, and on the banks of the Dnieper. Ros is the Lithuanian name of the river Niemen ; and hence the appellation given to the ancient Prussians—still borne by the German occupiers of their country—

---

[1] Schafarik, "Slawische Alterthümer," ii. 98.

viz., *Po-rousi*, or people dwelling on the banks of the Rous.[1] M. Reclus calls attention to the fact that the Arabian authors, at the end of the ninth and commencement of the tenth century, speak of the Russians of their time as a Slavonic nation divided into three groups, that of Kouyaba (Kiev), that of the Slavs, or Sloveni of Novgorod, and the family of Artsania, supposed to be identical with the inhabitants of the country of Razan, on the Oka, or the population of Rostov, in the government of Yaroslavl, not far from the Volga. If we weigh the testimony furnished by Byzantine, Arabian, and Jewish writers, and the results of the explorations of the Russian Kourgani, we must perforce acknowledge that at least at the close of the ninth century, there existed in the basin of the Dnieper, a Russian nation, tolerably compact, possessing certain industries and acquainted with the art of writing.[2]

The story of the three brothers, Rourik, Sineous, and Trouvor, who were invited by the citizens of Novgorod, has a very legendary air. Concerning the foundation of this town, we know nothing; its origin is lost in remote antiquity. Some writers have supposed that a large Finnish settlement existed on its site. Karamzin, however, does not think that it was a celebrated city before the time of Rourik. It is natural to suppose that there would be consider-

---

[1] Reclus, v., 302.

[2] A valuable collection of passages is given in the following work—Von Hammer, "Sur les Origines Russes, extraits de Manuscrits Orientaux," St. Petersburg, 1825.

able intercourse between the inhabitants of the north coast of Russia and the Norsemen. Oustrialov holds that some of the latter went to Byzantium through Russia, for we know that the Greek emperors had a body-guard of Varangians. But how did these brothers first come into the country? Were they invited, or did they make a piratical invasion? The national vanity of the Russian historians has led them to consider that these strangers were invited. The whole story bears a very suspicious resemblance to our own legend of Hengist and Horsa, and probably ought to be put upon the same footing. According to one of these accounts, they were summoned by Gostomîsl, a leading citizen of Novgorod. Karamzin thinks the whole story of this Gostomîsl very dubious. There is no mention of him in the chronicle of Nestor, or in the Stepennaïa Kniga of which I shall speak shortly. According to another legend, Rourik was the son of the Swedish king Ludbrat and his queen Oumila, the daughter of Gostomîsl, and was born at Upsala in 830. From all these stories we seem to learn one thing, viz., that a successful Scandinavian invasion occurred in the North of Russia. The very names of the persons introduced into the story, such as Gostomîsl, seem to show that it is a myth.[1] The three brethren, we are told, finally settled in the country,—Rourik at Ladoga, where the river Volkhov flows into the lake ; Sineous at Bieloe ozero (white lake), in the territory

---

[1] Does it mean, one who cares for guests, hospitable ?

of a Finnish tribe; and Trouvor at Izborsk, on Lake Peipous.

(2) The Poles.—The first authentic date of Polish history is the year 963, when a certain prince, Mieszko, was subjugated, and compelled to pay tribute to the German emperor, Otho I. Schafarik ("Slawische Alterthümer," i., 205) sees their name in the Bulanes of the geographer Ptolemy (*floruit cir.* 161), although there is another reading, Sulanes. The name seems to connect itself with the Slavonic, *pole*, a field, and thus would signify the dwellers on the plain, *cf.*, such names as Champagne. Jordanes (in the sixth century A.D.) mentions Slavs as inhabiting the banks of the Vistula, but with no definite nomenclature. It was probably about the sixth, or perhaps seventh century, that a people called the Lekhs settled near the above-mentioned river. This is certainly the oldest name which can be assigned to the Poles. The attempt of Schafarik to connect it with the Polish word *szlachta*, meaning nobility, cannot be considered successful; the latter word has been derived with greater show of probability from the German word, *Geschlecht*.[1] By the tenth century the name of Lekh was beginning to grow uncommon, and was gradually becoming superseded by the appellation of Poliani, or inhabitants of the plains. Nestor, however, knows both names, and distinguishes between two branches of the Poliane, viz., Poliane Liakhove on the Vistula, and Poliane

---

[1] Pïpin and Spasovich, 457.

Rousove on the Dnieper. When we have the first glimmer of light thrown upon the Poles as distinguished from the other Slavs, we find them broken up into different tribes, each under the rule of its chief. Dlugosz, their early chronicler previously mentioned, has drawn a pleasing picture of their primitive happiness, but it can only be looked upon as a rhetorical composition. He speaks of their having no riches, and arousing no jealousy or hatred among their neighbours; of their implicit obedience to the wishes of their chiefs, which had all the force of statutes; of their Arcadian simplicity and happiness.

(3) The Bulgarians.—Already at the commencement of the third century A.D. we find Slavs settled between the Danube and the Balkan. A constant immigration was going on till the middle of the seventh century, as these hordes were pushed further southwards by new invaders from the East. In 681 the Slavonic settlers fell under the power of a tribe of Bulgarians, a Ugro-Finnish race, if we follow the opinion of Schafarik, Drinov, and the best authorities. The origin of the Bulgarians is one of the vexed questions of ethnology. Some have made them Tatars; Raich, the Serb, held them to have been Slavs, and this view has lately been resuscitated by Professor Ilovaïski, the Russian historian, who seems to take special delight in breaking a lance against all the orthodox and well-grounded decisions of Slavistic. Kerstovich, a native Bulgarian writer, makes them also to have been Slavonians, but he puts the Huns

under the same head, and thus produces a great confusion of ethnology. The etymology of this name, Bulgarians, Bolgare, has not yet been satisfactorily explained. The theory which would connect it with the Volga is exploded. The original forms of the name, Burgari, Borgian, Wurgari, &c., show its analogy with forms like Onuguri, Uturguri, Kutriguri, and the appellations of other tribes. We thus see that the elements of the composition of the word are Bul and gari.[1] History tells us that Koubrat, a Bulgarian prince, shook off the yoke of the Avars, and that on his death his possessions were divided among his five sons. The eldest remained in the ancient settlement on the Volga, where the ruins of their former capital, Bolgari, are still pointed out to travellers. The third son, named Asparoukh, crossed the Dniester and the Dnieper, and first settled in a place called Onklos, a word in which Schafarik sees the old Slavonic *ongl, angulus,* between the Transylvanian Alps and the Danube.[2] From this place the Bulgarians pushed further south, as previously mentioned, till they reached the localities which they have ever since occupied, where they became mixed with the original Slavonic settlers. Drinov compares this fusion and importation of a new nomenclature to the mixture of the German Franks and the Gauls and the adoption by a branch of the Slavonians of the Finnish name

[1] Schafarik, "Slawische Alterthümer," ii., 169.
[2] See Professor Drinov's "Settlement of the Balkan Peninsula by the Slavs" ("Zaselenie balkanskago poluostrova Slavyanami," Moscow, 1873).

of their conquerors, whence the appellation Russian, as previously mentioned.

(4) The Serbs.—Somewhere about the beginning of the seventh century we find the Serbs settling, with the consent of the Emperor Heraclios, in what had been the ancient Mœsia. Our chief authority for their migrations is the Emperor Constantine Porphyrogenitus, but his account has a very mythical air ; and we need not puzzle ourselves with too close an accuracy about the heroes Klukas, Lobelos and Chorbatos, nor the sisters Tuga and Buga. The Serbs have, unlike the Russians and other Slavs, kept their old name, for we know from the ancients that Servi was one of the appellations which the Slavs gave themselves, whereas they were called Wends by their Teutonic neighbours. Procopius has quaintly turned this into Σπόροι, and informs us gravely that they were so called because they lived σποράδην. According to Schafarik this was originally the generic name of the Slavs : we find it in Pliny, Serbi ; in Ptolemy, the geographer, Serbi and Sirbi. In Vibius Sequester, a geographer who wrote in the sixth century A.D., they are called Servecii or Servetii. The roots of this word Schafarik finds in the Sanskrit *su*, to produce, and thus makes the name equivalent to the children. But this cannot be considered a very happy conjecture.

(5) The Bohemians or Cechs.—It is a mere geographical expression to apply the Celto-Germanic name of. the country of the Boii (Boiiheim) to the Slavs who occupied it afterwards. In the same way the English

D

are sometimes called Britons.   The name Cech has never been satisfactorily derived.   Dobrovsky wished to connect it with a word *ceti*, signifying to begin, and thus would make the name imply the original inhabitants.   Schafařik, however, does not endorse this etymology.   The land now occupied by the Cechs was, as previously mentioned, first held by the Celtic Boii, and afterwards by the Teutonic Marcomanni.   The Cechs are supposed to have arrived in the country between 451 and 495 A.D.

(6) Lusatian Wends or Sorbs.—The word Lusatia (German, *Lausitz*) is derived from a Slavonic root, signifying a low, marshy country.[1]   The term Wend applied to them by their German neighbours will be explained a little further on.

(7) The names Slovaks and Slovenes are made clear by their connexion with the word Slav, Slavonic, of which I shall now speak.

The name Slav does not occur in any written memorials before the time of Jordanes.   He says: "Quorum nomina licet nunc per varias familias et loca mutentur principaliter tamen Sclavini et Antes nominantur."   It is probably connected with the root *slovo*, the word, which is related to the Greek κλύω, and in some Polabish vocabularies we get the very interesting form *slivo*, which is further supported by the verb *slit*, used like the Greek κλυειν=to have a reputation.   The Slav thus comes to signify the intelligibly speaking man, as opposed to the (seemingly)

[1] Lug, or luza.   Cf. "A Sketch of Serbo-Lusatian History" (in Polish), by W. Boguslawski.   St. Petersburg, 1861.

dumb man, *Niemetz,* which in modern Russian and all other Slavonic languages has come to mean simply, the Germans; they being the nearest Gentiles, so to speak, with whom the Russians came into contact; another application of the old line,—

Barbarus hic ego sum, quia non intelligor ulli.

The tendency to seek a self-laudatory origin for their national name has led some Slavonic scholars to identify the word with *slava,* glory. Under any circumstances this word and *slovo* are from the same root. The word *slave* has, however, acquired another meaning in the languages of Western Europe. The devastating wars of the Germans in early days,—of Charles the Great, Henry the Lion, and Albert the Bear,—so harried with fire and sword the territories of the unhappy Slavs, and uprooted their occupants, that the European markets were glutted with captive Slavs, who thus added another word to our modern vocabulary.

The Slavs have never applied the name Wends to themselves; this is the appellation which they have received from their German neighbours. Even now the Finn calls Russia *Wennalaiset,* or the land of the Wends. To this day the Lusatians are styled Wends, and the name Windish is frequently given by the Germans to what would be more correctly called the Slovenish language. The name is connected by Schafarik with a root, *wenda* (Russ. *voda,* Lat. *unda*), and thus would come to mean the people dwelling by the water, the shores of the Baltic being one of the earliest homes of the

Slavs.   Tacitus talks of the nations of the Peucini,
the Venedi, and the Fenni ; and the Wendic mountains (τὰ οὐενεδικὰ ὄρη) are mentioned by the geographer Ptolemy.   The latter writer, who flourished
about A.D. 161, and whose work formed a text-book
even so late as the fifteenth century, has given us
a list of rivers and tribes in European Sarmatia
at considerable length.   Let us remember that by
Sarmatia the ancients signified all the country lying
east of the Vistula and north of Dacia, thus including
parts of Poland and Galicia, Lithuania, Esthonia,
and Western Russia.   The Tanais was considered to
form the boundary between Europe and Asia.

In Ptolemy the Baltic appears as part of the
Northern Ocean, but he is acquainted with the Vistula,
which he calls by its name.   He tells us that Sarmatia is inhabited by very widely-scattered races,
and that the Wenedæ are established along the
whole of the Wendish Gulf (οἱ τε οὐενέξαι πάρ' ὅλον
τὸν οὐενεδικὸν κόλπον).   The Winidæ are also mentioned
by Jordanes.

(8) Croat, Chorwat, Hrvat.—Schafarik derives this
word from the original name for the Carpathian
mountains, Chrbet, which, like the word Alp, may
be used to signify any mountain, as it literally means
a ridge or backbone, and occurs also in Russian.[1]
We must pay no attention to the mythical Chrobatos
of Constantine Porphyrogenitus.

[1] This explanation is also adopted by Professor Ljubic,
"Survey of Croatian History" ("Pregled Hrvatske Poviesti"),
Fiume, 1867, p. 6.

(9) Polabes, an extinct tribe, dwelling on the shores of the Elbe (Laba), as described in chapter x. of this work.

(10) Pomeranians, a Slavonic tribe, dwelling on the shores of the Baltic (*Po* and *More*, the Sea).

(11) Bosnia, so called from the river Bosna.   In connexion with which the name Herzegovina may be mentioned, which is a barbarism from the German *herzog.*   It was first used in the time of Stephen, one of the Servian princes, who acknowledged himself the vassal of the German emperors.

Before concluding these brief remarks on the origin of the nomenclature of the various Slavonic races, I may mention that at the end of the second volume of the invaluable " Slavonic Antiquities " of Schafarik, extracts are given from all authors directly or indirectly referring to the Slavs, from the time of Herodotus, who is supposed, with considerable probability, to allude to them as the Budini and Neuri, to the monk Khrabr, in the tenth or eleventh centuries. The Father of History has but a scanty knowledge of the north of Europe ; of the Baltic he tells us nothing, but he appears to have heard of the lakes of Ladoga and Onega, as he describes the Tanais as rising in a large lake.   He has, however, in his fourth book given us a very length) description of Scythia, especially the southern part, for of the northern he had but a vague conception. We know what different opinions have been held about the travels of Herodotus ; according to some extreme views he had traversed all the regions he describes; according to others, his own personal experience was but small, his narratives consisting mostly of tales drawn from merchants and the conductors of caravans, with whatever accumulation of gossip the traveller's love of the marvellous addressing an uncritical audience would add. Herodotus does not pretend to have been personally acquainted with all, or even the principal parts of Scythia; he had probably made a journey to Olbia on the Hypanis (Boug), and drawn his narrative from the garrulous and perhaps mendacious Greeks he met there.[1] Still we must be thankful for his curious, if fragmentary details.

I shall not discuss the question here as to whether the Scythians were a Mongolian or Indo-European race. The correct view would appear to be that the namé was applied loosely to a *colluvies gentium*, and this is the only way in which we can explain the very divergent accounts given of them.

Two tribes have been identified with the Slavs with considerable probability by Schafarik,—namely, the Budini and Neuri; of the former we are told that they formed a very numerous and powerful nation; also that they had blue eyes and red hair (Βουδῖνοι δε ἔθνος ἐὸν μέγα καὶ πολλὸν γλαυκόν τε πᾶν ἰσχυρῶς ἐστὶ καὶ πύῤῥον). They had a city in their territory called Gelonus, built entirely of wood; this erection of wooden buildings is eminently character-

---

[1] Cf. Rawlinson's Herodotus, iii., 41. The site of Olbia can still be traced about twelve miles below Nikolaev. Mounds mark the site, and many coins have been found there.

istic of the Slavs, as may be seen in Russia at the present day. In ancient times large parts of Moscow were built of wood ; hence the frequency of fires. Of the same material the temples of the gods were also constructed. The account given of the origin of this town by Herodotus is very curious. He tells us that the Geloni were anciently Greeks, who, being driven from their factories along the coast, fled to the Budini and took up their abode with them. The Budini, however, and Geloni spoke different languages. Schafarik claims these Budini as a Slavonic race, and thinks that the description of the country given by the historian exactly corresponds to Volínia and portions of White Russia. Besides Herodotus, the Budini are mentioned by Pomponius Mela, Pliny, Ammianus Marcellinus, and others. Ammianus has a horrible story to tell us about them : " Post quos Budini sunt et Geloni, perquam feri, qui detractis peremptorum hostium cutibus indumenta sibi equisque tegmina conficiunt, bellatrix gens." The whole of this part of Russia is full of marshes, and the northern portion of the country of a most unlovely character. The word Budini, Schafarik connects with a Slavonic root, meaning dwelling ; it would be the same as is found in Buda, the name of one of the parts of Pesth. Concerning the Neuri, Herodotus tells us that they were driven from their former quarters by a plague of serpents, and came and dwelt with the Budini. He further adds that they were conjurors (γόητες), and that both the Scythians and the Greeks who dwelt in Scythia asserted that every

Neurian once a year became a wolf during a few days, and at the end of that time was restored to his proper shape. He adds quaintly, " Though they say this they do not persuade me; still they do say it, and confirm their assertion with an oath." These people are placed by Schafarik on the river Boug, which traverses Podolia and empties itself into the Black Sea : there even at the present day we have a river named Nurev, and the surrounding country is called Nurska. The word *Nur* is claimed by Schafarik as genuinely Slavonic, and signifying land. It is, he says, so explained in the Dictionary of the Russian Academy. Besides this argument based upon language, he thinks that the Budini would not have received them unless they could claim a community of race. He also relies upon their superstition as another proof; the Russians of those parts (Volinia and White Russia) being much addicted to a belief in wer-wolves, to which the legend seems to refer. This, however, is a superstition widely spread throughout Europe. Karamzin rationalises the story after a singular fashion ; he considers that it arose from the fact that during the winter the Neuri dressed themselves in the skins of wolves ; others, believing both the Budini and Neuri to have been Finns, trace the legend to the great reputation formerly enjoyed by them as wizards. Thus we find that Ivan the Terrible, in his last illness, sent for several witches from Lapland that he might consult them. With reference to the serpents, some Slavonic scholars are inclined to consider them as used figuratively. The

Old Slavonic mythology is full of stories about serpents and dragons, as will shortly appear in my chapter on Bulgarian literature.

The Slavonic element among the Scythians of Herodotus has been well discussed by Dr. Kurd de Schlözer.[1] He agrees with Schafarik, that although the arrival of the Slavs in Europe was later than that of the invasions of the other Indo-European peoples, still by the time of Herodotus, the fifth century before our era, all the tribes known later under the name of Slavs had occupied European territory. The departure from Asia and arrival in Europe of a tribe so numerous would have produced a great commotion among the neighbouring peoples—a movement which certainly would not have escaped the notice of the Greek and Roman writers if it had happened at a period nearer to our era. In the curious tale given by Herodotus (iv., 5, 6), he sees with much reason an allusion to the Slavs. A hero named Targitaus has Jupiter for his father, and the daughter of the river Borysthenes for his mother. He had three children : Lipoxais, Arpoxais, and Colaxais, the youngest of the three. In their reign several golden implements fell from heaven,—a plough with its yoke, an axe, and a vase. The eldest of the brothers perceived them first, and approached to pick them up, but as he came near, the gold took fire and blazed. He, therefore, went his way, and the second coming forward made the attempt, but the

[1] " Les Premiers Habitants de la Russie : Finnois, Slaves, Scythes, et Grecs." Paris, 1846.

same thing happened again. The gold rejected both the eldest and the second brother. Last of all the youngest brother approached, and immediately the flames were extinguished; so he picked up the gold and carried it to his home. Then the two elder agreed together, and made the whole kingdom over to the youngest born.

Upon this Dr. Schlözer very truly remarks that such a legend could never belong to a nomad people, as the Scythians in the limited sense of the word were. We seem to have an echo of the stories of the peasants Mikoula Selianinovich, Piast and Premysl, and their labours with the plough. The theory that among some of the Scythian tribes grouped in such an obscure manner by Herodotus the ancestors of the Slavs may be found has been supported in recent times by Zabielin. He also thinks that their original settlement was in Volinia and White Russia. The blood of the inhabitants is probably purer there because the barrenness of the soil and the numerous marshes have turned away conquerors, whether coming from the north or the south.[1] The human bones which have been found under the ancient tombs or *kourgans* and the sites of fortified camps (*goroditcha*) in the governments of Chernigov, Kiev, Pskov, Novgorod, and St. Petersburg are accompanied by objects indicating a rudimentary civilization, which, according to the form of the skull, have belonged to a Slavonic race. The ancient burial customs so ·

---

[1] See Reclus, "Géographie Universelle," vol. v., p. 299.

familiar to us from the fourth book of Herodotus continued in these countries till the tenth or eleventh centuries, as the Byzantine coins prove which have been found in the kourgans, where the warrior rests with his arms and the corpse of the wife is still decorated with ornaments. Sometimes the obsequies were accompanied by the sacrifice of domestic animals, as the favourite charger or dog of the hero ; and his slaves, male and female, are also added. In one of these vast kourgans we meet at the same time with the calcined bones of human beings, horses, birds, fish, arms, implements and jewels. A large tomb of this description called the Chernaia Mogila (Black Tomb), near Chernigov, was explored by Samo-kvasov and described in the Russian Review, *Drev-naia i Novaia Rossia* (Old and New Russia), which unfortunately has now ceased to appear.

Besides the accounts given by Jordanes, and Procopius of the Slavs, which have been already frequently quoted, we get the curious description given by the Byzantine Emperor Maurice (582—602 A.D.), from which the following salient points may be selected.

He tells us that the Slavs in his time were very numerous and very fond of liberty : they were hardy and very hospitable, showing much delicacy of feeling in their attentions to their guests. Their women were especially noted for their fidelity to their husbands, which was so great that at the death of her husband the wife would frequently refuse to survive him. We are also told of them that they were in the habit of using poisoned arrows. Somewhat amusing is the quaint but rather incredible story told by Theophanes, who flourished about A.D. 817.[1] "On the following day three Slavonians by race but wearing no weapons were seized by the Romans; they had only harps in their hands. But the king asked whence they came and where was their dwelling, but they replied that by race they were Slavonians, and that they dwelt at the extreme of the western ocean, and that the Chagan had sent an embassy to them and presents to their rulers to join him in an expedition against the Romans. Their rulers, therefore, had commissioned them to make an apology to the Chagan, because it was not possible on account of the length of the journey to send him any troops. They moreover asserted that they had made a journey of eighteen months and had thus come upon the Romans. They said they carried harps, because they were unacquainted with the use of iron, and the emperor, having wondered at their stature and the strength of their bodies, sent them to Heraclea."

[1] See "Monumenta Poloniæ Historica," by Bielowski, p. 4.

CHAPTER III.

EARLY RUSSIAN LITERATURE.

THE old Russian literature may be divided into two classes :—

(1) Oral.

(2) Written.

Russian literature is very rich in national songs and legends ; and some of these, to judge by the allusions found in them, may claim very considerable antiquity. They are called by the native scholars Bîlini, which may be translated "Tales of the olden time," and have been divided into the five following classes :—

1. The Cycle of the Bogatîri Starshii, or Older Heroes.

2. The Cycle of Vladimir, Prince of Kiev.

3. The Cycle of Novgorod.

4. The Cycle of Moscow.

5. The Cycle of the Cossacks.

To these two more might be added—viz., those referring to the time of Peter the Great and the Modern Period, but in this work I can only allow myself brief allusions to them. The metres in which these bîlini are chanted are irregular ; the ear being apparently satisfied with the ictus on some particular syllables.

The study and collection of these poems only dates from the commencement of the present century. It may easily be imagined that they would have presented but little attractions to the Gallicised courtiers of the time of Catherine, a period when the French language seemed on the point of supplanting Russian as the medium of communication among the upper classes. We find the nobility corresponding almost entirely in this language, and very curious French they occasionally wrote, to judge by some of the specimens given in the Russian review, *Starina*. In 1804 a small collection was published, based upon a publication attributed to Kirsha (the abbreviation of Cyril) Danilov. These ballads had been taken down about the middle of the eighteenth century among the workmen in the iron-foundries of Prokofii Demidov, descended from the blacksmith of Toula, who had been enriched by Peter the Great. The songs met with much success : the Russians saw a past revealed to them of which they had had but little idea, and as the romantic school of literature began to develop itself under the influence of Zhukovski and Poushkin, and the somewhat *couleur de rose* history of Karamzin made its appearance, the legends were more than ever welcomed. The first edition contained only twenty-nine pieces, but the second, published in 1818, had sixty, and the year following there appeared at Leipzig a small work entitled, " Fürst Wladimir und dessen Tafel-runde, alt-russische Heldenlieder." Here translations of some of these poems are given, and, as M. Rambaud tells us, of some others of which the originals are now lost, so that the collection did not begin too early. From 1852 to 1856 Sreznevski, the eminent scholar, whose loss Russia is now deploring, was collecting them in the governments of Olonetz, Tomsk, and Archangel. Since this time the publication of these interesting poems has been going on, just as the impulse of the " Minstrelsy of the Scottish Border " gave rise to so many other collections.

As might naturally be expected in popular poetry, although the ballads themselves are ancient, the phraseology has become more and more modernised, and anachronisms are frequent. Thus we have allusions to guns and telescopes; and the Germans are mentioned at a time when the Russians could not have had any intercourse with them. We get the usual conventional epithets found in all epic and ballad poetry. The wine is "green"; the Prince is the "bright sun"; the earth is "damp"; the Tatar is the "unbeliever." Three is a magic number : the hero sleeps three and sometimes twelve days. When there is fighting it generally lasts three days and three nights. The heroes' drink is of three kinds,—wine, beer, and mead. Potyk plays three games of chess with the heathen king. Forty thousand is the invariable number of an army.[1]

A discussion on the origin of these bilini has been aroused by the work of Vladimir Stasov. Contrary to the opinion of the majority of Russian scholars, he considers that the lays are in their origin Oriental,

---

[1] Wollner, "Untersuchungen über die Volksepic der Grossrussen." Leipzig, 1879.

have been introduced into the country, comparatively speaking, recently, and have only undergone a few modifications to Russify them.

The heroes of the first cycle are mythical beings; their stature is gigantic, and their strength super-human. Among such may be mentioned Volga Vseslavich, Mikoula Selianinovich, and Sviatogor. Volga Vseslavich is represented as the son of a serpent. He is capable of undergoing all sorts of transformations like Proteus. Sometimes he is a wolf, sometimes a falcon. When the city of Kiev is about to be besieged by the King of India, or the Sultan of the Turks, according to the variants of the legend, Volga becomes a bird, flies to Constantinople, and hears all the plans of invasion under the Sultan's window. He and his drouzhina, or band, succeed in massacring the Sultan and exterminating his people. According to M. Rambaud, this is merely a legendary poem on the well-known expedition of Oleg against Constantinople, as narrated by Nestor.

In Mikoula Selianinovich, or Nicholas the son of the Villager, we have the glorified peasant. He corresponds to the Przemysl of the Cechs and Piast among the Poles. We see the republican and pastoral tendencies of the Slavs in the circumstance that a peasant is made the hero of a series of bilini. On one occasion Mikoula is met by Volga and his drouzhina, while ploughing; but when the warrior and his company attempt to lift the peasant's plough

[1] "La Russie Épique," p. 36.

and find themselves unable, he, with a single touch, raises it from the earth and hurls it to the clouds. Sviatogor is another of these legendary Titans; one story represents him as stretched at full length upon a mountain. Ilya Murometz, of whom I shall speak more anon, wishes to challenge him to battle, but his most formidable blows can hardly arouse the giant from his dream; he thinks that they are only pebbles falling upon him. At the third blow he turns and says to the hero, "You are brave as a man, remain brave among them; you will never be able to measure your strength with me. See what my size is; the earth itself cannot contain me; I have at last found this mountain, and rested on it."[1] We here meet with some of the well-known tales of our childhood.

I now come to the cycle of Vladimir, the prince of Kiev, which we must remember was the first seat of the Russian nationality, and is still a sacred place to the Russians, endeared as it is with so many historical associations. The great glory of this cycle is Ilya Murometz, whose achievements form the subject of many a picturesque lay. A Russian author has, with great force and beauty, applied the tale of Ilya Murometz to his own country. It has been the sleeping giant, full of strength and latent energy: "What ails Ilya? He is heavy, and we will make sport of his lumbering and unmanageable bulk." Meanwhile, ever stronger grows the giant, who at last

[1] Rambaud, "Rus. Épique," p. 42.

E

leaps up and stands in all the vigour of his massive frame to confront and confound his enemies.

Some have compared Vladimir with his Drouzhina to Arthur and his Round Table. There is something in the parallel, but it must not be pushed too far. We can hardly call the members of the drouzhina knights, and there are none of the aristocratic notions, prevalent in the West, to be found in the companionship. On the same seat sits a rich boyar, the son of a merchant, and Ilya Murometz, the peasant. To this cycle belong the heroes Dobrina Nikitich, Alesha Popovich (son of the priest), who conquered the gigantic dragon Tougarin, Soloveï Boudimirovich, Diouk Stepanovich, who crossed the Dnieper by a single leap of his horse, and others.

The cycle of Novgorod is not so rich in legends as that of Kiev, but nevertheless contains some very interesting bílini. The stories that are told bear out the accounts of the luxury and turbulence of the great Slavonic republic, such as it has been handed down to us in the chronicles, of which more anon. To this cycle belong the stories of Vasilii Bouslaevich and Sadko, the rich merchant. The great prosperity of Novgorod is familiar to all readers of Russian history; it formed one of the members of the Hanseatic League, and its geographical position was favourable as being on one of the old high-roads of trade. Moreover, it never fell under the yoke of the Tatars.[1] Ivan III.,

---

[1] "The celebrated saying, 'Quis potest contra Deum et magnam Novgardiam?' first occurs in Albertus Crantius, who wrote in the fifteenth and sixteenth centuries."—KARAMZIN.

however, was resolved to consolidate the Russian empire; he easily picked a quarrel with the refractory republic; in 1478 an end was put to the vech, or popular assembly, and the bell was carried off to Moscow, where it is still shown.

The fifth cycle deals with the autocracy. Among the events celebrated are the taking of Kazan in 1552, and the conquest of Siberia by Yermak the Cossack. Many are the lays treating of Ivan the Terrible, and the instrument of his cruelties, Maliouta Skourlatovich, who stood in the same relation to him as Tristan l'Hermite did to Louis IX. of France, being his intimate associate and the instigator of many of his cruelties.

The bílinas previously mentioned have lived for centuries on the lips of the peasants. It is not a little strange that the first ever committed to writing were copied out by one Richard James, an Oxford graduate, who was in Russia in 1619 as chaplain of the embassy. The manuscripts are preserved among the Ashmolean Collection, and have been printed by several Russian editors.[1]

As a specimen of these interesting poems, so little known in our own country, let us take the lay of the rebel who is to be executed, and who dies in a very penitent and devout frame of mind, grateful to his Tzar for punishing him :—

[1] See "Istoricheskie Ocherki Rousskoi Narodnoi Slovesnosti i iskousstva" (Historical Sketches of Russian Popular Literature and Art), by Bouslaev. St. Petersburg, 1861, vol. i., p. 470.

Ah ! my head, my dear head,
My head that long hast served me.
Thou hast served me, my dear head,
Thirty and three years.
Not swerving from my trusty steed,
Not turning my foot from the stirrup,
But, my head, thou hast not gained
Either glory or joy,
Nor good words for thyself,
Nor lofty glory.
Yonder along the Masnitzkaia,
By the gates of the Masnitzkaia
They are leading a prince, a boyar.
Before him walk priests and clerks :
They bear in their hands a great book ;
After them comes a troop of archers ;
They carry their halberds uncovered ;
At his right side
Walks the stern executioner,
In his hands he carries the broad axe,
At his left side
Goes his sister.
She weeps, as a river flows ;
She groans, as brooks murmur.
Her brother soothes her,—
Do not weep, do not weep, my sister.
Dim not thou with tears thy bright eyes,
Flush not thy white face ;
Nor make sad thy joyous heart.
What now dost thou wish—
For my lands, my estates,
My rich possessions,
My gold or silver ?
Or dost thou weep my ruined fortunes ?
Ah, my light, my dear brother,
I do not desire them,
Either thy lands or thy estates,

Or thy rich possessions,
Nor thy gold nor silver ;
Only I desire, brother,
To see thy prosperity restored.
To this answered her brother,—
Thou, my light, my sister,
Thou mayst weep, but tears avail not,
Thou must pray, but prayers avail not.
Thou mayst entreat the Tzar, nor does that avail thee.
God to me has been full of pity,
The Tzar has been full of mercy ;
He has ordered them to sever my traitorous head
From my sturdy shoulders.—
They took the prince to the lofty scaffold,
To the place appointed.
He prayed to the Saviour, to the miraculous picture ;
He bowed low on all sides,
Farewell, world, and pious people,
Pray for my sins,
For my heavy sins.
Hardly could the people see him
When his treacherous head was cut off
From his sturdy shoulders.

The following curious poem gives an account of
the expedition of the Cossack Yermak, by which
Siberia was made subject to Russia. I have translated it quite literally, with a slight abridgment here
and there to avoid the constant repetitions :—

On the glorious steppes of Saratov,
Below the city of Saratov,
And above the city of Kamîshin,
The Cossacks, the free people, assembled ;
They collected, the brothers, in a ring ;
The Donski, Grebenski, and Yaitzki,
Their hetman was Yermak, the son of Timofei ;

Their captain was Asbashka, the son of Lavrentii.
They planned a little plan.
The summer, the warm summer, is going,
And cold winter approaches, my brothers.
Where, brothers, shall we spend the winter?
If we go to the Yaik, it is a terrible passage;
If we go to the Volga, we shall all be considered robbers;
If we go to the city of Kazan, there is the Tzar—
The Tzar Ivan Vasilievich, the terrible.
There he has great forces,
There, Yermak, thou wilt be hanged,
And we Cossacks shall be captured
And shut up in strong prisons.
Yermak, the son of Timofei, takes up his speech,—
Pay attention, brothers, pay attention,
And listen to me—Yermak.
Let us spend the winter in Astrakhan;
And when the fair spring reveals herself,
Then, brothers, let us go on a foray;
Let us earn our wine before the terrible Tzar.

Accordingly, when the winter was over, and the warm summer had come, Yermak again addresses his companions:—

Ha, brothers! my brave Hetmans!
Make for yourselves boats,
Make the rowlocks of fir,
Make the oars of pine!
By the help of God we will go, brothers;
Let us pass the steep mountains,
Let us reach the infidel kingdom,
Let us conquer the Siberian kingdom,
That will please the Tzar our master.
I will myself go to the White Tzar,
I shall put on a sable cloak,
I shall make my submission to the White Tzar.
Oh! thou art our hope, orthodox Tzar,

Do not order me to be executed, but bid me say my say,
Since I am Yermak, the son of Timofei,
I am the robber Hetman of the Don;
'Twas I went over the blue sea,
Over the blue sea, the Caspian ;
And I it was who destroyed the ships ;
And now, our hope, our orthodox Tzar,
I bring you my traitorous head,
And with it I bring the empire of Siberia.
And the orthodox Tzar spoke ;
He spoke—the Terrible Ivan Vasilievich :
Ha ! thou art Yermak, the son of Timofei,
Thou art the hetman of the warriors of the Don.
I pardon you and your band,
I pardon you for your trusty service,
And I give you the glorious gentle Don as an inheritance.

The conquest of Siberia was effected by the brigand Yermak at the head of 850 men, Russians, Cossacks, Tatars, and Polish and German prisoners ; he defeated the Khan Kouchoum, and took possession of his capital, Sibir. This Slavonic representative of Pizarro and Cortez, as M. Rambaud calls him,[1] did not long survive his imperial master ; while trying to swim across the river Irtîsh he was drowned by the weight of his armour in the year 1584.

The following lines on the burial of Ivan the Terrible are curious :—

Why, bright moon, father moon,
Why dost thou not shine as of old time,
Not as of old time as before?·
It happened to us in Holy Russia,
In stone-built Moscow, in the golden Kremlin,

---

[1] " Histoire de Russie," p. 240.

In the Ouspenski Cathedral
Of Michael the Archangel,
They beat upon the great bell,
The sound echoed over the whole damp mother earth.
All the princes and boyars came together,
All the warrior-people assembled
To pray to God in the Onspenski Cathedral.
There stood a new-made coffin of cypress-wood.
In the coffin lies the orthodox Tzar—
The orthodox Tzar, Ivan Vasilievich the Terrible.
The life-giving cross stands at its head ;
By the cross lies the imperial crown ;
At his feet his terrible sword.
Every one prays to the life-giving cross ;
Every one bows to the golden diadem ;
Every one looks with trembling at the terrible sword.
Around the coffin the wax-lights burn ;
Before the coffin stand all the priests and patriarchs ;
They read and sing the valedictory hymn ;
They sing farewell to our orthodox Tzar—
Our Terrible Tzar—Ivan Vasilievich.

The bilini are carried on through the times of Boris Godunov and the False Demetrius to the days of Peter the Great, when they seem to have gained fresh vigour, being inspired by the glories of the great regenerator of his country. Want of space alone prevents me from giving *in extenso* the very spirited ballad of the good boyar Nikita Romanovich and Maliouta Skourlatovich, infamous in Russian history. There is a great repetition of lines and epithets, as in all Russian ballad poetry. Nikita demands the death of the infamous favourite.

> Ah ! 'tis thou art our Lord, Tzar Ivan Vasilievich
> I do not want thy trusty steed,

I do not want thy cloak of marten's skin.
I do not want thy golden chest ;
Give me only Maliouta Skourlatov—
Order me, Lord, to slay him.

There is also a touching poem handed down about Xenia Godunov, the unfortunate daughter of Boris. She laments her dear chamber and happy life, while Boris Godunov still reigned. This poem is undoubtedly a contemporary production. .

The scope of my work will not allow me to extend these notices till the glories of the reign of Peter the Great, but the following short poem on the taking of Azov in 1696 is interesting. Something like a metrical version has been attempted :—

Ah ! ye soldiers, mournful soldiers,
Day or night how little rest ye !
Late at eve was order given :
All night long their weapons cleaning,
Ready stood at morn the soldiers.
'Twas no golden trumpet sounded,
'Twas no silver flute that echoed,
'Twas our Tzar, our noble father.
Come, my princes, come, my boyars,
Come and tell me ! now take counsel
How to take Azov directly.
Silent princes were and boyars ;
Tears he shed, our Tzar, our Father ;
Tell me, ye dragoons, my soldiers
Give me now a steadfast counsel,
How to take Azov, the city.
Like as bees with gradual humming,
Spake the true dragoons and soldiers :
" Cost what may, Sire, we will take it."
Set the sun in blood-red splendour,

Rose the bright clear moon thereafter,
Rose the dawn and forth they ventured
To the city, Azov glorious.
To the walls of white stone shimmering.
From the rocks no stones were rolling,
They were foes that swift descended;
But upon the fields no snow-flakes:
Corpses there of foemen slaughtered.
'Twas not rain that swelled the torrent,
'Twas the blood of Turkish foemen.

A favourite hero in many of these ballads is the robber, Stenko Razin, who was executed at Moscow in 1671. He is spoken of with great admiration :—

The glorious quiet Don is troubled
From Cherkask to the Black Sea.
All the circle of the Cossacks is disturbed,
We have no longer a hetman ;
No longer Stepan Timofeievich,
Called Stenko Razin.
They have taken the good youth,
They have bound his white hands,[1]
They have taken him to stone-built Moscow,
And on the glorious Red Square
They have cut off his rebellious head !

So, also, in another poem :—

Come forth ! come forth ! thou bright sun !
Come forth over the lofty mountain ;
Over the green oak-grove ;
Over the dwelling of the good hero, Stephen Timofeievich,
Called Stenka Razin !

---

[1] "White" is here merely a conventional epithet, and constantly occurs in the Russian ballads.

Come, come, bright sun !
Warm us, poor people ;
We are neither thieves nor robbers,
We are only the workmen of Stenka Razin !

The composition of these poems has not ceased in our own time, but the race of minstrels seems passing away before modern improvements. The cycle of Cossack songs must be treated of separately, as it more properly belongs to Malo-Russian literature.

Russia is very rich in popular poetry. Not only are there bílini, but stores also of religious songs, and such as have to do with various festivals of the year. These latter are called "stikhi." Most of them are supposed to be very ancient, and to belong to the period when Christianity was first introduced into Russia. Some of them have been collected by Bezsonov, and will be found in his "Kalieki Perekhozhie, or Wandering Psalm-singers."

Let us take the following as a specimen of these compositions :—

THE LAMENTATION OF THE SINFUL SOUL.

The sinful soul laments
Before the image of the Saviour ;
The sinful soul bemoans,
Expecting for itself eternal torment.
How can I, the soul, go
To the awful judgment of God at His coming ?
To the sinful soul avail
Neither property nor wealth ;
There is no ransom for the sinful soul,
Either in gold or silver.
Neither friends nor brothers

Can help the sinful soul,
Only tears and repentance
Can help the sinful soul ;
Only prayers in the midnight,
Soft deeds of mercy.
By these the sinful soul delivers itself
From terrible, eternal agony.
By these does the sinful soul gain
The heavenly kingdom.
Great is the name of the Lord on the earth.

Or the following lines from a poem on the day of judgment :—

Now is it time for the soul to rest,
Now is it time for the soul to return,
Now is it time for the soul to weep,
Before the coming of the angels ;
Then the earth will tremble,
And the stone-built cities will be thrown into ruins,
And the founts and streams flow forth ;
Through the skies the seas will be thrown into commotion,
And the moon turned into blood,
And the sun and the moon grow dim,
And the stars shall fall from the heavens upon the earth.
Then the angels and archangels shall be afraid,
The cherubim and seraphim shall tremble,
And all the powers of the heaven shall be shaken.

And so on ; but the piece is in reality little more than a version of the very words of Scripture. The following, however, has more originality :—

THE SOUL'S FAREWELL TO THE BODY.

The sun is about to set ;
The red sun has set.
The soul has departed from the body ;
Departing, she thus addresses it :—

> Farewell, farewell, thou white body,
> Thou goest, O white body, to the damp earth,
> To the damp earth to be dissolved :
> To the damp worms to be devoured ;
> I, the soul, go to Christ himself,
> To Christ himself, the righteous Judge.

There are also the Obradnia Piesni, songs on fête days and other occasions, under which head come the many Russian wedding-songs.

As a specimen of one of the Russian bridal-songs let us take the following, which is not without a certain elegance. I have been compelled to omit some of the repetitions, which are tedious to read, however agreeable they may be when chanted as a refrain :—

> Thou broad street !
> Thou green grass !
> Who has trodden the green grass ?
> They have come for the Lord's wooing ;
> They are seeking the beautiful damsel.
> Ask ye, ask ye,
> Of her near companions,
> How seemeth, how seemeth
> Our Anna Mitrevna ?
> In stature she is slender and tall;
> In face white and ruddy ;
> Her eyes are like the bright falcon's ;
> Her brows are like the black sable ;
> She has a braid of hair
> Down to her silken girdle.

It is this long braid of hair which distinguishes the maiden from the married woman. It is untied with much ceremony at marriage. Many of the songs

sung on these occasions are of great antiquity.
Among the common people the want of a written
literature has been partly supplied, as is so often the
case, by the abundance of the oral and traditional.
We will conclude our extracts from the Russian
national songs with the following pretty little piece :—

> I the trusty youth went
> And took refuge by the gentle Don,
> And I asked the ferrymen,
> Take me to the other side ;
> I wish to see my father and mother,
> To give my blessing to my little children, the orphans ;
> To tell my dear wife that she must wed another, or live as a
> widow,
> For I am sick and weary.
> My beating heart ails ;
> Death will soon come to me,
> And then I shall say,
> Bury me where three roads meet—
> To Petersburg, Moscow, and glorious Kiev ;
> Put at my head a golden cross,
> At my feet a green pine.[1]

Here also must be included the Koliadki, or songs
sung at Christmas-time. The derivation of this word
has been a great puzzle to scholars. Some connect
it with *kolo*, a ring. It is, however, more probably
to be derived from the Latin Kalendæ, which perhaps came into the Russian language through the
Greek ritual, just as *pogan* (paganus) and other similar
words have been introduced. If I were to quote

[1] I have been compelled to cut down some of the lines and
redundant epithets of this little song, but nothing has been
added.

some of the surmises of the Slavonic scholars about
this word, it would reflect but little credit on their
philological skill. The number of Latin and German
words (especially relating to religious matters) to be
found in the Old Slavonic is cited by Kopitar as evidence to support his theory that the home of the Old
Slavonic was Pannonia; thus *tserkov*, German *kirche*,
oltar, altar, *post*, fast, *pop*, *pfaff*, *pekl* and *peklo* from
pech, a word used by the Germans of the eleventh
century for hell; *srieda*, the middle, used for Wed-
nesday, exactly as the Germans call it Mittwoch;
tsesar, Cæsar, the Frankish pronunciation of the
Middle Ages, whence the modern Tzar, incorrectly
written Czar, and finally *otzet*, vinegar, from the
Latin *acetum*. Moreover, the influence of Gothic or
Germanic words may be traced in *penaz*, from the
mediæval German *pfenning*, *knaz* from *chuning*, and
ouseraz from the Gothic *ausahrings*, which has become
in modern German *ohrring*. A very curious word is
the old Slavonic *velblad*, which is taken from the
Gothic *ulbandus*, which is, again, corrupted from the
Greek ἐλέφας. In Slavonic, however, by some confusion, the word has come to mean camel. So also
the Slavonic *steklo*, glass, must have been adopted
from the Gothic *stikls*. These words, as well as those
relating to the Church, are supposed by Schafarik
and Thomsen to have been borrowed from the
Goths, when the Slavs dwelt near them east of
the Vistula, and on the shores of the Black Sea.[1]

[1] See Thomsen, quoted *supra*, p. 26.

The common word in the Slavonic languages for
king, *korol, kral*, has a curious derivation, viz., from
the name of Karl the Great (Charlemagne). The
primitive Slavs, living in their communes, forming
a democratic agricultural society, knew nothing of a
king, but took the word from the great monarch
who impressed his individuality so vigorously upon
them by his severities. The word knout, which
has become among us a very symbol of the
so-called Tatar barbarism, is, no doubt, an Indo-
European word, the same as our knot, old Norse
knutr ; and perhaps the common Slavonic *kniga*,
book, is connected with the old Norse *kenning*,
learning, our ken, cunning. Many other interesting
instances are given in Tamm's "Slaviska Lå-
nord från Nordiska Språk" ("Slavonic Loan-words
from Northern Languages"), Upsala. The great
importance of the study of the Slavonic languages for
comparative philology was fully recognised by Bopp
and Schleicher. Their position in the Indo-European
family may be clearly seen by the table given in
Schleicher's "Compendium," p. 9. The "Comparative Grammar of the Slavonic Languages," by Professor Miklovich of Vienna, is the monumental work
in which the relation of each of the Slavonic languages
to the others can be traced.

But to return to the Russian ballad-stores. Mention
must also be made of the *podbloudnia piesni*, literally,
songs relating to the dish, sung to a favourite
mode of divination among peasant girls by means
of objects concealed in a dish. This forms an

amusement of the winter evenings from Christmas till Twelfth Night. On New Year's Eve is sung the song of Ovsen, a sort of god of the New Year, who brings fruitfulness with him. As the young men who go about on this occasion scatter oats, the whole ceremony probably derives its name from the custom, as *oves* (pronounced *avyos*) is equivalent to oats. There are also *Khorovods*, or songs accompanied by dancing. Many specimens of the refrains chanted on these occasions may be found in the common Russian song-books. They are frequently pretty, and not merely quaint, and must astonish those who are prepared to find only barbarism among the lower classes of Russia.

The Russian peasant is surrounded with ceremonies and superstitions from his very cradle. Among no people in Europe have customs and traditions lingered so much : hence the rich field which Slavonic nations offer in folk-lore and folk-song.[1]

And here a few words may be introduced on the subject of Slavonic mythology, which, even up to the present time, is in a somewhat confused state. A very good summary of what is known of it, written in a sober fashion, will be found in the little work of M. Louis Leger, "Esquisse Sommaire de la Mythologie Slave," Paris, 1882.[2] The two most

---

[1] For much curious information on Russian superstitions and songs the reader must be referred to the valuable work of Mr. Ralston, "The Songs of the Russian People."

[2] A more elaborate work, but full of wild theories, is "Wissenschaft des Slawischen Mythus," Lemberg, 1842, by Hanus. There is also another by Schwenk.

F

important sources of information on the deities of the
Slavs are Procopius and Helmold. The former says,
"They believe in one god only, the fabricator of
lightning, and think that he rules everything (*Perun*),
and they offer to him oxen and all kinds of sacrifices.
They know nothing about fate, nor do they think it
has any influence in human affairs. But when death
is at hand, or they are seized by illness, or are getting
ready for war, they promise that they will offer a
sacrifice to the god as a thank-offering for their lives
if they escape. And if they do escape they carry out
the promised sacrifice, and think that they purchased
their preservation at this price. They worship rivers
and nymphs and certain other deities, and sacrifice
to all of them, and draw their divinations from these
sacrifices."[1]

In all Sclavonic languages the name of God is
Bog, which is thus explained by Miklosich :[2]—" *Bog*
is identical with the Sanskrit *bhaga*, master,—properly,
distributor. It is an epithet of God, and the proper
name of a Vedic divinity; old Persian, *boga*, old
Bactrian, *bagha*, God; the Indian *bhaga* signifies
also prosperity, happiness. It is not easy to deter-
mine if it is the first or the second sense which has
served for the point of departure of the Slavonic
word ; the words *bogati*, rich, and *oubogi*, poor, can
be cited in support of the second meaning." Besides
the Greek and Latin author previously mentioned

---

[1] Procopius, as quoted in Schafarik, "Slawische Alterthümer,"
vol. ii., p. 661.

[2] As quoted by M. Leger, p. 9.

for the gods of the Slavs of Novgorod and Kiev we have the Russian chroniclers as authorities. For Poland, Bohemia, Servia, Croatia, and Bulgaria, there are no early documents, except, perhaps, occasional fragments of songs containing allusions to heathen deities and their worship. Traces are to be found of the *cultus* of the sun under the name of Dazhbog, son of Svarog, the god of the sky; and Cyril, of Tourov, alludes to the time when the Slavs worshipped the elements.[1] The fabricator of lightning or thunder, spoken of by Procopius, may, without doubt, be identified with Peroun, who is known to have had a statue at Novgorod by Lake Ilmen, and also at Kiev. In the treaties concluded in the tenth century between the Russians and the Byzantine Greeks, the Russians are found swearing by Peroun, and Veles, the god of flocks, according to Nestor. Although the idol of Peroun was destroyed by Vladimir, the hero of the bilini, when Christianity was introduced in 988, yet the god was transmuted into the saint Ilya (Elijah), who has become the saint of thunder, and perhaps is in some way connected with the tradition of Ilya Murometz, of whom I have already spoken.

It is Ilya who produces the thunder as he rolls through the skies in his chariot of fire. Veles, the god of flocks, has become St. Basil, and the festival of Koupalo, the god of the summer solstice, has been naturally changed into that of St. John. A kind of

---

[1] Cited by Leger, p. 13.

god of the winds was Stribog, whose name has been preserved by the chronicler Nestor, and the author of the prose-poem on the expedition of Igor, to be spoken of afterwards. There is also a goddess Lada, said to have been a Slavonic Venus, whose name is occasionally met with in the refrains of songs. The great god of the Baltic Slavs was Svantovit, who was worshipped in the island of Rügen, once Slavonic territory. Besides these are Triglav, the three-headed god, Radigost, and others.

Among the more picturesque of these Russian superstitions may be mentioned the *lieshie*, or wood-demons; the *vodiani*, or water-sprites; and *rousalki*, or naiads, corresponding in some particulars to the Servian *vilas*. There is also the *domovoi*, or house-spirit, a kind of Robin Goodfellow, who is represented as a dwarf, and has his habitation in the stove. The Eastern Slavs are richer in all these beliefs than the Western, as might have been expected from their comparative remoteness from the great European centres. The ignorance of the peasantry and the scantiness of printed literature explain the abundance of popular song. We find that condition among Slavonic peoples in which popular poetry (in its strictest sense) is possible. Every member of the family, down to the humble Lusatian Wend, almost smothered by his German neighbours, can boast a fine flower-show both of lays and legend. It was beautifully and truthfully said by Schafarik, that wherever there is a Slavonic woman there also is a song.

So much then for the Russian bîlini or legendary poems, which were treated with contempt by scholars till within the last fifty years. The attention paid to popular literature throughout Europe awoke also the curiosity of the Russians, who were ignorant of the great treasures which they possessed. Ample justice has, however, now been done to them in the collections of Ribnikov, Kirievski, Hilferding, Barsov, Bezsonov, and others. Of the Skazki, or National Tales, there are good collections by Sakharov, Afanasiev, and others. In the old-fashioned days the ladies were lulled to sleep by their female serfs who narrated to them these quaint legends. The stories told to Poushkin by his nurse, Arina Rodiovna, are said to have quickened his genius, and Lermontov has recorded his regret that he had not more often kindled his torch at the same light. In his piece entitled "Song about the Tzar Ivan Vasilievich, the Young Oprichnik, and the Bold Merchant Kalashnikov," he has given us an excellent imitation of a bîlina.[1]

II. We now come to our second division, viz., the written literature, which I shall carry as far as the period of the reforms introduced by Peter the Great at the close of the seventeenth century.

The celebrated Ostromir Codex (1056–1057), the earliest monument of Slavonic literature of which the date is known, is a Russian recension of an old Bulgarian original, and had therefore better be left

---

[1] For a more detailed account of the Russian Skazki, see the excellent work of Mr. Ralston, " Russian Folk-Tales,' London, 1873.

till we come to consider the old Bulgarian or
Palæoslavonic literature. Belonging to the year
1073, we have the Izbornik Sviatoslavov, or Miscellany of Sviatoslav. This manuscript is preserved
in the Synodal Library of Moscow. It was written
by John the Deacon for Prince Sviatoslav, and is a
translation from the Greek. The contents of this
curious collection are not merely theological,—
philosophy, rhetoric, and other branches of learning
are also handled in it, and it is styled by Bouslaev[1]
a kind of Russian encyclopedia. We must remember
that it was from Constantinople that early Russia
drew its civilisation. The next important monument
of the language is the " Discourse concerning the Old
and New Testament " by Ilarion, Metropolitan of
Kiev. This curious treatise is based on a parallel
between the Old and New Testament under the
names of Hagar and Sarah. It has an historical
interest inasmuch as it contains an elaborate pane-
gyric of Prince Vladimir of Kiev, the hero, let us remember, of one of the cycles of bilini, who in the tenth
century introduced Christianity into Russia. Another
interesting sermon or discourse of the same kind is
that by Theodosius, a monk of the Pestcherski cloister
of Kiev on the Latin or Varangian Faith. In this,
as Bouslaev says, we may see what the early Russians

---

[1] Rousskaia Khristomatia (Russian Chrestomathy), 2nd
edition. Moscow, 1877. This valuable work is entirely devoted to the early memorials of the language, which are chronologically arranged. Bouslaev also published an Historical
Grammar.

thought of the Roman Catholic religion. A few words may here be said about Kiev, which is one of the sacred places of Russia. This ancient city was visited, according to Nestor, by St. Andrew and on the spot where he fixed the cross, a magnificent cathedral now stands dedicated to him. The Pestchers-kaia Lavra, that is, the Monastery of the Catacombs, contains the bodies of many of the Russian Saints and other historical persons including Nestor himself. Kiev is a great place for pilgrimages, and is visited annually by about 300,000 persons. Besides the work above mentioned, Theodosius wrote some other *Pouchenia*, or Instructions, characterised by their simplicity of style and practical nature, among others one on drunken-ness. Another writer was Luke Zhidiata, appointed bishop of Novgorod in 1036, who has left a short but very interesting " Discourse to the Brethren."

With Nestor, a monk of Kiev (born about the year 1056, died about 1114), begins the series of Russian chronicles. He appears to have been well acquainted with the Byzantine historians. We find many legends mixed up with his work ; the style is frequently highly coloured and poetical so that we cannot help suspecting that he has incorporated bílini which had been lost, just as the Polish historians, Gallus, Kadlubek, and Dlugosz, did. Prosaic details alternate with such passages ; historical events are mixed up in some of the Russian chronicles with details of the weather and the narration of portents. We are thus reminded of our own Anglo-Saxon chronicle. As a specimen of the style of Nestor let us take his quaint account of the death of Oleg, which has formed the subject of a spirited ballad by the Russian poet, Poushkin :—

"And Oleg lived, having peace on all sides, ruling in Kiev.   And Oleg remembered his horse, whom he had entrusted to others to feed, himself never seeing him.   For a long time ago he had asked the wizards and magicians, ' From whom it is fated that I should die ?' And one of the magicians said to him : 'Prince, the horse which thou lovest and upon which thou ridest shall be the cause of thy death.'   Oleg receiving this into his mind said, ' I will never ride the horse nor see him any more.'   And he ordered them to take care of the horse, but never to bring it to him again ; and several years passed, and he rode him no more, and he went among the Greeks.   And he returned to Kiev, and stayed there four years, and in the fifth he remembered his horse, by whom the soothsayers had predicted that Oleg would die, and, having called the oldest of his grooms, he said : ' Where is my horse, which I enjoined you to feed and take care of ?'   And they said : ' He is dead.' And Oleg smiled and found fault with the soothsayer and said : ' The wizard spoke falsely and it is all a lie ; the horse is dead and I am alive.'   And he ordered them to saddle his steed for he wished to see the bones of the horse.   And he came to the place, where the bones and the skull lay unburied.   And he leaped from his steed, and said with a smile : ' How can a skull be the cause of my death ?'   And he planted his foot on the skull, and out darted a snake.

and bit him on the foot, and from the wound he fell
sick and died. And all the people lamented with
great lamentation and carried him and buried him
on the mountain, called Stchekovitza. There is his
grave to this day, and it is called 'the grave of Oleg.'
And all the years of his reigning were thirty-three."
This curious story is found in other parts of Europe,
besides Russia; it belongs to the common stock of
Aryan mythology. As an eye-witness Nestor could
only describe the reigns of Vsevolod and Sviatopolk
(1078–1112); but he gathered many interesting details
from the lips of aged men, two of whom he especially
mentions, Giorata Rogovich, an inhabitant of Novgorod, probably a merchant, who furnished him with
information concerning the extreme north of Russia,
Pechora, and other places; and, secondly, Jan, an old
man ninety years of age, who deceased in 1106,
and was son of a certain Vishata, the voievode of
Yaroslav, and grandson of Ostromir, the Posadnik,
for whom the celebrated Codex was written.

The chain of the chronicles extends in almost un-
broken continuity to the days of Alexis Mikhailovich,
the father of Peter the Great. Of the two breaks
which occur the first is in the time of Vasilii, or Basil,
son of Dmitri Donskoi, and the second in the days
of Ivan the Terrible (1534–84). In a note to the
first volume of his history (St. Petersburg, 1818,
p. xxxii.), Karamzin tells us that there are upwards of
a thousand of these annalists preserved in Russia, to
say nothing of short compendiums. Every town of
the least importance had its annalist, and Novgorod,

the great, boasted of several. A good edition of these chronicles was published at St. Petersburg in 1846, including Nestor, who has been translated into Polish, Cech, German, and French,[1] but not into our own language. It is necessary to study them in order to understand Russian history, and we can see by his notes what extensive use has been made of them by Karamzin. But to return to Nestor, there are several manuscripts of this interesting work ; the oldest which has been preserved (the Lavrentievski) dates from the year 1377. Thus, unfortunately, we have none that are contemporary. Besides writing this chronicle, he compiled lives of the Russian Saints, Boris and Gleb, and the Igoumen Theodosius. A certain school of Russian critics, headed by Professor Ilovaïski, has attempted to throw doubt on the genuineness of this important work, but he has been completely refuted by Pogodine. Among the continuators of Nestor were monks of Kiev, Volïnia, Pskov, Novgorod, and Souzdal. The annals of Pskov are full of the quarrels of the people with the neighbouring Germans, and their proud mother-city, Novgorod. In the year 1510 the independence of the former city was annihilated by Basil, the father of Ivan the Terrible, and it is in the following manner that the writer of the chronicle laments his downfall :—

"Then disappeared the glory of Pskov and our city was captured not by those of another faith, but by those of our own faith. Who would not weep and groan

---

[1] A new translation is promised by M. Leger.

about this? O glorious and great city of Pskov, for what dost thou lament and weep? And the beautiful city of Pskov answered, How can I help weeping and grieving about the desolation which has befallen me. A many-winged eagle has flown to me with lion's claws and has taken from me all my beauty and wealth and carried off my children." Of the same kind are the Imperial Book (Tzarstvennaïa Kniga) and the Genealogical Book (Stepennaïa Kniga) so called because it gives the seventeen degrees of the generations of the imperial family from the time of Vladimir I. We can thus see that there is plenty of material for Russian history, only these compilations want sifting and reducing to shape.

The early Russian travellers are worthy of some attention. First of these must be mentioned the Igoumen Daniel, who visited the Holy Land in the time of the Grand Duke Sviatopolk Mikhail (1093–1113). The Byzantine Emperor at the time was Baldwin I. Daniel was probably a monk from the government of Chernigov, as may be inferred from his comparing the Jordan with the Snov, which flows through that province. A later traveller was Athanasius Nikítin, a merchant of Tver, who visited Golkonda and the Dekkan in 1470, and left an account of his journey.[1] Anastasius writes as follows:—"I started

---

[1] "Travels of Athanasius Nikítin," translated by Count Vielhorski, and edited for the Hakluyt Society by R. Major, in "India in the Fifteenth Century." There is also a valuable monograph on the subject by Sreznevski.

from the church of our Holy Saviour of Zlatoverkh, with the kind permission of the Grand Duke Michael Borisovich and the Bishop Gennadius of Tver, went down the Volga, came to the convent of the holy life-giving Trinity, and the holy shrines of Boris and Gleb, the martyrs, and received the blessing of the Igumen Macarius, and his brethren. From Koliazin I went to Ouglich, thence to Kostroma, to the Knez Alexander with an epistle." He took a horse with him through all his travels, and when in India he says : "At Joneer the Khan took away my horse, and having heard that I was no Mahometan, but a Russian, said, 'I will give thee the horse, and a thousand pieces of gold, if thou wilt embrace our faith, the Mahometan faith ; and if thou dost refuse I shall keep the horse and take a thousand pieces of gold upon thy head.' He gave me four days to consider, and all this occurred during the Fast of the Assumption of Our Lady, on the Eve of Our Saviour's Day (Aug. 18th). And the Lord took pity on me because of His holy festival, and did not withdraw His mercy from me, His sinful servant, and allowed me not to perish at Jooneer among the infidels. On the eve of Our Saviour's Day there came a man from Khorassan, Khozaiécha Mahomet, and I implored him to pity me. He repaired to the Khan in the town, and praying him, delivered me from being converted and took from him my horse. Such was the Lord's wonderful mercy on the Saviour's day."

He also makes the following pious reflections at Dabul : "And there it was that I, Athanasius, the sinful servant of God, bethought myself of the Christian religion, of the Lent fastings ordained by the holy fathers, of the baptism of Christ, and of the precepts of the apostles, and I made up my mind to go to Russia. May God preserve the Russian land. God preserve this world and more especially from hell; may He bestow His blessings on the dominions of Russia and the Russian nobility, and may the Russian rule increase."

There is also a narrative of the adventures of two merchants sent by Ivan the Terrible, viz., Korobeinikov and Grekov, with a present of 77,000 florins to the patriarchs of Constantinople and Alexandria, and to the monks who guarded the Holy Sepulchre, desiring them to pray without ceasing for the soul of his son, whom he had killed with his iron staff in a state of ungovernable fury. A modernised version of this narrative was published at Moscow in 1830, by Ivan Mikhaïlov. Vladimir Monomakh, who was Grand Duke from 1053 to 1125, composed, after the Byzantine fashion, an " Instruction " (*Pouchenie*) for his sons, which is curious for the picture of the manners of the times which it presents.[1] The following extract will give an idea of the piece : " In war be vigilant ; be an example to your boyars. Never retire to rest till you have posted your guards. When you travel through your provinces, do not allow your attendants to do injury to the

---

[1] This interesting memorial of the ancient Slavs is printed in extenso in Bielowski, "Monumenta Poloniæ Historica," i., 864.

inhabitants. If you find yourself afflicted by any illness, make three prostrations to the ground before the Lord; and never let the sun find you in bed." "At the dawn of day my father and all the good men did thus, they glorified the Lord. They then seated themselves to deliberate, or to administer justice to the people, or they went to the chase, and in the middle of the day they slept, which God permits to man as well as to the beasts and birds. As for me, I accustomed myself to do everything that I might have ordered my servants to do. Night and day, in the summer heat and winter cold I knew no rest. I wished to see everything with my own eyes. Never did I abandon the poor or the widows to the insolence of the powerful. I made it my duty to see the churches and the sacred ceremonies of religion, as well as the management of my household, my stables, and the hawks and falcons, with which I hunted." He afterwards recounts his various expeditions against the enemy, and the perils he had undergone in the chase. It is interesting to us Englishmen to know that Vladimir married Gyda, a daughter of Harold, who fell at Senlac. Passing by the writings of Cyril, the bishop of Tourov, we come to the well-known "Story of the expedition of Prince Igor" (*Slovo o polkou Igoreve*), which is a kind of prose bílina (some modern scholars have attempted to construct it in rhythmical form), which narrates an expedition of the year 1185. The manuscript volume, which contained this production, came originally from the

monastery of the Saviour at Yaroslavl, but was unfortunately burned in the conflagration, which took
place at Moscow in the year 1812. Luckily the piece
had been printed, but very carelessly, by Count
Mousin-Poushkin, and a transcription was also found
among the papers of the Empress Catherine II. Concerning the authenticity of this prose-poem, there has
been a controversy, which would occupy too much
space to be discussed here. The chief difficulties
have been the prose-poetical style, and the many
expressions which seem to show that the author was
acquainted with the classical writers and poems of
chivalry. Moreover, there is a strange mixture of
heathen and classical allusions. This M. Courrière
in his "Histoire de la Littérature contemporaine
en Russie," explains in the following fashion. He
supposes that the song of Igor was composed by
a bard, who formed part of the drouzhina of the
Grand Duke. "This militia, by reason of its origin
and warlike character, was but little under religious
influence. Like the people it had faithfully preserved
the antique traditions of the ancient bohatîri: it
modelled its *piesni* on the old legends." Something
like the same mixture is found in the "Discourse of
a Lover of Christ, and Advocate of the True Faith,"
printed by Bouslaev in his Chrestomathy.

A few extracts from the "Slovo" will give some idea
of its style. The expedition of Igor, prince of Novgorod Severski in Chernigov, is undertaken against the
Polovtzes, a Tartar tribe in the south of Russia. He
thus addresses his troops, "I wish to break my lance

in their remote steppes, to lay my head there or to drink up the Don from my helmet." The numerous army assembles : " The horses neigh on the Soula, the thunder of glory resounds in Kiev, in Novgorod are heard the trumpets, the standards wave in Poutivl : Igor awaits his dear brother Vsevolod." Vsevolod describes his warriors in the following florid manner, for the whole piece is full of oriental hyperbole : " Their bows are strung, their quivers are open, their swords are sharpened, they bear themselves in the field like grey wolves, they seek honours for themselves and glory for their prince." Igor hastens to assist his brother. We are told that the earth was deluged with blood and strewn with carcasses : there was no more supply of the *wine of blood*. In fact, there is a profusion of the grim metaphors which give such ghastliness to some of the Anglo-Saxon poems. The wife of Igor, Yaroslavna, the daughter of Yaroslav, is represented as weeping and anxious at Poutivl : " I will fly like a cuckoo over the Danube. I will dip my gloves of beaver skin in the river Kayala : in the morning I will wash the bleeding wounds on the brave body of my prince. . . . O glorious Dnieper, thou forcest thy way by the rocks through the territory of the Polovtzes. Thou didst bear on thy waves the barks of Sviatoslav against the host of Kobiak,[1] bring, lord, my beloved one to me so that I may not any more send him early my tears by the sea. . . . . O bright, very bright sun ! to all thou art warm and

---

[1] Alluding to a previous expedition of Igor against Kobiak, prince of the Polovtzes, in 1171.

beautiful; why, lord, hast thou darted thy burning rays on the beloved warriors? Why in the desert without water, in their thirst dost thou direct on them thy rays? why dost thou make their quivers useless, through their sufferings? Wherefore, O powerful wind, with thy light wings, didst thou waft the arrows of the Khan against the warriors of my love? Was it not enough for thee to make the blue sea swell and to float the vessels by its undulations?" As Igor is coming back sailing on the river Donetz, the author invests the river with life and makes it address the hero, "There is no little glory for thee, Igor, and vexation to the Khan, and rejoicing to the Russian land." The prince answers, "It is no little boast to thee, Donetz, when thou floatest Igor on thy waters." The rhapsodist winds up in the following way, "It is bad for the head to be without the shoulders, and bad for the shoulders without the head. Happy is the land and many the people triumphing in the rescue of Igor. Glory to the Princes and their Host." So ends this strange production, which in many places resembles the Irish prose-poems, such as the description of the Battle of Clontarf, in "The War of the Gaedhill with the Gaill," and "The Battle of Magh Rath."

I am compelled to pass over several lives of saints and religious discourses, and the legendary stories of the "Tzar Solomon," drawn from Byzantine sources, to come to the Zadonstchina, a prose-poem, very much in the style of the "Story of the Expedition of Igor." The former piece celebrates the great victory gained

by Dmitri Donski over the Tartars at the Battle of
"Koulikovo Pole,"—the field of woodcocks.   It was
first published by Undolski in 1852.   It is said to
have been composed by a monk named Sophronius.

The story of Drakoula (Poviest o Drakoulé) is a
collection of anecdotes concerning a very cruel prince
of Moldavia, who lived in the beginning of the fifteenth century.   According to Bouslaev the work
became more popular in Russia during the reign of
Ivan the Terrible on account of the parallel which
could be drawn by the Russians between his atrocities
and those of the Moldavian prince.   Here we first
find the following highly dramatic story.   "On one
occasion some ambassadors came to him from the
Turkish Tzar.   They entered and bowed before him,
but, according to custom, did not take their hats
from their heads.   Whereupon he asked of them,
'Wherefore act ye thus?   Do ye come to a great
prince and act so shamefully?'   But they answered
and said, 'The laws of our land hold this custom.'
But he replied, 'I also have a mind to make stronger
your custom, and do ye stand firmly to it.'   And he
ordered his attendants to take iron nails and nail their
hats to their heads."   This tale is told by Collins, the
English physician to Alexis Mikhailovich, in his interesting book on Russia, of the Tzar Ivan the Terrible,
and he is said to have acted in this way to a French
ambassador.   But there is an earlier authority.   Heylyn, in his Microcosmos, Oxford, 1629, says (p. 346),
"And truly there is no nation so kindly entertained
amongst the Russians, both prince and people, as the

English, who have many immunities not granted to other nations. The cause I cannot but attribute to the never-dying fame of our late Queene, admired and loved of the Barbarians; and also to the conformable behauiour of the English in generall, which hath been so plausible, that when Wasiliwich or Basiliades nayl'd the hat of another forraine ambassador to his head, for his peremptorinesse, he at the same time vsed our S. Thomas Smith with all curtesie imaginable."

And here, perhaps, would be a fitting place to say a few words about the various codifications of the Russian laws.

(1) The Rousskaia Pravda of Yaroslav, which is preserved in the Chronicle of Novgorod.[1] In this we see that the early Slavs, before they had undergone the evil influence of the Tatars, had very much the same institutions as those prevalent among other European nations at the time: for instance, the trial by wager of battle, trial by ordeal, and circuit of judges.

The following enactments of this early code are worth our attention :—

If a man were murdered, his relations might take the life of the murderer; if there were no relations, atonement must be made by payment of a sum of money into the treasury. There is a graduated list of penalties, varying, of course, according to the rank of the person slain. The penalty for murdering a woman is only half of that for the death of a man.

[1] " Das älteste Recht der Russen," von Joh. Ewers. Dorpat, 1826.

Nothing need be paid for killing a slave, if he gave provocation; if he were slain without any reasonable pretext,—a point which was no doubt very arbitrarily settled,—compensation for his loss must be made to the master. According to the scale of fines settled in these laws, we can form an accurate idea of the gradations of ranks then existing in the Russian principalities. First came the Boyars; in the second rank soldiers, persons attached to the court, landowners, and merchants; in the third, slaves belonging to the Grand Dukes, the Boyars, and the Monasteries. These slaves were originally, in most instances, captives in war and their descendants, but there were many other ways in which a man might become a slave,—*e.g.* insolvent debtors, and those who, being free, married slaves. If the murdered could not be found, the district in which the crime was committed was assessed. Injury to limbs was also atoned for by pecuniary compensation, heavy damages being laid for pulling the hair out of a man's beard. A regular scale of fines was also imposed for blows. If, after having struck a freeman, a slave conceals himself, and his master does not deliver him up, the latter must pay twelve grivnas to the person injured, who has the right of putting to death the slave who has committed the offence, wherever he shall find him. A burglar caught at night, *flagrante delicto*, might be slain by the master of the house.

Whoever stole a horse forfeited his liberty. "So important," adds Karamzin, "was this animal, the true servant of man in war, in agriculture, and in

travel." The penalty, however, for stealing an ox
was only a fine. One curious enactment is another
proof of the jealousy with which the possession of a
horse was guarded. If any one rides another man's
horse without having obtained its owner's leave, he
shall pay a penalty of three grivnas. According to
Karamzin a similar law prevailed among the Low
Germans of Jutland. The law of succession is not
very clearly stated in this code. Males appear to
have been preferred to females, and the youngest son
was always to take the father's house, as being less
able to provide himself with a livelihood.

(2) The Laws of Ivan III.

(3) The Laws of Ivan IV. the Terrible.—The
Stoglav·and Soudebnik.

(4) The Ordinance (*oulozhenie*) of the Tzar Alexis
Mikhailovich, father of Peter the Great. The three
first of these codes are printed at full length in the
very convenient work, edited in Bohemian, at Prague,
by Dr. Hermenegild Jirecek, and entitled "Svod
Zákunuv Slovanskych " (Collection of Slavonic Laws).
The law-book, or Soudebnik, of the Tzar Ivan III.
was published in 1497. When Herberstein, the
ambassador from the emperor of Germany to Muscovy, visited the country in 1517, he was made
acquainted with some of the enactments of this code,
and has given a translation in his very interesting
work, " Rerum Muscovitarum Commentarii," of
which so many editions appeared during the sixteenth century. Herberstein was one of the earliest
and one of the most intelligent travellers in Russia.

The second work of importance is that of Giles
Fletcher, "Of the Russe Commonwealth," Lond.,
1591. This, the first edition, has now become very
scarce, as by order of Elizabeth it was suppressed
owing to the candid and severe remarks made
upon the emperor and the country by the author.
Elizabeth at that time was very anxious to be on
good terms with Ivan on account of the advantages
of the Russian trade, of which the English had for
many years the monopoly.[1]

The Soudebnik of Ivan IV. is founded upon that
of his grandfather. The ordinance of the Emperor
Alexis is a much more copious document. The
original manuscript of this code is still preserved at
the Kremlin, written upon a series of rolls, as is frequently the case with Slavonic manuscripts, and preserved in a casket, in which it was placed by order
of the empress, Catherine II.

In the year 1553 a printing-press was set up in
Moscow, and here was printed, in 1564, the first book,
—an Apostol, as it is called by the Slavs,—*i.e.*, a book
containing the Acts of the Apostles and the Epistles.
The chief printers were Ivan Fedorov and Peter
Mstislavetz. In other Slavonic countries the art of
printing had been introduced much earlier. Thus
we have Bohemian books printed in Gothic letters at
Pilsen in 1468 and 1475, and in Cyrillic by Sveipolt Fiol
at Cracow in 1491. About the year 1525 there was a

---

[1] See the interesting work, "England and Russia, 1553–
1593," published at St. Petersburg in 1875, both in Russian
and English, by Youri Tolstoi.

press at Vilna, and as early as 1548 Ivan the Terrible
had invited printers from Germany, but did not succeed in securing their services.

The labours of Fedorov and his companion were
destined to be of but short duration.   The efforts of
those who earned a living by copying books, and the
prejudices of the superstitious, prevailed.   The printers
were driven out of Russia, and found a refuge in
Lithuania, having lost their protector, Macarius, the
Metropolitan of Moscow, who died in 1564.   Ivan
Federov was warmly received by Sigismund III. of
Poland, and printed several books in that country,
among others the well-known Bible of Ostrog in 1581.
A copy of this rare book is preserved in the British
Museum, and actually came from the library of Ivan.
It was brought from Russia by Sir Jerome Horsey.
On the fly-leaf is the following memorandum in
Horsey's own hand :—" This Bibell in the Slavonian
tonge had owt of the Emperor's librari."

Some very interesting details about the progress of
the art of printing in Slavonic countries are given by
Pipin in his often-cited history.   He shows us (as
might have been expected) how much more active
the presses were in the western and southern Slavonic
countries than in the principality of Moscow.   Up to
the year 1600 only sixteen books had been issued
by the Moscow press, but in the west and south, 67 ;
up to 1625, by the Moscow press, 65 ; and by the
western and southern, 147.   In Great Russia, or, as
it was then called, Muscovy, there was only one press
at the capital, whereas in the other countries they were

frequently to be found in small towns and even at monasteries.   Besides the presses already mentioned, at Lemberg a book was printed in 1574, at Kiev in 1614, and at Chernigov in 1646.

As the early-printed Slavonic books are great rarities, the following facts may interest the curious :— The first primer was printed at Vilna in 1596; afterwards, at Moscow, two by Bourtzov in 1634 and 1637, and a Slavonic Greek and Latin Primer by Polikarpov in 1701.   The first Greek Slavonic grammar, called Ἀδελφότης, was printed at Lemberg in 1591 ; the second, the Slavonic grammar of Lavrentii Zizanii, at Vilna, in 1596; the grammar of Smotritzki followed this.   The first Palæoslavonic and Russian grammar was published by Berinda, at Kiev, in 1627.   The first grammar of the Russian language appeared at Oxford in the year 1696 by Henry Ludolf, brother of the author of the " History of Æthiopia."   It was written, no doubt, on account of the great curiosity excited everywhere by the adventures of Peter the Great, the most conspicuous lion of the time.   The types with which this book was printed are still in the possession of the Clarendon Press ; they are, however, very far removed from the elegance to which Cyrillic printing has been brought in Russia and some other countries.

One of the most curious books of the period of Ivan the Terrible is the Domostroi, or Book of Household Management, said to have been written by the Monk Sylvester, although this has been contradicted.   This ecclesiastic—if he were the author—was at one time in great favour with Ivan, but having offended him, was banished by the tyrant to the Solovetzki monastery, where he died. The work was primarily addressed by the priest to his son Anthemus and his daughter-in-law Pelagia, but as the greater part of it was of a general character, it soon became used in all households. This father of the Church is most comprehensive in his details; he discusses religious duties and descends even to the details of the kitchen and the mysteries of cookery. We get many glimpses into social life among the early Russians in this book, and see the humiliating position in which women and children were placed in the family. The wife is to be constantly weaving and making clothes, with the assistance of her domestics. But even in her management of them she can hardly move a step without the directions of her husband. Her greatest honour consisted in attending to his wants: in fact, she was under an Oriental despotism. Personal chastisement might be inflicted upon her for her faults. Sylvester, if we are to trust the account of himself, must have been a benevolent man. He thus writes to his son: "I have freed all my slaves; they now live in their own houses and are full of good wishes for us. Many orphans and poor people I have nourished from their childhood, both at Moscow and Novgorod. I have taught them to write, to paint *icons* (sacred pictures), to copy books, or to earn their living by some other trade; and thy mother has brought up poor girls, has taught them to work, trained them for the duties of a household, and having prepared them has settled them in marriage. Many of these we have trained are now priests, or clerks, or work in shops." The seclusion of women was to be broken through by Peter the Great when he established his assemblies after the manner of the French. Sylvester appears in his work as a rigorous conservative, and an opponent of all foreign innovations.

About this time, Macarius, the metropolitan of Moscow, composed the Chetii-Minei, or Monthly Readings, a book which contains extracts from the Greek Fathers arranged for every day· of the week. The compilation of this work is said to have occupied him twelve years.

An important writer of the time of Ivan the Terrible was Prince Kourbski. Andrew Mikhailovich Kourbski, descended from the princes of Yaroslavl, was born about the year 1528. In his younger days he distinguished himself as a soldier, and fought at Kazan and with the Livonian knights. But, having quarrelled with Ivan, he fled to Poland, where he was well received by Sigismund Augustus. He died in 1587 or 1588. Immediately on his flight from the country he commenced an angry correspondence with Ivan, reproaching him for his many cruelties. The story is well known how he deputed his faithful servant, Ivan Shibanov, to convey one of these epistles to Ivan, who, while he read it, kept striking the feet of the unfortunate messenger with his iron staff till they streamed with blood.[1]

[1] This occurrence has formed the subject of a ballad by Count A. Tolstoi.

Many of the compositions of the tyrant himself have been preserved, not the least curious of which is the letter which he wrote to Cosmas and the Brotherhood of the Cyrillian Monastery on the White Lake (Bieloe Ozero).

A very interesting work is the chronograph, as he styles it, of Sergius Koubasov, the son of a boyar of Tobolsk. In the first quarter of the seventeenth century he compiled this record, which extends from the foundation of the world to the election of Mikhail Romanov. The early part is taken from the Byzantine chroniclers, but the most valuable is that which commences with the reign of Ivan the Terrible, because the author then writes from his own personal knowledge. Not the least curious part of his book is where he gives us descriptions of the appearance of the Tzar and members of the Imperial family. Thus he tells us that Ivan the Terrible was tall and ugly, with a long flat nose and grey eyes ; lean, but with broad shoulders.[1] A more lovely picture is given of the unfortunate Xenia, daughter of Boris Godunov, who was cruelly thrust into a monastery by the conqueror, the false Demetrius. Thus we are told that she was a girl of wonderful sense ; of a fresh healthy complexion ; large dark eyes, very bright, but especially so when she shed tears. This is altogether a most curious book, and must make us regret that the chronicle of Prince Mstislavski, which he

---

[1] A more favourable description, however, is given of Ivan by Sir Jerome Horsey, in his " Diary," preserved in the British Museum.

showed to Horsey, according to the diary of the latter, and which contained his account of contemporary events, has been lost.

A very important work is the sketch of the Russian Government and the habits of the people, written by one Koshikhin (or Kotoshikhin, for the name is found in both forms), a renegade *diak*, or secretary, which, after having lain for a long time in manuscript in the library of Upsala, in Sweden, was edited in 1840 by the historian Soloviev. Owing to some political intrigues, Kotoshikhin was compelled to leave his country. He was executed at Stockholm about 1669 for the murder of his master. His book is of great value as a picture of the manners of the time ; it is also important as a good piece of early Russian prose-writing. According to Soloviev, the work of Kotoshikhin circulated extensively in Sweden in a Swedish translation. He is thus spoken of by the author of this version : " Fuit profecto solers animo atque etiam ingeniosissimus inter suos coæquales et conterraneos." It appears that during his residence in Sweden he went by the name of Ivan Selitzki. I take him altogether to have been a remarkable man for his time. The picture of his native country drawn by Kotishikhin is not a very favourable one. He tells us of the frequency with which the torture was applied, and how in its agonies the wretched victims accused all kinds of persons, who were themselves in turn visited with it. The boyars, he says, are all ignorant men, and even in the Tzar's *douma*, or council, "sit silently stroking their beards, and make no reply when there is need of their advice." In the details of domestic life we see many Asiatic customs ; at the long banquets and receptions of guests there were endless ceremonies : the richly-embroidered Oriental robes which were worn were without any real elegance. Corpulence and a thick beard were universally admired. The women lived apart, and never made their appearance in the men's assemblies, nor were they ever seen by any one except their nearest relations. Marriages were arranged by the parents as a commercial speculation, and the bridegroom had no opportunity of becoming personally acquainted with his bride. She was only shown to his mother, or some near female relation, and on these occasions they sometimes put a stool under her feet to make her appear taller, or instead of her they brought a handsome female slave ; and in the same way they married to the bridegroom an elder sister instead of a younger, who was more handsome. " Nowhere," says Kotoshikhin, "are such deceptions played with regard to young women as in the Empire of Muscovy." The disappointed husband would frequently persecute his wife till she retired into a monastery. On this account law-suits sometimes occurred between relations, and there were disputes about the marriage portion. As might be expected, Kotoshikhin has but little to tell us about the lower orders. The wretched peasantry, with the outrages heaped upon them for centuries, are merely silent figures in these panoramas of the old Russian life ; we learn more about them from

such books as Giles Fletcher's, in the time of Ivan
the Terrible. Nor has he much to say about the
Church, which, recruited mainly from the lower orders,
has never shown a bold and independent front in
Russia. His talk is of the nobles, of their ignorance
and corruption, and he recommends education as the
great remedy, and education by sending the sons of
leading men to be trained in foreign countries.
During his short reign (1598–1605), Boris Gòdunov,
a far-seeing, and for his time enlightened, man, sent
eighteen students to be educated out of Russia.
Some of these went to France, others to Lübeck
and England. Of the fate of those who went to
France nothing appears to have been heard, but it
is supposed that they never returned, and the same
remark applies to the students at Lübeck. The reign
of Boris was followed by the episode of the troubled
rule of the false Demetrius. Russia was in all the
agonies of internecine war. But after Vasilii Shouiski
had ascended the throne, application was made to
the burgomaster of Lübeck to send them back. There
is no reason, however, to believe that they ever returned. I now come to those sent to England, four
in number. These were committed to the charge of
John Meyrick, a member of the English factory at
Moscow, and were named respectively, Grigoriev,
Koshoukhov, Davîdov, and Kostomarov. When
they were sent for after the Russian troubles, Elizabeth
had been succeeded by James I. In 1613, an embassy came from Mikhail Romanov, the new emperor,
one of the objects of which was to bring the students

back; but they refused to go, and the English Government does not appear to have made any effort to
compel them. Nor was another attempt, eight years
afterwards, more successful. Of their subsequent fate
little is known, but that they remained English
subjects, and one of them, Nicephorus Grigoriev,
was ordained a clergyman of the Church of England.[1]
Professor Brückner has added further details, for
which we are indebted to his interesting " History
of Peter the Great," now in course of publication in
Russia. He tells us that another of these Russian
" children " served in Ireland as secretary to the
Government, and a third busied himself with commercial pursuits in India, the trade of which was just
beginning to be opened to the English. The Russian
who became an ecclesiastic seems to have shown
repugnance to his native country; we are told that
he thanked God on account of the English who had
taken him out of Russia, and uttered many abusive
expressions about the orthodox faith. The descendants of these Russians are probably still living among
us. But, for a long time, any Russian who praised
foreign countries, or wished to visit them, was regarded
as a traitor. In the time of Michael Romanov, Prince
Khvorostin was accused of heresy and treason because
he desired to visit foreign countries, and made the

---

[1] I have thought these facts so curious for us Englishmen as
to warrant this digression. They are taken from an article,
"The First Russian Students" (*Pervíe Rousskie Stoudentí*),
by A. Arseniev in the excellent review, *Historical Messenger*,
July, 1881.

remark that "everybody at Moscow was a fool."
The false Demetrius, whose short reign terminated
in such a sanguinary fashion, gave great offence by
ridiculing the ignorance of the boyars, and promising
to let them visit foreign countries so that they might
get themselves educated. In the times of the Tzars
Michael and Alexis, the wise views of Boris and
Demetrius were ignored. Olearius tells us, that when
a certain merchant of Novgorod wished to send his
son into foreign countries to get him educated, the
Tzar (Alexis) and the Patriarch forbade him.[1] A
hundred years after Boris, the great introducer of
Western culture into Russia, Peter, attempted the
same thing with more successful results.

But already, even during the reign of Alexis, the
father of Peter the Great, there were signs of the
empire being brought under European influence.
Many foreigners entered the Russian service, and
in 1649 the *oulozhenie*, or great code of laws, was
promulgated, which is divided into twenty-five chapters, and was based partly upon the earlier codes of
Ivan III. and IV., and partly upon the laws of the
Byzantine emperors.

A curious work which has come down is the
"Directions for Falconry" (*Ouriadnik Sokolnichia
Pouti*),—always a favourite amusement with the
Russians,—compiled by order of the Tzar Alexis Mik-
hailovich. To this period also belong the works of
the first Panslavist, Youri Krizhanich, who, although

---

[1] "Istoria Petra Velikago," A. Briknera, p. 201.

a Serb by birth, wrote in Russian. His "Critical Servian Grammar" (with comparison of the Russian, Polish, Croatian, and White Russian) is still preserved in manuscript at Moscow. , Very little is known of the life of Krizhanich. He was a Roman Catholic priest, who, upon some accusation which has not been ascertained, was banished to Tobolsk, in Siberia, where he finished this laborious work. He himself has placed at the end of the manuscript "pisano v Sibiri" (written in Siberia). This obscure and unrecognised philologist showed a great deal of insight into his subject, and anticipated many of the views of Vouk Stephanovich. His curious work on the "Russian Empire," which constitutes his claim to be called the earliest advocate of Panslavistic doctrine, was edited by Bezsonov at Moscow, in 1860.[1] The picture drawn by the learned Serb of the condition of Russia is by no means a flattering one. Soloviev speaks of it as exhibiting a "national bankruptcy in an economical and moral sense." So gloomy is the description, that were not the pages of the book glowing with love for Russia, we might well believe that the author wrote under the influence of national animosity. Such is, however, very far from being the case. The great remedy suggested for the country by Krizhanich is education and adopting the improvements of the West. "The other nations, not in one day or year, but little by little, derived

---

[1] In the present century, the idea of panslavism, the *bête noire* of so many of our Western statesmen, was revived by the Bohemian poet, Jan Kollar.

H

instruction from each other, and so we may also learn
if we persevere." These words came at a good time ;
for one of the great characteristics of the reign of the
Emperor Alexis was the tendency shown by Russia
to look towards the West : the ice of barbarism was
gradually melting away, and everything was to be
ready for the great reformer, Peter.

Other works which may be mentioned are the "Account of the Siege of the Monastery of the Troitza,"
near Moscow, by the Poles, and "The Life of the
Patriarch Nicon," by Shousherin. Nicon, as my
readers will doubtless remember, was the indefatigable advocate of Church authority in the reign of
Alexis Mikhailovich, and the head of the commission
for correcting the Slavonic version of the Scriptures,
the alterations in which led to the sect of Staro-
obriadtzi, now very numerous in Russia.   He
was born at Nizhni Novgorod in 1605, the son of
humble parents.   After having been for some time
a monk in the Solovetzki Monastery on an island
in the White Sea, he visited Moscow in 1646, and
by his learning attracted the notice of the Tzar
Alexis.   In 1648 he was made Metropolitan of
Novgorod, and in 1652 Patriarch of Moscow.   He
now set himself about his great task of correcting
the Slavonic version of the Scriptures.   In order to
procure a good collection of manuscripts, he de-
spatched the hieromonach Arsenii Soukhanov to
Mount Athos and the East.   This emissary brought
back about 500 manuscripts, which formed the
nucleus of the now celebrated Synodal Library.   In

1655 and 1656 he summoned two councils of the Church, at which the newly-translated service-books were promulgated, and the old ones called in. This led to the great schism of the Staro-obriadtzi (viz., followers of the old ritual), which has lasted till the present time, a large section of the community refusing to accept the corrected books. Nicon afterwards fell into disgrace, and was degraded by the Tzar to the position of a common monk. He died at Yaroslavl, in 1681. Besides his labours with the sacred books he also edited a series of Russian chronicles.

I shall close my account of early Russian literature with some mention of Simeon Polotzki (1628–80), tutor to the Tzar Feodor, son of Alexis, who was an indefatigable writer of religious and educational works ; but his productions can now only be of antiquarian interest. He is of some importance as having been one of the first to introduce the Russians to the culture of the West, which he had gained by his studies in the University of Kiev, then a part of Polish territory. He appears to have come to Moscow about the year 1664. He wrote several theological works, such as the " Garland of Faith" (*Vienetz Vieri*), and composed poems and religious dramas (*e.g.* " The Prodigal Son, Nebuchadnezzar," &c.). Perhaps the most amusing are his quaint verses on the new palace built by the Tzar Alexis at Kolomenskoe. He also executed a poetical version of the Psalms. Polotzki seems to have had great educational influence among the Russians, and it was in this

sphere that his work principally lay. Professor
Zabielin in his interesting work on " The Domestic
Lives of the Early Russian Tzars," has told us of the
system of education observed in the imperial families
and among the boyars, but his accounts are so
minute that probably no one but a reader taking
deep interest in Slavonic subjects would have patience
to wade through them.   With Polotzki closes the old
period of Russian literature : with the reforms of
Peter the Great, Western influence began and the new
era was inaugurated by Lomonosov.

CHAPTER IV.

EARLY MALO-RUSSIAN AND WHITE RUSSIAN LITERATURE.

IT would be impossible in a little work like the present, the scope of which is not philological, to go into the vexed question of the origin of the Malo-Russian, and whether we are to consider it to be a language or a dialect. It will be sufficient here to quote the great names of Miklosich and Schleicher in support of the former opinion. The Little Russians subject to the Tzar, together with the Rusniaks or Ruthenians, who constitute the bulk of the Austrian province of Gallicia, amount to 16,370,000. The authority over this people in earlier times alternated between the Russians and Poles. One of the earliest capitals of Old Russia was Kiev, still an object of great reverence. Its political glories lasted till it was devastated by the Tatars. If this city had remained the capital of Russia, Malo-Russian would undoubtedly have become the national language. At the present time its orthography is by no means fixed, which is embarrassing to the student. In the books published at Lemberg we find modifications of the Cyrillic alphabet, so as to express some of the peculiar sounds of the language. Its vocabulary is very curious and quite a mine for the philologist, but up to the present time its lexicography has been much neglected, and the activity of the press of Kiev was checked in the reign of the Emperor Alexander II., probably owing to the revolutionist propaganda from Galicia. The whole question is stated in " La Littérature oukrainienne proscrite par le Gouvernement russe, Rapport présenté au Congrès littéraire de Paris 1878," by M. Dragomanov. Still writers in this language are fairly active, and Lemberg is the centre of their labours. The works of Shakspeare are now in course of being translated into Little Russian. When the Lithuanian princes conquered south-western Russia, part was incorporated with their dominions, but in 1386 Lithuania was joined to Poland by the marriage of its prince, Jagiello, with Hedwig, the Polish heiress, who consented to the union on political grounds.

The Cossacks so often mentioned in connexion with the Little Russians were at one time divided into two great families, those of the Don and those of the Dnieper. The former were incorporated with Russia as early as the days of Ivan the Terrible ; the latter, long nominally subject to the Poles, broke out into rebellion under Bogdan Khmelnitzki about the middle of the seventeenth century, who finding that he could not make head against the Polish generals, went over with all his followers to Alexis Mikhailovich, the father of Peter the Great. The Western Cossacks established themselves on some island of the Dnieper where they founded a military republic called the *Sech*. Their numbers were recruited from renegade

Poles, Little Russians, and Tatars, and their sub-
jection to Poland was little more than nominal. The
Cossacks of the Dnieper are frequently called Zapor-
ozhki, or Cossacks beyond the waterfalls. They are
first mentioned in Polish history in the year 1506, in
the time of Sigismund I.,[1] and their first hetman (a
corruption of the German *hauptman*) was Przeclaw
Lanckoronski.[2] In 1518, at the diet of Piotrkow, a
subsidy was granted them on condition of their
defending the Polish frontiers against the Turks.
Another hetman, Daszkiewicz, fashioned them into
something like a regular body of militia. But it was
King Stephen Batory, one of the bravest and most
efficient kings who ever reigned in Poland (1576–
1586), who thoroughly realised how useful they might
be made. By him their forces were divided into six
regiments of one thousand men each, and various
officers put over them. In the war waged by Batory
against Russia in 1586, they performed prodigies of
valour; at the same time as the king rewarded them
for their achievements, he took care that they were
kept in proper discipline. One of their hetmans,
Podkova (in Little Russian, Pídkova [3]), having dis-
obeyed his orders, he caused him to be seized and

---

[1] See "The Cossacks of the Ukraine," by Count II.
Krasinski, London, 1848.

[2] This word was probably borrowed from a Low German
source. It has become Ataman in Russian.

[3] He is said to have gained this name, which signifies, both in
Russian and Polish, a horseshoe, on account of his extraordinary
strength, he having repeatedly broken a horseshoe in two with
his fingers.

beheaded. Some of the *doumi*, or national songs, relate to this chief. The great strongholds of these sturdy freebooters were the islands of Khorchitza, Sednev, and Kaniov ; they fortified themselves by a ring of chariots bound together with iron chains and a deep trench, and they were always plentifully supplied with ammunition. They elected their own hetman amidst festivities, in which much drunkenness prevailed. He had authority over them only in war, and if he conducted a campaign badly or otherwise displeased them they could put him to death. They ate their food at public tables, like the Syssities of the ancients, and no women under pain of death were allowed in the *Sech*. Their corsair incursions were performed in light vessels, called *chaiki*, which could contain from thirty to sixty men, and were armed with cannon ; with these they committed devastations up to the very walls of Constantinople. In these respects they may be compared with the vikings of an earlier period. In the time of Sigismund III. dissensions began to arise between the Polish nobility and the Cossacks. Moreover, Sigismund, who in many respects resembled Ferdinand II. of Austria, was a very zealous Roman Catholic, and made desperate attempts to convert the Cossacks, who belonged to the Greek Church. In 1596 they revolted *en masse*, but were defeated by Zolkiewski, and their chief, Nalivaiko, the subject of many a lay, was condemned to death and executed.[1]   I have already

[1] The manner in which this was accomplished shall be left in the Latin of a chronicler, not certainly of the most Ciceronian

alluded to the secession which took place in the middle of the seventeenth century under Bogdan Khmelnitzki.

While treating of the literatures of the Russian dialects, it will be as well to include here the White Russians in the governments of Mohilev, Minsk, Vitebsk, and Grodno. The old literature of these parts of the present Russian Empire is, as may be imagined, somewhat scanty. Nor, indeed, is it very easy to mark out in the early period what must be considered strictly belonging to Great and what to Little Russia. Thus, according to some, "The Story of the Expedition of Igor," mentioned in the preceding chapter, is more properly Little Russian, and Wiszniewski, taking his stand upon the fact that Kiev and the southern part of Russia belonged in the early period to the Poles, has even ventured to include it in his "History of Polish Literature." First, we have the Law Book (*Soudebnik*) of the year 1468, and the Lithuanian Statute compiled in the years 1522–29. The White Russian Chronicles are small and scanty, and are generally found in the same collections as those which relate to Eastern Russia.[1] A stimulus was given to Little Russian

elegance -"Varsaviam adductus . . . . neque permittebatur somnum capere, sed si quando declinabat oculos in somnum, peditibus ad id vigilantibus, obtusa parte securis monebatur vigilantiæ. Tandem vero equo candenti impositus fuit ac candenti corona coronatus."

[1] There are some valuable documents in the White Russian Archives (Bielorousskii Arkhiv), of which unfortunately only one volume appeared in 1824, edited by Grigorovich.

literature by the press set up at Cracow by Sveipolt
Fiol, where the first book was printed in Cyrillic
letters in 1491. Little Russia, we must remember,
belonged then to Poland. Fiol seems to have been
born in Poland of German parents. His press was
very active, but he fell at last under the censure
of the bishop of Cracow, who suspected him of
Hussitism or an inclination to the Greek Church,
certainly heresy in some form, in consequence of
which he afterwards retired to Hungary. Towards
the end of the fifteenth or beginning of the sixteenth
century we have a translation into Little Russian of
the Song of Solomon, and about the years 1556–1561
a version of the four gospels was made, the so-called
Peresopnitzki Translation.[1] The chief interest, however, in these dialects of the Russian language must
be derived from their oral, and not their written, literature, at all events for the early period with which
we have to do on the present occasion.

The Malo-Russian is very rich in *skazki* (National
Tales) and in songs peculiar to this people is the
"Douma," a narrative poem in most respects corresponding to the Russian *bílina*. In 1819, Prince
Tzertelev published a small volume of these under
the title "Attempt at a Collection of Ancient Songs
of Little Russia." This was followed by the editions
of Maksimovich and Metlinski, but all these works,
although showing considerable learning, have been
thrown into the shade by the elaborate publication of

---

[1] See Pipin and Spasovich, "History of Slavonic Literature," i., 326.

MM. Antonovich and Dragomanov, of which, unfortunately, only one volume and a portion of the
second has as yet appeared. Here the songs are
arranged chronologically, and accompanied by copious
notes.

To give some idea of the great quantity of these
poems, I cannot do better than cite the divisions
under which they are grouped by M. Dragomanov.

(1) Songs of the period of the *drouzhina* and the
Princes. These relate to the early, independent days
of the Little Russians, but towards the latter part of
the period fresh elements begin to enter. The Malo-
Russians had been partly amalgamated with the Lithuanian Principality, and, when that was united with
Poland in the sixteenth century, they found themselves face to façe with alien masters with whose
government they felt no sympathy, and there must be
added to this the appearance of the Turks and Tatars
on their confines. Under these circumstances was
developed the Cossack period (Kozachestvo), which
represents one of continued struggles with the Polish
pans and the Roman Catholic religion, in consequence
of which we have the well-known revolt of Bogdan
Khmelnitzki, and a large part of the Cossacks transfer
their allegiance to the Emperor Alexis.

(2) The Cossack period of the National Songs
is very rich. The *doumî* chiefly deal with the sufferings and imprisonment of Malo-Russians among the
Turks and Tatars, as we see by such a title as the
following: "Captivity and Blinding of Kovalenko by
the Tatars." Raids of the description mentioned

in this poem were very common. Thus Professor
Dragomanov cites from an old chronicler an account
of a fray in 1667 when "the horde carried off many,
some of whom were ploughing and some sowing.
They say that of heads of families alone, besides
wives, children and servants, there were taken 8,064."
The Polish chroniclers are full of accounts of these
raids, and the sufferings of the miserable villagers.
Some of the songs treat of the purchase of the slaves
from captivity, and other ways in which they are
rescued.

The Lays of the third period are classed under
the heading of "Songs of the Days of the Haidamaks." This last word is said to be Turkish in origin,
and to signify a robber. The Haidamak somewhat
resembles the Bulgarian *heyduk* and the Greek
klepht. He is a patriot who has joined bands of
robbers as the only means of liberating his country.
The Haidamaks form the national party in opposition
to the Polish magnates and the Jews, who have always
been so unpopular in these parts of Russia. Under
this period comes the massacre of Human, when
many Jewish children were slain by Gonta. Shevchenko, the chief poet of the Ukraine, who died in
1861, has made this the subject of a powerful *douma*.
Vigorous it certainly is, but the details are too horrible
to make an agreeable poem. The other two divisions
of the Cossack songs given by Professor Dragomanov
are too modern to be brought within the scope of
my book. Peter the Great was very severe upon the
Malo-Russians in consequence of the rebellion of

Mazepa, who joined Charles XII.   In the new
volume published by M. Dragomanov, " Political
Songs of the People of the Ukraine," Geneva, 1883,
we have many poems lamenting the decay of Cossack
independence, as, for instance, in a song of the year
1709 :—

> Oh ! a bomb flew from the Muscovite field,
> And fell in the midst of the Sech ;
> Oh ! although the glorious Zaporogues have fallen—
> Yet their glory has not fallen !

Catherine II. went further; in 1765 the hetmanship
was abolished and in 1775 the *Sech*, or military
republic, previously described, destroyed.

As a specimen of the elegance and simplicity of
these Cossack songs, I append the following :—

> By our *sloboda* (quarter, habitation),
> Grows corn mingled with tares.
> A young girl was reaping the corn,
> And was binding the little sheaves.
> There appeared a Cossack
> On his black horse.
> Go on reaping, sweet maiden,
> Bind up the little sheaves.
> The Cossack mounted on a hill,
> Letting his horse roam over the valley,
> And he himself fell asleep for a time.
> The young maiden came,
> And plucked some grass,
> And threw it at his face,—
> " Beware of sleeping, Cossack,
> Thou wilt find thy horse no more.
> The Turks and Tartars have come,
> And have taken thy horse, reins and all."

Ah ! the Turks know me well,
They will not catch me.
If they take my horse—I shall get another,
But if they take thee, I shall find no other.[1]

Interesting collections of the national legends have
been published by Koulish and Roudchenko, and
are very interesting for the study of comparative
mythology. The songs of the Choumaki, or wandering
pedlars, have also been committed to writing. In
Little Russia the itinerant minstrel or *Kobzar* (so
called from the *Kobza*, a rude kind of guitar, which he
carries, very much resembling the Servian *gousla*) is
still to be met with, although unfortunately becoming
daily rarer. At the congress of *literati*, which met a
few years ago at Kiev, Ostap (Little Russian for
Eustathius) Veresai, a wandering minstrel, performed
before the assembled guests. To the reader unacquainted with the Slavonic languages, the work
entitled " Les Chants historiques de l'Ukraine," by
Professor A. Chozdko, may be recommended. It is
only recently that the Russians have realised the
value of their popular poetry, and now collection after
collection appears. Had they waited a little longer
it would have been too late. There is much tenderness
and delicacy of expression in these pieces, and they
ought to be better known to Western readers. The
territory of Little Russia, which, till recently, was almost
a *terra incognita* to the Russians themselves, has been
made more familiar by the writings of Gogol and
Shevchenko. The former has published many tales

[1] "Dragománov," i., 141.

illustrating Little Russian life; he uses, however, the Great Russian language. Tales have also been written by Kvitka and Grebenko, and by a lady (Mme. Markovich) who writes under the *nom de guerre* of Marko Vovchok. How rich the whole country is in legends and folk-lore may be seen by the work of M. Dragomanov, "Little Russian Popular Traditions and Tales" (*Malorousskia Narodnia predania i Razskazi*).

Professor Bodenstedt, who has translated many of the Little Russian *doumi* into German, thus expresses himself on the general character of these compositions :—"In most Little Russian songs a strange, fascinating melancholy prevails : the mother takes a sorrowful leave of her beloved son, who is going into the field, from which she does not expect to see him return ; the deserted sister weeps over her fallen brother, who was her former protector, nurtured and comforted her, and now, like a lonely orphan, she laments among strangers ; the old Cossack bewails the loss of his youth, when he went to the war in goodly array, and fought with wild Tatars, and was beloved by gentle maidens. The influence of woman is seen everywhere ; as in the history of the Oukraine we find many other features of the knighthood of the Middle Ages. The Little Russian lives in the closest communion with nature ; from her the beautiful similes which we find in his songs are borrowed. Has the Cossack fallen on the field, the eagles, his brothers, fly to him and speak comfort to the dying hero ; are his eyes closed, the cuckoo sings his grave-song

from the flowering elder-tree. Every brave warrior
is a 'noble falcon'; he follows the enemy as a bird
chases its prey through the air. From the blowing
of the wind and the murmur of the waves, from the
neighing of his horse and the beating of its hoofs, he
can foretell the future." This picture, as drawn by
the worthy professor, may seem to some a little
idealised, but we must remember that the habits
of the Little Russians were very different from those
of the Great Russians, who have absorbed them.
No doubt, time has destroyed many of these characteristics, but to go no further back than to the days
of Clarke—the traveller at the beginning of the present century,—we find more of the spirit of chivalry
among the Little Russians than among the Musco-
vites. Clarke, who labours under the most aggra-
vated Russophobia, superinduced by the ill-treatment
which he received at the hands of the Emperor
Paul, has nothing but praise for the Cossacks of the
Oukraine. Their hospitality, simplicity, and honesty
are his constant themes.

The literature of the White Russians is but scanty
and almost entirely oral. Collections of their songs
have been published by Shein, Bezsonov, and others.
In 1844 a small volume of Rural Poems (*Piosnki
Wiesnacze*) was printed at Vilna, in Latin letters in
what was called the "Slavono-Krevitchian" dialect.
This, however, is none other than White Russian.
The Krivitches (mentioned by Nestor) were an ancient
tribe inhabiting these regions. There is a good
dictionary by Nosovich, and the dialect is gradually

being brought under proper philological treatment.
As regards the country of the White Russians, it is
certainly one of the least interesting parts of Russia,
both on account of the dulness and monotony of the
scenery and the poverty of the inhabitants.

It is often very difficult for the philologist when
examining the few religious books and others published
in early times in the White Russian territory to say
exactly what the dialect is.   As is always the case
where a language is but little cultivated, we get a
great many forms.   Thus the foundation of the
language of most of these books is Palæoslavonic,
but Polonisms abound.   The Lithuanian Principality,
which attained a considerable degree of political importance before its union with Poland, employed the
White Russian dialect for diplomatic purposes.   No
document whatsoever has come down to us in
Lithuanian, as Professor Nil Popov informs us in
an article in the Russian *Critical Review*.   In the
White Russian dialect, mixed with much Palæoslavonic, Francis Skorina translated some of the Old
Testament, which he published at Prague between
the years 1517–19, and the Acts and Epistles at Vilna
in 1525.

CHAPTER V.

EARLY BULGARIAN LITERATURE.

In a previous part of my work, I have alluded to the various theories on the subject of the Old Slavonic language. As the view taken here will be that the Old Slavonic is identical with Old Bulgarian,[1] I shall now treat of the earliest codices in this language, and the Glagolitic will be taken first.

1. The Codex of Assemani, so called from the monk who brought it from a Greek monastery on Mount Libanon. It is now in the Vatican. It has been edited by Racki, a distinguished Slavonic scholar. It contains extracts from the Gospels for each day of the year; by some it is considered to belong to the eleventh, by others to the thirteenth century.

2. The Codex called Glagolita Clozianus, because it originally belonged to Count Cloz of Trent. It contains homilies by SS. John Chrysostom, Athanasius, and Epiphanius. It was edited by Kopitar at Vienna

---

[1] I am prevented by the scope of this work from giving here the reasons which seem to me to justify this opinion. The reader who cares to pursue the subject further must consult Scheicher, "Die Formenlehre der Kirchenslawischen Sprache," pp. 28, 29; or Miklosich, "Altslovenische Formenlehre in Paradigmen, Einleitung."

in 1836. It was supposed by him to be of the eleventh century.

3. The Four Gospels, found by Grigorovich in a monastery on Mount Athos, of the eleventh century. This is a quarto manuscript containing 172 parchment leaves. The beginning and the end are wanting; leaf 134, on which the Gospel of St. John begins, is written in Cyrillic.

4. Another Codex of the Gospels found in the Monastery Zographus on Mount Athos. According to Grigorovich, it belongs to the twelfth. century. This manuscript has been edited with great care by Professor Jagić, of St. Petersburg, one of the most eminent of modern Slavists.

5. A fragment of the gospels belonging to M. Mihanovich, a manuscript in quarto, containing two leaves of parchment, with notes in Cyrillic.

6. The Palimpsest of *Boyana*, discovered by Grigorovich in the town of that name, near Sophia, a quarto manuscript containing a hundred and nine parchment leaves; it includes the gospel of Saint Mark, written in Cyrillic, according to M. Courrière, with occasional traces of Glagolitic. It would be impossible in a work like the present to give a complete list of the Glagolitic Codices. I have therefore chosen the most important.

The most ancient manuscript in the Cyrillic character is the Ostromir Codex, already alluded to; it was written by the Diak Gregory according to the order of Ostromir, the *posadnik*, or governor, of Novgorod. This valuable manuscript was ori-

ginally preserved in the cathedral of St. Sophia,
at Novgorod, but was found at the close of the
last century in a room of one of the imperial
palaces by Yakov A. Drouzhinin, where it had lain
for some time, having been probably brought for
the inspection of the Empress Catherine. By him
it was taken to Alexander I., by whose orders it was
preserved in the Public Library at St. Petersburg.
It has been edited by the well-known Slavonic scholar,
Vostokov. This fine manuscript is written in large
uncial characters, with the headings of the chapters in
golden letters; it also has ornamental capitals and
portraits of the four Evangelists.

7. Some Legends and Homilies, which have been
edited by Miklosich under the following title " Monumenta linguæ Palæoslovenicæ e codice Suprasliensi,"
Vienna, 1851. The manuscript is assigned by the
learned professor to the eleventh century. It is called
the " Codex Suprasliensis " because it was formerly
preserved in the abbey of the Basilian monks at
Suprasl, near Bialystok, in Poland. It is a manuscript
of the highest importance on account of the purity
of the language. It is to be regretted that some of
the leaves have been lost; but before this misfortune
befel it a transcript of the whole manuscript was
made by the indefatigable Kopitar, and this is luckily
preserved.

The question is a very interesting one, but perhaps hardly to be solved exactly :—How much of the
Scriptures did the Slavonic apostles translate? It
seems probable that the whole of the gospels were

rendered into Slavonic.   Some have asserted that the
Old Testament was also translated, but this appears
unlikely, since no ancient codex of it exists or has
ever been proved to have existed,[1] and as to the
New Testament, the Apocalypse must certainly be
excepted.   In the time of Nestor, the Proverbs of
Solomon certainly existed in a Slavonic translation.
The book of Wisdom, Ecclesiastes, the Prophets, and
Job were translated in Servia in the thirteenth or fourteenth century; the Pentateuch in Russia or Poland
somewhere about 1400.   It is certain, that towards
the close of the fifteenth century the whole Bible was
already translated into Palæoslavonic.   According to
Dobrovsky, the different parts of it were not collected
till after 1488, when the Bohemian Bible of Prague
was printed.   The Slavonic Bible was arranged on
the model of this, and what was wanting was at that
time supplied.   There is at Moscow a complete
codex of the whole Bible of the date of 1499.   The
text of the translation was not disturbed till the celebrated recension of Nicon, in the time of the Emperor
Alexis, of which I shall shortly speak.

Mention may also be made of the Psalter of
Bologna, which is assigned to the twelfth century.
The Book of the Gospels of Rheims, called in
French the "Texte du Sacre," has had a very curious
history.   It was upon this book that the kings of
France were accustomed to take the oath at their
coronation at Rheims before the Revolution.   The

[1] "Historical View of the Slavic Language" (*sic*), by Mrs.
Robinson (*Talvj*), Andover, U.S., 1834, p. 28.

manuscript was magnificently bound in a cover of plates of gold, ornamented with precious stones. When in 1717 Peter the Great visited Rheims, it was exhibited to him among the other curiosities of the place, and he recognised that it was written in some Slavonic language. In 1789 an Englishman, Thomas Ford Hill, having been shown some Glagolitic manuscripts in the Imperial Library at Vienna, at once declared that they were written in the same characters as the mysterious book of Rheims.

The matter would soon have been sifted, as the curiosity of Slavonic scholars had been excited, when the Revolution broke out in all its fury. The wonderful book disappeared, carried off, no doubt, on account of its precious exterior. Nor could any trace of it be found, and its loss was naturally deplored by Slavonic scholars, as they imagined that it might have contained leaves of the highest antiquity and of priceless value. Sylvestre de Sacy and Kopitar made all possible search for it, but without success. How it ultimately turned up I am unable to state, but it was recognised by the philologist Stroiev, of course stripped of its gorgeous environment. The book was found by Paplonski to consist of two parts—1st, Cyrillian in a Serbo-Russian dialect, written, according to the inscription at the end, by St. Procopius at Prague in 1032 ; but this statement is a mere fabrication, and must have been added by a later hand. 2nd, Glagolitic of Cech origin, and dating no further back than 1325. Kopitar seems to have made out the history of the volume in the "Slavische Bibliothek" very satisfactorily. He thinks that it was purchased by the German Emperor, Charles IV., under the impression that it was really written by St. Procopius; about 1451 it seems to have got to Constantinople, and to have been bought there by a French cardinal, who presented it to the cathedral at Rheims. The theory of Zherebtzov that it was taken to France by Anne, daughter of Yaroslav, who married Henry I., is groundless.

As the copyists of the various old Slavonic manuscripts were Bulgarians, Servians, or Russians, they introduced forms from their own languages. This makes it difficult to classify thoroughly the Palæoslavonic texts. But, according to their characteristics, I have for the most part spoken of them under their several languages. The disciples of Cyril, and Methodius appearing in Bulgaria in the reign of the Tzar Simeon (892–927), which has been called the golden age of Bulgarian literature, soon busied themselves with the spread of the Christian religion and the production of books. The Tzar Simeon himself appears as a literary man. To him is assigned the translation of 135 sermons of St. John Chrysostom, under the title of " Zlatostroui," the oldest manuscript of which dates from the twelfth century.

Among writers of Old Bulgarian literature may be mentioned Clement, John the Exarch of Bulgaria, and the translator of John Malala. Clement, who is styled, in the titles of his works, the Slavonic Apostle, has left a great many works, chiefly sermons and panegyrics of saints. He died in the

year 916. To a monk, named Gorazd, is assigned
a "Life of St. Methodius." A very fertile writer of
the time of Simeon was John, called the Exarch
of Bulgaria; among his works may be mentioned
the "Shestodnev" (Book of Six Days), containing
a commentary on the early chapters of Genesis,
which treat of the Creation; a translation of the
Greek grammar of Damascenus, also of the dia-
lectics and philosophy of the same author. The
"Shestodnev" is compiled from the writings of Basil
the Great, John Chrysostom, and others; but the
Exarch shows himself to be well acquainted with
Greek philosophy, and quotes Plato, Aristotle, and
others. Wherever he does so it is to oppose their
false heathen opinions. In the prologue to his work,
John the Exarch alludes to the Tzar Simeon; in the
beginning of the sixth discourse he describes the
grandeur of the royal palaces, the temples, and the
greatness of the tzar himself.[1]   At this time Ochrida
was the capital of the Bulgarian kingdom. Mention
must also be made of Bishop Constantine, said to
have been one of the disciples of Cyril and Methodius, who translated many of the discourses of
Athanasius and St. John Chrysostom. Among his
writings is a prayer in rhyme, in which he speaks of
the baptism of the Slavonic race throughout the
world. According to Pípin, this is the first known
piece of Slavonic poetry composed by a literary man
—in contradistinction to the popular and oral verse

---

[1] Pípin and Spasovich, 55.

so much in vogue among Slavonic peoples. Especially important is the notice of the monk Khrabr, which has been alluded to in the first chapter of this work. Here we have some interesting information on the origin of the Slavonic alphabet as invented by Cyril, and allusions to the earlier forms of writing in use among the Slavs. Khrabr wrote, as he says, at a time when men were still living, who had seen Cyril and Methodius, and therefore he himself must have flourished in the tenth century.

It would be impossible, in a short work like the present, to enumerate all the translations of Byzantine authors. Certainly, if the Old Slavonic literature was not very original,—and we must remember that very little of our own in the Middle Ages is,—it was very active. The "Sbornik," or Miscellany, alluded to under the head of Russian literature as that of Sviatoslav, because copied out for him in 1073, was compiled in the time of Simeon. This is almost an encyclopædia, and contains a great deal of multifarious learning mixed with extracts from the fathers. It fully partakes of the nature of the Byzantine literature of the time,—a literature of extracts and anthologies.

Of the chroniclers more minute mention seems to be necessary. The Greek author, John Malala, exists in a Slavonic version, which in many respects exhibits the characteristics of a paraphrase, as there are frequent additions from other sources. The translator is supposed to have been the Presbyter Gregory, and his period the golden age of the Tzar Simeon. In the twelfth century it was already made use of by the Russian historical writers.   There is also the chronicle of George Armatolus, of which two Slavonic versions exist, one of which was used very much by Nestor. There is even an opinion that one of these versions was executed in Russia.   Besides these we have the Chronicles of Constantine Manassias and Simeon Metaphrastes in Slavonic versions.

The apocryphal books already mentioned form a curious feature of the old Slavonic literature.   They are chiefly assigned to the sect of the Bogomiles, founded by the priest Bogomile, who lived in the time of the Bulgarian Tzar Peter, and to the priest Jeremiah, who, perhaps, was only the collector of them.   These apocryphal pieces contain strange mixtures of Christian belief and heathenism, on such subjects as the following : " The Tree of the Cross," " How Christ Ploughed," &c.   M. Léger cites the eminent Orientalist, Joseph Derembourg, as his authority for the statement, that the originals of most of these legends must be sought in the Midrasch of the Talmud.

Professor Jagić has shown how, in one of these stories, the name of Virgil has been introduced in his mediæval character of a magician.   The word occurs in such a corrupt form, that it had quite escaped the notice of scholars, just as it lies hidden in the Welsh word for alchymy and chemistry,—namely, *fferylliaeth* or *fferylltiaeth*.[1]

[1] See "Lectures on Welsh Philology," by Professor Rhys (p. 205).

Besides the lives of the saints and translations of the fathers of the Greek Church, there are legendary stories of Alexander the Great and the Trojan War, the stories of Barlaam and Yoasaf, of Stefanit and Ikhilat, and the fantastic tale of the Tzar Solomon and Kitovras. Many of these, including the previously mentioned apocryphal books (*lozhnia knigi*) have been recently edited for the "Early Russian Text Society."

However little original merit these works may boast of, they must always be interesting to the antiquarian and philologist,—and, if we except some great names, such works formed the staple of all European literature during the Middle Ages.

Unlike the Russians and Serbs, no specimens of Bulgarian laws have come down to us, although Suidas has preserved some fragments[1] in a Greek translation. We get, however, a very interesting glimpse into the customs and institutions of the Bulgarians in an indirect way. They received Christianity in the time of Boris, called by the Byzantines Bogoris, who was baptised under the name of Michael, A.D. 864. A great instrument in his conversion is said to have been his sister, who had been thirty-eight years a captive at Constantinople. He extirpated idolatry among his subjects with much cruelty, and as soon as he had accepted Christianity, seems to have been anxious to enter into relations with the Latin

[1] See the quotation in "Written Laws of the Southern Slavs" ("Pisani Zakoni na Slovenskom Jugu") of Professor Bogisic, Agram, 1872.

church, led probably to do so by the hereditary
antipathies existing between the Bulgarians and
Greeks.   He accordingly sent his brother to Rome,
and submitted one hundred and six points to the pope,
embracing every question of discipline, ceremony, and
morals.[1] We can see from these questions, that
among the Slavonised Bulgarians many customs
prevailed (*e.g.*, polygamy) unknown to the Slavs, who
were of a purer stock.   Under Krumus or Kroum, a
subsequent prince, the Greek Emperor Nicephorus
undertook three expeditions against the Bulgarians,
in the last of which he was slain (811).   His head
was carried triumphantly on the point of a spear, and
the skull, enchased with gold, became a favourite
drinking vessel at the Bulgarian feasts.   The Tzar
Simeon, previously alluded to, had been educated at
Constantinople and attained such proficiency in the
learning taught there that he ordinarily went by
the name of the Half Greek ('Ημίαργος).   Gibbon
acknowledges that during his long reign of more than
forty years Bulgaria assumed a rank among the
civilised powers of the earth.   Simeon frequently
defeated the Byzantines and twice took Adrianople.
His victories were, however, tarnished with great
cruelty, for we are told that he ordered the noses of
all the prisoners to be cut off, and sent the Byzantine
soldiers thus mutilated to Constantinople.[2]   In 921

---

[1] See Milman's "Latin Christianity," vol. iii., p. 250., ed.
1867.   The answers of Nicholas (who occupied the papal chair
from 858 to 867) are exceedingly curious.

[2] Finlay, "History of Byzantine Empire."

Simeon advanced to the very walls of the imperial city : the palaces and many villas around were burned, and the Bulgarian monarch retired laden with plunder. He made his appearance again two years afterwards, and the Byzantine emperor, Romanus I, now thoroughly humbled, was compelled to consent to an interview outside the walls and had the mortification of listening to the triumphant shouts of his Slavonic enemies and witnessing the pomp of their sovereign. According to Finlay, Simeon retired to his own kingdom laden with the plunder of the provinces and the gold of the Emperor.

With the subjugation of the Bulgarians by the Turkish Sultan, Amurath or Murad (1360-1389), the Old Bulgarian literature, in the restricted sense of the term, ceased. We now come to their oral literature. I know of no earlier collection than that of Bogoev,[1] published at Pesth in 1842, a work which I have not seen, but have found mentioned in the "Chansons Populaires Bulgares Inédites" of Dozon. Its publication was probably owing to the great interest aroused throughout Europe by the Servian ballads collected by Vouk Stephanovich.

A volume of Bulgarian National Songs, collected by the Brothers Miladinov, Demetrius and Constantine,

---

[1] "Bulgarski Narodni Pesni i Poslovitzi" (Bulgarian Nationa Songs and Proverbs). See also an article in the "Bohemian Magazine" (*Casopis Ceského Musea*) for 1847, where we find that this Bogoev published other works at Odessa. He would appear to be the same as Ivan Bogorov who has published a Bulgarian-French Dictionary.

was published by Constantine at Agram in 1861.
This is the work issued under the auspices of Bishop
Strossmayer, who has done so much for Slavonic
literature.   In his preface Constantine Miladinov
speaks of the great wealth of popular song among
his countrymen.   He tells us that from one young
girl alone, at Struga, he collected 150 beautiful songs.
The fate of these brothers was very melancholy, and
is curious as helping us to form an idea of the
system of the Turkish Government.   After the publication of the ballads at Agram in 1861, Constantine
Miladinov returned to Bulgaria.   He joined his
brother Demetrius at Struga, in Macedonia, on the
Albanian frontier, where the latter was exercising the
profession of a tutor.   Soon afterwards an order came
from the Turkish Government that they were to
be sent to Saloniki (Thessalonica), and thence to
Constantinople.   Here they were accused of treason,
information having been laid against them by some
of the Greek priests, who are in perpetual collision
with the Bulgarians on theological grounds, because
some of the poems in their collection contained
satirical allusions and attacks upon the Turks and
Greeks.   One of the pieces which especially gave
offence is to be found on page 113 of the book,
entitled " Stoyan and Patrik "; it recites the achievements of a certain Bulgarian hero, named Stoyan,
against the Turks and Greeks.[1]   In consequence of

[1] For much of my information on the Brothers Miladinov I
have been indebted to some interesting articles which appeared
in the " Bohemian Literary Journal " (*Casopis Ceského Musea*),

these charges the brothers were condemned to imprisonment for life. When the news of their detention reached foreign countries, the patriotic Bishop Strossmayer exerted himself for their liberation by means of the Austrian consul at Constantinople, and the Russian Government also assisted in the demand. The Ottoman authorities were at length compelled to send an order for their release, but when the decree sanctioning their liberation reached the prison they were found dead. They had been secretly murdered; it was in this way that the Turks evaded the pressure put upon them. Constantine had not reached the age of thirty years, Demetrius was a little older, and left a wife and two children in great poverty.

I may here mention "National Songs of the Macedonian Bulgarians," collected by Stephen J. Verkovich. Of this one volume was published at Belgrade in 1860. The book is edited in Servian, and a Bulgaro-Servian vocabulary is added. In his preface, Verkovich tells us that 270 of the songs were written down from the recitation of a woman, named Dafina, at Seres, in Macedonia. This fact must be considered as proving, in an interesting way, how poems may be orally preserved in a country where printed books are very scarce. My readers should compare the remarks of Mr. Gladstone in his valuable Homeric Primer.[1]

in 1866, written by a native Bulgarian—Velyo D. Stoyanov. In the poem, which is now before me, the Greeks are called *loukavi*—treacherous.

[1] See page 41 of that work.

Such accounts as this of the memory of the Bulgarian woman greatly assist his theory.

A second part of the collection of Verkovich has not appeared, and he has since tarnished his fame by the publication of the Slavonic Veda (*Veda Slovena*), at Belgrade in 1874. This book is a mass of fabrications; the pieces printed contain allusions to the deities of the Indian mythology and traditions of Orpheus, the object being to exaggerate the antiquity of Slavonic tradition. The work is calculated to discredit for a long time any fresh collections of Slavonic oral literature.[1]

In 1875 appeared the very interesting collection of Bulgarian songs published by Auguste Dozon. These were entirely new to the literary world, and had been either collected by the editor himself, or communicated to him by his friends. From the volumes of the Brothers Miladinov and M. Dozon a fair idea may be formed of Bulgarian folk-lore and mythology.[2] To these may be added the Bulgarian National Miscellany (*Bulgarski Narodni Sbornik*) of Basil Cholakov, published at Bolgrad, in Bessarabia, in 1873.

As might be expected, the country is well worthy of attention from the curious traditions and local customs which abound. As among the Serbs,

---

[1] See the severe criticism by Jagić in the "Archiv für Slavische Philologie," vol. i., Part III., p. 576.

[2] Some of the Bulgarian National Poems have been translated into German. Bulgarische Volksdichtungen, ins Deutsche übertragen von Georg Rosen. 1879.

the chief legendary hero is Marko Kralevich, who
reminds us in so many particulars of the Russian
Ilya Murometz. A great number of poems are devoted
to him in the Miladinov Collection. The lyrical
pieces, which treat of the affections, show considerable
tenderness, and are by no means devoid of elegance.
In this respect they may be compared with the
Cossack Songs of Little Russia. Many lays relate
to the Vilas, or Samovilas, who figure among the
Russians as *rousalki*, or water-nymphs, and also
among the Servians. They are represented as of
a malignant nature, and feeling great jealousy of
female beauty. In the story of Neda and the Samovila,[1] Neda has gone to the cool fountain (*stoudna
voda*), and has accidentally trodden upon the yellow
flowers of the Samovila, who tells her that she must
surrender her black eyes. In the ballad of the fair
Stana and the Samovila,[2] we are introduced to the
comely maiden arranging herself with rustic pride
for church on Easter-Sunday (*Veligden*, literally, the
Great Day). Her mother enjoins her not to go
too early to the church for fear the young priests
(*giatzi*) should make love to her ; at this Stana is
offended, takes her white veil, goes into the garden,
and sits down under a rose-tree. She is met by a
malicious Samovila, who ends by tearing out her
black eyes.

We have also another lay, showing the malignity
of the Vilas connected with the great hero, Marko
Kralevich.

[1] "Miladinov," p. 6.   [2] Ibid., p. 5.

K

Marko wandered by the green forest,
He wandered three days and three nights.
He could not find water,
Either to drink or to wash,
Neither for himself nor for his swift horse.
Then says Marko Kralevich—
" Ah, forest, Dimna forest,
Thou hast no water that I may drink,
And wash myself.
May the wind harass thee !
May the sun burn thee ! "
The forest of Dimna replied to Marko,—
" Ah ! Marko—ah ! brave hero.
Do not curse the forest of Dimna,
Curse the old Samovila,
Who has taken the seventy springs
And has carried them to the top of the mountain.
She sells a glass of water,
One glass for black eyes."

Hereupon the hero addresses his trusty steed, who, in the Servian legends, is called Sharatz, and has as much sympathy with his master as the more celebrated horses of Achilles. They go in pursuit of the Vila, and the hero becomes master of the seventy springs.

A terrible lay concerning the Samovilas is given by Miladinov as taken down from oral recitation at Panagiouritche. Here we have something of the same sort as the legend, which occurs in Modern Greek, Rouman, and Servian, of the master-builder, Manole, given in the Servian ballads under the name of the " Building of Skadar," and also in Stanley's " Rouman Anthology." A Samovila builds a castle, " not in the sky, not on the earth ; she builds it in the dark clouds, and it is built from young warriors, fair girls, and black-eyed wives." Students of comparative mythology will not need to be reminded of the wide circulation of this curious Aryan legend. On another occasion we are told how a girl demands back her brother from a Samovila, who has enchanted him, as Vivien did Merlin. The angry Samovila carries off the youth into the air and tears him into thousands of little pieces, "of which the greatest might easily be carried by an ant."

It is but rarely that we find any kindly acts assigned to these creatures. Their mischievous activities, however, may occasionally be defeated by the energy of man. Thus the mysterious peasant, Jovan Popov, conquers one of these supernatural beings, and takes her home as a wife : but, after having given birth to a son, she succeeds in escaping to the inaccessible retreats which are frequented by creatures like herself. Jovan Popov reminds us very much of the Russian hero, Mikoula Selianinovich, mentioned in a previous chapter of this work.

I give a few extracts from this ballad, literally translated :—

Jovan Popov has gone ploughing at Easter.
When he had gone half his journey
There appeared a Samovila of the mountain,
And stopped him in his path.
" Go back, Jovan Popov,
Do not plough on Easter Day."
Jovan answered softly,—
" Fly away, Samovila,
Lest I descend from my swift steed,

Lest I catch you by your auburn hair,
And bind you to the tail of my swift horse.

*   *   *   *   *

The Samovila grew angry,
She let fall her auburn hair
And caused his swift horse to stumble,
That she might drink his black eyes.
Ivan Popov became angry ;
He caught the Samovila by her auburn hair
That he might bring her home.,
From afar he calls to his mother,
" Come forth, dear mother,
I bring you a bride, a Samovila."

The Samovila is detained as a wife, and a child
is afterwards born to the marriage, but the fairy
manages to escape at last.

At once rushed forth the Samovila ;
She took the child,
And said haughtily to Jovan,—
" Oh ! hero, Jovan Popov,
What ! did you think
That you could keep a Samovila,
A Samovila for your love ? "

Dragons and serpents play a very important part
in all these stories, and are subdued by heroes, as
in the fine Russian *bilina*, which tells us of Dobrína's
battle. The horse also is frequently introduced as
an agent, and is represented with wings. The dragons
fall in love with women and carry them off. On
page 10 of Miladinov's book, we have a poem in
which Perdan, who had been left an orphan, fights
three days and three nights with two dragons, who

eventually overpower him. In one poem (Dozon, page 7) a female dragon takes the form of a bear, a favourite animal in the legendary poetry of so many countries. Some of the lines in this piece are very picturesque; it begins as follows :—

> His mother said to Stoyan,
> " Stoyan,—my son, Stoyan,—
> Whilst thou wert my son, with thy mother,
> Thou wert fair and ruddy.
> Since thou hast parted from thy mother
> Thou art a pale yellow,
> Like a yellow orange,
> And like a green bush.
> Hast thou, my son, evil companions ?
> Or are the shepherds rude to thee ? "

To this the son replies that he has no bad associates, nor is he ill-treated by the shepherds, only at night a she-bear comes to him and calls him her sweetheart.

> To Stoyan his mother said,
> " This is not a savage bear ;
> It is Elka, the she-dragon."

The mother counsels him to ask craftily the she-dragon to tell him of some plants which will create aversion when a person is anointed with their juice, alleging as a reason that a certain Turk has conceived a passion for his young sister, and he wishes to make him hate her. Elka tells Stoyan the names of the magic plants ; they are boiled in a pot by the mother at midnight.

It was not the sister of Stoyan she anointed,
But Stoyan himself.
When even came,   •
Lo ! the she-bear came,
She came from afar and cried out,—
" Stoyan, dear Stoyan,
How easily you have deceived me,
And separated me from one whom I loved."

In the ninth piece given by Dozon, we have a
young girl borne away by a dragon in a chariot drawn
by horses.   The whole legend, the magic cauldron
and the car, reminds us forcibly of the Greek story
of Medea :—

You marry me, mother, you betroth me,
But you do not ask me, mother,
If I wish to marry or not.
A dragon loves me, mother ;
This evening will come
Dragons with white horses,
Dragons with golden chariots,
Little dragons with golden cradles.
The forest, without any wind, will be laid low ;
The village, without fire, will be burnt.
Barkings will be heard, but no dogs appear.
Her mother said to Dimitra,
" Why did you not tell your mother,
That she might pour water upon you,
On an enchanted fire in an enchanted cauldron?"
Hardly had the mother ceased speaking
When the forest was laid low without any wind,
The village was burnt without fire.
A barking was heard although there were no dogs,
And then they carried away Dimitra.

Sometimes the dragons come in the forms of winds

and clouds. The beautiful Rada is carried off while at a fountain.[1]

Birds, as in all mythologies, play a very important part among the Bulgarians. With the Slavs, the falcon (*sokol*) is always considered the symbol of a young man. Ravens also figure constantly : thus intelligence of the disastrous battle of Kosovo is brought by two ravens. In a poem, on page 165 of M. Dozon's collection, a young man is turned into an eagle. He is constantly being scolded by his mother on account of his love for a girl named Malamka, whereupon he prays to God to turn him into an eagle, grey and white (*sivo bielo*),—

> So that I may fly up aloft
> And they may think me lost.
> And then I may descend in the form of an eagle
> Into the garden of Malamka.
> And God had pity upon him,
> And changed him into an eagle,
> And he flew aloft,
> And then descended
> Into the garden of Malamka ;
> Malamka was transplanting flowers, &c. &c.

Cholakov gives us many curious incantations used by *baiachki*, or sorceresses, against diseases, and the nine female divinities called *ourechnitzi* (M. Dozon makes them three in number, and calls them *narech-nitzi*), who at the birth of a child prophesy its fate. Among the spirits of the elements are the Youdas ; these are also of an evil nature, and probably derive

[1] Dozon, p. 12.

their name from Judas, the betrayer, for in Slavonic countries, as elsewhere, we have a curious confusion of Pagan and Christian superstitions. Peroun, the god of thunder, has been mixed up with Elijah, or Elias (St. Ilya).[1] Veles, the god of cattle, has been converted into St. Basil, and Sventovit has probably been metamorphosed into St. Vitus, originally a Sicilian saint. These Youdas are represented as exercising a malignant influence upon the human race. Their songs, like those of the Sirens of Greek fable, have an intoxicating effect; listeners lose their reason, and if they wish to preserve themselves must stop their ears. Miladinov identifies these spirits with others called Stii. Of a mischievous character also are the Violitzi and the Lamias, beings borrowed from the ancient and modern Greek mythology, with which the Slavonic has much in common. Two considerable ballads on St. George and the Lamias are given by Miladinov. As in Russia, so in Servia and Bulgaria, we have a host of poems sung by wandering minstrels on the feast days of certain saints. I have already alluded to Bezsonov's Russian collections, called " Wandering Psalm - singers " (*Kalieki perekhozhie*), published at Moscow in six parts in 1860–62. Here we find many a curious mediæval legend worked up into a rhythmical form.

[1] In the Miladinov Collection we have the ballad of St. Elias and the Nine Lamias (*Svete Ilia i devet Lamii*). For information on these subjects see Ralston, " The Songs of the Russian People" and " Russian Folk-Tales."

Now and then among these Bulgarian ballads we come upon one which expresses forcibly the wretched thraldom under which the country long groaned. Probably many more might have been collected, but the responsibilities of publishing them were too serious. We have seen what a fate was brought upon the Miladinovs by a few satirical lines. The most striking of these is the story of the " Young Janissary and the Fair Dragana," given in the collection of the latter. The Janissary, who in his early youth had formed one of the victims of the tribute of flesh which the unfortunate Christians were obliged to pay to their conquerors after having sacked a village and committed great atrocities, carries off a female captive, whom he finds out to be his own sister. As this ballad is a very interesting one, I add a literal translation of it.

THE JANISSARY AND THE FAIR DRAGANA.[1]

The land of the Wallachians is desolated,
The land of Wallachia and Moldavia,
Moldavia and all the Dobrudja,
Some run up and some run down
From the cruel Turk and the terrible Magyars.
They were cutting to pieces the old and making slaves of the
        young.
They were taking the maidens selected from the rest,
And made them youthful slaves,
And young men also they chose.
And they made the young men Janissaries.
Wherever they passed the villages were burnt.

---

[1] Miladinov, p. 124.

The men they enslave, the villages they burn.
They crossed the white Danube :
They drew up their ranks near Yetropoli,
They spread abroad their blue tents.
They divide the pillage of the broad plain,
The young girls and young men.
To some of them two or three fall as a portion.
To the young Janissary has been given
Only one young girl, the fair Dragana.
And he led her into his white tent,
And when it was late in the evening,
The young Janissary was sitting in the court-yard.
He looked down, he looked up.
Out of the black earth a blue fire burns,
But from the blue sky a rain of blood falls.
The young Janissary was frightened,
So that he called to fair Dragana,
And said sadly to Dragana,—
" Oh ! Dragana, my slave,
I will ask you to tell me truly,
Have you a brother or have you a sister ?
Have you a father, have you a mother ?"
But Dragana answered him clearly,—
" I have a father, I have a mother ;
I have a brother, I have a sister."
" Where is thy brother ? has he been carried into slavery ? "
Dragana answered him sadly :
" When they came to the Wallachian land
The Turks killed the young Bulgarians,
And my brother was taken by that army.
Now thirty years have passed [1]
Since I saw my brother."
" Oh ! Dragana, my slave,
If thou seest him, canst thou recognise him ?"

---

[1] The ballad-singer seems careless about his chronology in
making Dragana rather older than one would imagine.

"If I see him, I shall recognise him
By his wounded head, by his broad chest."
But the Janissary asked Dragana,—
"What is there on thy brother's head?"
"My brother has a mark from a sword;
He was wounded in a cruel battle."
But the Janissary asked Dragana,—
"What has your brother on his broad chest?"
"My brother has a scar on his breast,
Having been wounded by an arrow in the cruel battle."
And the Janissary bared his chest,
His white chest, and his wounded head,
And to Dragana he said sadly,—
"Arise, sister, let us go home,
Let us go home, let us see our mother."

Just as Greece has a multitude of ballads treating
of her *klephts* and *pallicares*, so the Bulgarians have
songs on the *haiduks* or brigands, who are celebrated
as our forefathers sang the exploits of Robin Hood
and Little John, and the French rustics of last century
the knaveries of Mandrin. Slavonic literature has a
great deal to tell us about these heroes : to go back
to the earlier days, we have Solovei, and in later times
Stenka Razin, Vanka Kaïn, and Pougachev, the bold
robber of the Yaik, who nearly overthrew the empire
of Catherine II.[1] M. Dozon complains that the
Bulgarian brigand is a far more vulgar hero than the
Servian. In many instances, certainly, he is but a
cowardly assassin; vices, however, of this sort are
just those with which a race becomes inoculated that
has long groaned under an iron yoke : it will never

[1] See Rambaud, "La Russie épique."

do to allow conquerors to argue the moral incapacity of their slaves by citing against them the vices which they themselves have engrafted. In the nineteenth poem of M. Dozon's collection we have a sister, Draganka, joining her brother, Ivancho, who has turned *haiduk*, in stealing some money in course of transmission from the Sultan's exchequer :—

> And Dragana was angry,
> She went after the convoy.
> She first turned to the right,
> Then again to the left,
> And she has massacred every one,
> All the fair-haired Cossacks,
> Three hundred deli-bashis,
> And she has seized hold of the treasure.

Popular sympathy is always with the brigands, and at the gallows he is very anxious that he should die with dignity. A very curious poem of this sort is included in M. Dozon's collection (page 48) of which the following is a literal translation :—

> Poor, poor Stoyan,
> They have watched him on two roads,
> On the third they have caught him.
> They got ready black cords,
> They fastened his white hands,
> And they brought Stoyan
> To the house of Jovan the priest.
> The priest had two daughters,
> And the third was Gioula, his daughter-in-law.
> Gioula was making butter
> At the little door of the garden :
> The daughters were sweeping the court.
> They said to Stoyan,—

"Oh ! Stoyan, poor fellow,[1]
To-morrow they will hang you
At the Sultan's palace,
So that the Sultana may see the spectacle,
And the Sultan's children."
Stoyan says to Gioula,—
"Gioula, daughter-in-law of the priest,
Are these girls sisters-in-law,
Or are they only neighbours ?"
Gioula answers Stoyan :—
"Oh ! Stoyan, poor fellow,
Why do you ask whether they are sisters-in-law or not,
Or whether they are neighbours ?"
Stoyan says to Gioula,—
"Gioula, daughter of the priest,
Tell the youngest,
Since they will hang me,
To wash my shirt,
To unfasten my hair.
For it pleases me, O Gioula,
When they hang a fine young fellow
That his shirt should be white,
That his hair should float in the wind."

Occasionally these robber-songs take a higher tone, and show something more than the coarse materialism of a life of thieving, which is only to be terminated by the halter. There is a poetry about these " dedicated beggars to the air " with their " looped and windowed raggedness." M. Dozon cites with justifiable approbation the beautiful little song which may be found on page 37 of his collection. The following

---

[1] Or, more literally, "Oh ! Stoyan, poor fool !" The words are, *Mori Stoyane gidio.* The first is the Greek μῶρος, the last is Turkish.

is a strictly literal translation; the original reminds
one of some of the best klephtic ballads :—

> Liben, the young hero, cried out
> On the summit of the old mountain,
> Liben bade adieu to the forest,
> To the forest and fountain he spake—
> " Oh, Wood ! oh, green Wood !
> And, oh ! cool Spring,
> Dost thou know, Forest, dost thou remember
> How often I have wandered over thee,
> Have led my young heroes,
> Have carried my red standard?
> I have made many mothers weep,
> Deprived many brides of their homes.
> Even more little orphans have I made,
> So that they weep, Forest, they curse me.
> Farewell, Forest, farewell,
> For I shall go home,
> So that my mother may betroth me ;
> May betroth and marry me
> To the daughter of the priest,
> The priest Nicholas."
> The forest never speaks to any one,
> And yet it spake to Liben.
> " Liben, thou hero, Liben,
> Enough hast thou wandered over me,
> Hast led thy chosen youths,
> Hast carried thy red standard
> On the summit, on the old mountain,
> By the cool thick shade of the trees,
> By the dewy green grass.
> Thou hast made many mothers weep ;
> Thou hast deprived many brides of their homes,
> Thou hast left more little children orphans,
> So that they weep, Liben, they curse
> Me, voivode, on account of thee.

Till this time, Voivode Liben,
The old mountain was thy mother,
The green forest was thy bride,
With tufted foliage adorned,
Refreshed with the sweet breeze.
The grass gave thee a bed,
Thou wert covered by the forest-leaves,
The clear waters gave thee drink,
The forest-birds sang to thee.
For thee, Liben, they spoke,[1]
Rejoice, young hero, with thy companions.
For with thee the forest rejoices,
For thee the mountain is glad,
For thee the stream is cool.
But now, Liben, thou biddest adieu to the mountain,
Thou dost desire to go home,
That thy mother may betroth thee,
May betroth thee and marry thee
To the daughter of the priest,
Of the priest Nicholas."

Surely never were the sympathies between nature
and man more beautifully expressed than in this
delightful song, which has all the freshness of its
native woods and mountains upon it. If we could
only do away with the savage accessories, the cruel
stories about widows and orphans, it might be taken
for one of Wordsworth's pictures. The part played
by women in these exploits of brigandage does not
form a theme for song, as far as I am aware, among
the Servian collections of Vouk Stephanovich and
others, yet it is frequently introduced into the Bul-

---

[1] Stories of persons who could understand the language of
birds and wild beasts are very frequent among Slavonic tradi-
ditions, especially Servian and Bulgarian.

garian ballads.   M. Dozon mentions only four pieces
of a similar nature among the modern Greek songs.
One of these is the well-known lay, beginning :—

Ποιὸς εἶδε ψάρι 'ς τὸ βοῦνο καὶ θάλασσα σπαρμένη ;
Ποιὸς εἶδε κόρην εὔμορφη 'ς τὰ κλέφτικα 'νδυμένη;

Who ever saw fish on a mountain, or the sea sown like a field?
Who ever saw a lovely girl who had dressed her as a *klepht?*

A poem entitled " Sirma Voivodka," on a heroine
of this kind is given in the collection of Miladinov.
Demetrius, one of the brothers, speaks of having
known this woman at the age of eighty at Prilip, and
having heard from her own lips the recital of her
adventures.

With the popular poetry our remarks on Bulgarian
literature must close, as modern compositions (and
they are indeed but scanty) do not come within our
scope.

CHAPTER VI.

THE EARLY LITERATURE OF THE SERBS, CROATS, AND SLOVENES.

THE Serbs belong to the eastern division of the Slavonic race, as will be seen by the table given in my first chapter. Their language is for all practical purposes identical with that of the Croats and Dalmatians. It also stands in very close relation to that of the Slovenes. Some have proposed to give these people the generic title of Illyrian, probably suggested by classical associations and the souvenirs of the short-lived Napoleonic kingdom of 1809. The name, however, has not become permanent, and, if used at all, only obtains among scholars.[1] This great Illyrian family is not only divided politically,—some of its members being subjects of Austria, and others independent, for the few left to Turkey since the treaty of Berlin are not worthy of mention,—but also theologically, the chief creeds being those of the Greek and Latin Churches and the Protestants being comparatively insignificant in number. There is, also, a considerable sprinkling of Mahomedans in Bosnia and Herzegovina, where the language is strictly

---

[1] Cf. "Grammatik der illirischen Sprache," by Ignaz Berlić. Agram, 1850.

L

Servian, and many of those whose ancestors went over
to the Mussulman faith have kept their Slavonic
names and Slavonic customs.   This change of belief
took place soon after these provinces were overrun
by Turkey, the landed proprietors being anxious to
preserve their estates and influence.   The religious
divergence has led to a farther separation in the
alphabets employed, those of the Greek Church
naturally preferring the Cyrillian, and those of the
Roman the Latin.   This causes a deplorable confusion
and a chaos of orthographies.   Some take Vouk's
modified Cyrillian alphabet.   About forty years ago
an attempt was made by Dr. Ljudevit Gaj, the
founder of the so-called Illyrian school of literature,
but his efforts were only partially successful.

As in the present work we have only to do with the
older Servian literature, I shall extend my notice no
farther than the period of the extinction of Servian
nationality at the battle of Kosovo (1389).

The earliest composition which has come down to
us in the Illyrian language (to use the generic term)
is the production of an unknown priest of Dioklea,
now Duklja, a mere collection of ruins, formerly the
capital of south-western Illyria, on the river Moraca.
Hence he is called in Latin Anonymus Presbyter
Diocleus, or in Illyrian Pop Dukljanin.   He must
have lived about the middle of the twelfth century, as
the chronicle in verse compiled by him extends to
the year 1161.   The poem itself consists of about
1,165 lines.   Like our own rhyming histories, it is
tedious and is interesting only as a literary monument.

It is printed by Kukuljevic Sakcinski, in the Archives for South Slavonic Literature ("Arkiv za povêstnicu Jugoslavensku "). Agram, 1851. The early period of Servian literature has been investigated with great care by the celebrated Schafarik. I cannot, however, follow him here in his minute enumeration of all the oldest documents to be found in the Servian language, such as the inscriptions on coins. I shall·select the most important, and may mention here that there are Servian recensions of many of the chief works of Palæoslavonic literature, translations of Saints John Chrysostom, Gregory, and others.[1]

The following demand special notice.

(1) The Life of St. Simeon by his son St. Sabbas, the first Archbishop of Servia. This was written about the year 1210, but unfortunately is only preserved in a manuscript of the seventeenth century. Besides this we have a "Tipik " (collection of statutes) by him for the monastery of Studenitza, where he was an Igoumen. St. Sabbas enjoys a great reputation among his countrymen for his labours in the education of the people. He was the founder of the celebrated Khilander Monastery on Mount Athos, in the year 1192.

2. The History of St. Simeon and St. Sabbas by Dometian, compiled in 1264, and preserved in a manuscript of the fourteenth century; for the copy

[1] The oldest documents of the Servian language, properly so called, which have come down to us, are a letter of Koulin, the Ban of Bosnia, in 1189, and the letter of the Tzar Simeon Nemanya to the monastery of Khilander on Mount Athos.

must certainly have been written between 1350 an
1400. Dometian (or Domitian) was a monk of th
cloister of Khilander. It has been printed sever;
times, the latest edition being that of Danichich,
scholar to whom we are indebted for an admirabl
lexicon of the old Servian, indispensable to all student
of this interesting language.

3. The "Rodoslov," or Lives of Servian kings an
archbishops, compiled by Archbishop Daniel, wh
died in 1338. Here are contained the lives of King
Radoslav, Vladislav, Ourosh, Dragoutin, Quee
Helena, Miloutin, Ourosh III., and Stephen Dou
shan. After his death his book was continued b
an anonymous writer or writers in the work entitle
"Tzarostavnik." "The Rodoslov" has also bee
edited by Danichich (Agram, 1866). I must te
the reader that neither elegance of style nor vigou
of narration will be found in these production;
They are written in an involved and confused mar
ner, and the language differs very much from th
modern Servian, being, in fact, a kind of ecclesiastica
Slavonic, greatly modified by Servian influences. Th
prose is, however, as good as anything of the kind i;
our own country at a similar period.

4. The Life of Stephen Dechanski, founder c
the monastery called after him, written by Gregor
Tzamblak, an Igoumen of the same monastery.

5. In 1394, we have the code of laws of Kin,
Stephen Doushan, one of the earliest specimens c
Servian legislation. This can only be compared i
importance with the "Rousskaia Pravda" of Yaroslav

mentioned in a preceding chapter. These laws have been much praised for their humane and civilised spirit in many respects, especially their encouragement of hospitality. Some of the punishments, however, which they sanction, appear barbarous at the present time. Take the following as instances :—

" Whoever sells a Christian (slave) to a man of any other faith shall have his hands cut off and his tongue cut out.

" If a nobleman commits an assault on another nobleman, he is to have his hands and nose cut off; if a peasant commits an assault on a nobleman, he is to be hanged.

" If slaves assemble together in a riotous manner, they are to have their ears cut off and their eyebrows singed off." [1]

The Servian chroniclers, such as they have come down to us, are at best but scanty, and confined to very dry details. They end, for the most part, with the sixteenth century, when the country had long been under the yoke of the Turks. Whenever their style becomes less meagre, it is sure to grow florid, and it would be dangerous to receive some of the

---

[1] These laws were first published from the manuscript by Raich, in his " History," at the close of the last century, since which time they have been edited by Schafarik and Miklosich. I have used the convenient little edition printed by Novakovich at Belgrade (" Zakonik Stephana Doushana, Tzara Srpskog "), 1870. Macieiowski, a Pole, has written an excellent history of Slavonic legislation, of which there is a German translation. As these sheets are passing through the press, the death at Warsaw of this veteran is announced at the age of 90.

stories which they give us as authentic history. Thus
we are told, that after the battle of Kosovo, "one
Vojvode, Kraimir, begged Bayazet to permit him to
hold a silver basin that the noble head of his tzar
should not fall on the earth. Prince Bayazet was
so surprised by this extraordinary evidence of the
noble's loyal love to the czar that he granted his
request."[1] There is a very curious version in Servian
of the "Alexander Sage," one of the many forms
of this interesting mediæval legend. It was edited
with notes by Novakovich, and originally published
in the Glasnik (Messenger), a valuable Servian
literary journal, to which I may here take the occasion of expressing my great indebtedness. After the
fall of the Servian monarchy at the Battle of Kosóvo
in 1389, the written literature of Servia during some
centuries is but meagre, although the activity of the
Dalmatians to a certain extent compensated for it.
There was, however, a noble ballad literature living
orally among the people in the midst of their deplorable degradation. They did not forget that they
were once a nation. I will now speak of these
ballads, that are inferior to none which any other
European people can show. Some of the earlier
Dalmatian poets had alluded to such compositions,
and even introduced extracts from them into their
works, but the first attempt to collect them for the
use of the people was made by the Franciscan
monk, Andrew Kacic-Miosic, a Dalmatian, who died

[1] Cited by Madame Miyatovich, p. 31.

in 1783.   Here was clearly a man in advance of his
age, for such poems were altogether alien to the
artificial French taste, which was then dominant
throughout Europe.   Percy's "Reliques," which may
be said to have created the modern romantic school
of poetry, which rapidly spread from England to
Germany, were not published till 1765.   The collection of Miosic was printed at Venice in 1756
under the title of "Razgovor ugodni naroda Slovin-
skoga" (Recreations of the Slavonic People).   Many
of the poems were composed by Miosic himself, and
the old ones were very much tampered with by him.
It is to be regretted that such should have been the
case; but we must remember that Percy did not publish all the specimens in his collection in their original
form, and Allan Ramsay, both in his "Evergreen"
and "Tea-Table Miscellany," altered the Scotch
poems almost *ad libitum*.   It has been left for our
century to witness a severe fidelity in the reprints of
early authors, and the transcriptions of oral poetry.

That the Serbs must have had their national
songs from very early times, we may infer from the
travels of Nicephorus Gregoras,[1] who, in the year
1325–26, came to King Stephen Ourosh IV. of Servia
as ambassador from the Byzantine Emperor An-
dronicus the Elder.   He notices that some Serbs
attached to his suite sang "tragic songs celebrating
the great exploits of their national heroes."   As M.
Pipin remarks, this is important, because it shows the

[1] See "Kossovo," by Madame Miyatovich, p. 33 ; also Pipin
and Spasovich, i., p. 263.

existence of a national epic among the Serbs before the Battle of Kosóvo. In the description of an
embassy sent from Vienna to Constantinople in 1531,
a certain Kouripeshich, by birth a Slovene, speaks of
hearing songs sung in honour of Milosh, who slew
the Sultan Murad.

Extracts also began to appear in some of the
Dalmatian poets of the sixteenth century. The first
Western scholar who called attention to them was
the Abbé Fortis in 1794, but they were not well
known till the publication of the four volumes of
Vouk Stephanovich Karajich in 1814 ("Narodne
Srpske Pyésme") at Leipzig. Many of these were
translated into German by Theresa von Jacob,
afterwards the wife of Professor Robinson of America,
who wrote under the pseudonym of Talvj (" Volks-
lieder der Serben," Leipzig). Soon afterwards an
English version of some of the most remarkable
appeared from the pen of Dr. (afterwards Sir John)
Bowring, with an elaborate introduction. The ren-
derings, however, it must be confessed, are diffuse
and inaccurate. Bowring had a very imperfect knowledge of the Servian language, and Mrs. Robinson
roundly taxes him with having translated from her
German version. The selection published by the
present Lord Lytton in 1861 is also of no value, as
the pieces have been translated through the medium
of the French. The small work of Mme. Mijatovics
(Miyatovich), entitled "Kossóvo," published in 1881
in London, is in every way accurate, and will
give much valuable information to those desiring

to make a closer acquaintance with these interesting productions.

The metre of the Servian poems is the unrhymed trochaic, rendered familiar to Englishmen by Long-fellow's "Hiawatha"; it seems the natural rhythm of people in a rude state of civilisation with poetical instincts, occurring besides in the old Bohemian frag-ment, "The Judgment of Libusa" (Libusin Sond), and also in the Finnish Epic, the "Kalewala," to say nothing of many others.

In a little work like the present a minute analysis of these remarkable songs cannot be attempted. They are sung to an instrument with one string called a gousla, of which a representation may be seen prefixed to the first volume of Vouk's collection. It is a sort of guitar, and in shape resembles one half of a pear cut in two. No doubt the melody of the language, as in Italian, greatly assists all these *im-provisatori*. It is certainly a curious phenomenon, that in modern times we should find a class of Homeridæ chanting to such primitive music the heroic achievements of their ancestors. A great deal of this kind of poetry is still being composed, as many of the songs relate to comparatively modern events, especially the exploits of Peter the Great and Napoleon I. Madame Miyatovich, in the interesting work already cited, has given a curious picture of the modern Servian bard, as he is still to be found:—

"During the meeting of the National Assembly, I had the opportunity of hearing a certain peasant,

Anta Neshich, recite in blank verse, to numerous audiences outside the Assembly Room, the whole debate on the bill for introducing the fresh monetary system into Serbia, concluding with the final acceptation of the bill. The poet put the debate on the Budget into the same taking form, to the great delight of his many auditors. Anta Neshich, from Ripany, a village about fifteen miles from Belgrade, was himself a member of the Assembly, and this fact of course did not make his recitations outside the walls less interesting to his auditors."

She tells us, subsequently, that "according to Serbian tradition, the two sons of the last Serbian ruler, Despot George Brankovich (who reigned from 1427 to 1456), after having been blinded by order of Sultan Murat II., took up the profession of wandering minstrels. The blind princes, with gousla in hand, travelled from city to city, from castle to castle, singing songs of the 'good old time.'" The talent for improvisation is very widely spread among the Serbs. We are told that even the beggars make their petitions in this way, and the wailing over dead bodies, or by graves, is in a kind of rhythmic chant. The metrical form is much more accurately kept up among the Serbs than the Russians or Malo-Russians. We shall see that it is among the members of the eastern branch of the Slavonic languages we get this wealth of popular poetry. Bohemian is poor, and Polish hardly boasts anything at all.

To the majority of readers the cycle which treats of Knez Lazar and his fate at the Battle of Kosóvo, will

prove the most interesting. Very beautiful is that in
which Militza, the wife of Lazar, in order to save
some scion of her race, entreats her brothers, one
after another, to stay from the battle, but they are
all eager to go.

In the following translation something like the
metre of the original has been attempted :—

> Lazarus, the Tzar, at supper sitting,
> Had his wife, Militza, there beside him.
> Spake to him the Tzaritza Militza,—
> " Lazarus, Tzar, thou golden crown of Servia,
> Thou dost wend the morrow to Kosóvo,
> Taking with thee voievodes and servants,
> Leaving no one here within the palace.[1]
> Thou dost lead my nine beloved brothers,
> My nine brothers, the nine Yougovichi.
> Of my brethren leave me but one only,
> Leave me but one brother still to swear by."
> To her answers Lazarus, prince of Servia :
> " Queen Militza, wife and best belovëd,
> Whom of all thy brothers art thou asking
> That in our white palace I should leave thee ?"
> " Leave me Boshko Yougovich," she answers.
> Thus to her speaks Lazarus, prince of Servia :
> " Queen Militza, wife and best belovëd,
> On the morrow when the white day breaketh,
> When the day breaks and the sun has risen,
> When the city gates are wide thrown open,
> Hie thee to the portals of the city,
> There the band of warriors parading
> On their fiery steeds will grasp their lances,
> Near them Boshko Yougovich, thy brother,

---

[1] I have occasionally ventured to omit lines in order to condense the poem. The forms " voievode " and " voivode " have
both been used as suited best the metre.

Bears the standard of the Cross before them.
Take thou from me words of salutation,
Bid him give the flag to whom he pleaseth,
Bid him stay with thee within the palace."
On the morrow, when the day had broken,
When the barriers of the town were opened,
Queen Militza hied her to the portals,
Took her stand at entry of the city,
Saw the warriors all parade before her—
Bosko Yougovich among the warriors,
On his steed and all with gold resplendent,
And Christ's glorious banner downward flowing.
And there comes the Tzaritza Militza,
Lays her hand upon the palfrey's bridle.
At the gates she reaches to her brother,
Thus with gentle accents doth address him :
" Boshko Yougovich, alas ! my brother,
Lo ! the Tzar hath granted my entreaties,
And thou needst not journey to Kosóvo.
To thee doth he send his choicest blessing,
Let whoe'er thou pleasest take the standard,
At Kroushévatz with me thou shalt linger,
I shall have a brother leal to swear by."
To his sister Yougovich replieth :
" To thy palace white return, fair sister,
But I shall not backward journey with thee,
Still my faithful hands shall clutch the standard,
Tho' the Tzar should give me e'en Kroushévatz.
Never may the army on me gazing
Call me Boshko Yougovich, the craven,
He who has not dared to seek Kosóvo
In Christ's honour there his blood to lavish,
Yea, and for his holy faith to perish."
Thus he spoke and sped him through the portal.
After him came Youg Bogdan, the aged,
And the seven Yougovichi with him,
Upon all the seven in order calling,

Never answer she nor look receiveth.
Yet a little longer time she waiteth,
And there cometh Yougovich Voïno
Leading proudly forth Tzar Lazar's horses.
And the steeds are decked with golden housings,
And she throws her arms around her brother,
And doth in these words at once accost him :
" Oh, my brother, Yougovich Voïno,
Thou art granted to my close entreaties,
And the Tzar doth send thee kindly greeting !
Give the horses to what chiefs thou choosest
Thou with me shalt rest thee at Kroushévatz,
I shall have a brother still to swear by."
To her Voïno Yougovich replieth :—
" O my sister, to thy white tower hie thee.
Never backward goes a noble warrior,
Never leaves the coursers of his master,
Even when he knows that death awaits him.
Let me, sister, go unto Kosóvo
For the Holy Cross my blood to lavish,
Dying for my faith and with my brothers."
Thus he spake, and quickly passed the portals.
And the Tzaritza, when she beheld him,
Fell upon the cold stones in her anguish,
Fell half-lifeless on the chilly pavement.
And anon there came Lazar the glorious,
And when he beheld his wife Militza
From his manly visage tears were flowing.
Gazing to the right hand and the left hand,
Goluban he called, his trusty servant.
" Goluban, my servant, tried and faithful,
From thy swan-white horse descend, I pray thee,
By her fair white hands take thou thy lady ;
Lead her back unto the lofty palace,
There I pray thee by God's grace to tarry.
Go not thou to battle at Kosóvo,
Rest thee with the Tzaritza in the palace."

From his horse the serving man descended ;
Down his white cheeks tears full fast were pouring,
From his snow-white steed forthwith descends he,
By her white hands takes his mistress fallen,
Takes her straight unto her lofty palace.
But his heart's desire he cannot conquer,
He must hie him to Kosóvo's battle,
He hath mounted straight his snow-white palfrey,
He hath ridden swiftly to Kosóvo.

It was at the Battle of Kosóvo (the field of black-birds) that the Serbs were utterly defeated by the Turkish Sultan Murad on the 10th of June, 1383. No event has been more celebrated in the national songs than this. Many are the lays to tell of the treachery of Vouk Brankovich and the glorious self-immolation of Milosh Obilich, who stabbed the conqueror on the battle-field. One of the lays tells us how the news of the result of the battle was brought by two ravens. The shroud made of silk embroidered with gold, with which his Tzaritza Militza covered the body of her husband, is still preserved in the cloister of Vodnik in Syrmia ; and a tree which the beloved queen planted is still shown to travellers at Zupa. One of the ballads deals with the discovery of the head of Lazar after the battle,[1] and its miraculous appearance.

I will conclude with one more specimen of the cycle of the Battle of Kosóvo, which shall be given in a literal prose version :—

[1] For many interesting details, see "Travels in the Slavonic Provinces of Turkey," by Mackenzie and Irby, i. 182 ; also the book of Madame Miyatovich, previously mentioned.

The maiden of Kosóvo rose early ;
She rose early on Sunday,
On Sunday before the bright sun,
Tucked up her white sleeves,
Tucked them up to her white elbows.
She carries white loaves on her shoulders,
In her hands two golden goblets,
In one cold water,
In the other ruddy wine,
She goes straight to the plain of Kosóvo ;
Then the maiden wanders over the battle-field,
Over the field of the noble Prince.
She goes among the bleeding heroes,
When she finds any living
She bathes him with cold water ;
She gives him the red wine sacramentally,
And feeds him with white bread.
Fate conducted her
To the hero, Paul Orlovich,
The young standard-bearer of the Prince,
And she found him, still living,
Though his right hand was cut off.[1]
His ribs are all broken,
And she takes him from the gory stream,
She bathes him with the cool water,
She gives him of the red wine. .
When the heart of the young man revived,
Paul Orlovich spake :
" Dear sister, maiden of Kosóvo,
What great need hast thou
That thou disturbest heroes in their blood
Whom dost thou, young as thou art,
Seek in the battle-field?
Is it a brother, or a brother's son,

---

[1] I have ventured to condense this poem by omitting a line occasionally.

Or dost thou seek an aged parent ? "
The maiden of Kosóvo said :
" Dear brother, unknown soldier,
I seek no one related to me.
Neither a brother, nor a brother's child,
Nor an aged father.
Dost thou know, O strange warrior,
When Prince Lazar gave the sacrament to his host,
At the beautiful church, Samodrezha,
By the hands of thirty monks, three weeks ago?
Last of all came three valiant chiefs ;
One was the Chief Milosh,
The other Ivan Kosanchich,
And the third Milan Toplitza.
I was there at the gates,
As the voivode Milosh passed by—
As handsome a youth as any in this world :
His sabre trailed along the ground,
A silk cap, ornamented with feathers, he wore :
On the hero a variegated mantle,
About his neck a silk handkerchief.
He looked around and cast his eyes on me,
He loosened the variegated mantle,
Loosened and gave it to me.'
' Take, maiden, the variegated mantle,
By which you will remember me ;
By the mantle think upon my name.
See, I go to perish, my love,
In the camp of the noble Prince.
Pray God, my dear love,
That I return whole from the camp,
And that good fortune may come upon you.
I will marry you to my Milan,
My Milan, my dear friend,
Who is my sworn brother ;
By the highest God and St. John ;
At thy wedding I will be groomsman.'

After him came Ivan Kosanchich,
As handsome a youth as any in this world,
On his finger a golden ring;
He looked round and gazed on me,
From his hand he took the ring of gold,
From his hand, and gave it me.
' Take, maiden, the ring of gold,
By which you will remember me,
And by the ring think of my name.
Lo ! I go to perish, my love,
At the camp of the honourable Prince.
Pray God, my dear love,
That I come back from the camp sound,
And a good fortune may befall thee.
I will marry thee to my Milan,
My Milan, my dear friend,
Who is my sworn brother,
By the highest God and St. John,
I will conduct thee as a bride.
After him came Milan Toplitza,
As handsome a youth as any on this earth,
On his arm a golden bracelet.
He looked round and gazed on me,
From his arm he took the golden bracelet,
From his arm took it and gave it me.
' Take, maiden, the bracelet of gold,
By which you will remember me,
And by the bracelet think of my name,
For I go to perish, my love,
At the camp of the honoured Prince.
Pray God, my dear love,
That I return safe from the camp,
That good fortune may befall thee,
I will take thee for my true love.'
And the three warriors went.
These now to-day I seek on the battle-field."
And Paul Orlovich said :—

M

" Dear sister, maiden of Kosóvo,
Dost thou see, love, those war-lances,
The highest and the thickest ?
There flowed the blood from the heroes,
To the stirrups of the good horse,
To the stirrups and to the girths,
And to the silken girdle of the hero.
There they have all fallen :
Go now to thy white house,
Stain not with blood thy skirt and sleeves."
When the maiden heard these words,
Tears flowed on her fair face ;
She went to her white house,
And mourned from her white throat,
Ah, unhappy one, what a fate has come to thee !
" If, unhappy woman that I am, I touch the green pine,
Soon will the green tree be withered."

Besides the historical persons who figure in the
ballads, there is the great legendary hero, Marko
Kralevich, who, like the Russian Ilya Murometz, has
many of the characteristics of a supernatural being.
He lives a hundred and sixty years, and no sword or
club can kill him.   His victories, chiefly over the
Turks   and   Hungarians,   are   told   in   the   most
exaggerated phraseology.   It is the incarnation of
manhood and prowess which we find in the popular
poetry of all nations.   At last, in the glory of his
strength, Marko perishes on the field of battle, but
the circumstances of his death are enveloped in
mystery.   According to some he was conveyed from
the scene of strife to a secret cave, where his wounds
were healed, and where, like our own Arthur in his
" isle-valley of Avilion," he lies hidden, destined to

appear on some future occasion to rescue his people from their oppressors. Almost as mysterious a being as the hero himself is his horse Sharatz, who was presented to him by a vila or fairy. I have already alluded to the Samodivas and Samovilas of the Bulgarians. The songs of these mysterious beings are of such bewildering sweetness, like those of the sirens of old, that men who listen will eventually lose their reason; on the other hand, they are capable of human passions, and we find them enamoured of Servian and Bulgarian heroes, and luring them away. Sometimes, also, they carry off the fair maidens of a district, as in the story of "Kilmeny," the best thing written by the Ettrick Shepherd. Many of the love-songs and poems relating to domestic life are exquisite, and show great refinement of feeling. All this must necessarily be a source of amazement to those who are prepared to find in the Serbs only a barbarous people. After the death of Vouk Stephanovich a supplementary volume was published by his widow, which her husband had left prepared for the press ("Srpske Narodne Pyesme iz Herzegovine. Vienna, 1866"). A good collection of songs of the Montenegrins ("Tzrnogortzi") was also edited at Leipzig in 1857 by Milutinovich, under the pseudonym of Choubr Choikovich. We cannot hope for a much further prolongation of this delightful period of popular poetry in Slavonic countries. Such productions only emanate from a people conscious of great national struggles and national triumphs, before naïve emotions and fresh feelings have been flattened down to a dead level by cosmopolitanism and the matter-of-fact of science.

Vouk Stephanovich himself never visited Bosnia and the Herzegovina ;[1] a circumstance which he very much regretted, as these are two great nests of Slavonic song. Those which he published were taken down by others and communicated to him. But since his death a little volume of Servian national songs from Bosnia was published at Sarayevo in 1867 by Bogolub Petranovich ("Srpske Narodne Pyesme iz Bosne"). Here the lays, many of which are very beautiful and of a truly idyllic character, are thickly interspersed with Turkish words. From this volume the following sweet little lyric seems worthy of being extracted :—

Oh ! beautiful maiden,
Why dost thou hide thyself from me ?
Do not hide thine eyes from me,
I may know thee
By thy sheep.
Thy sheep are white,
With marks on the white.

Oh ! beautiful maiden,
Do not hide thine eyes from me.
I may know thee
By thy lambs,
Thy white lambs,
With marks on the white.

----

[1] " Pipin and Spasovich," i. 279.

Oh ! beautiful maiden,
Do not hide thine eyes from me,
I may know thee
By thy white kerchief.
Thy white kerchief is
Embroidered with purple.

Oh ! beautiful maiden,
Do not hide thine eyes from me,
I may know thee
By thine embroidered robe. ,
Thy robe is embroidered,
Ornamented with gold buttons.

Oh ! beautiful maiden,
Do not hide thine eyes from me,
I may know thee
By thy tall stature,
Slender and tall,
Like a green palm.

Oh ! beautiful maiden,
Hide not thine eyes from me,
I may know thee
By thy white face—
Thy face is white,
Ruddy on the white.
I will take away thy kerchief,
Look at thy black eyes,
And kiss thy white face.

Later collections of Servian poetry have appeared
by Rayachevich and Ristich. The great scholar
Miklosich has written a work on the national poetry
of the Croats ("Beiträge zur Kenntniss der Slavischen
Volkspoesie. Die Volksepik der Kroaten "). A collection of songs and epic fragments is given in this

work, most of which are devoted to the topics on which Slavonic song seems never to grow weary, viz., the sad episode of the battle of Kosóvo. Miklosich remarks very truly, that although the modern Croatian lays have adopted the metre now so much in vogue in Servia, yet at one time they could boast of one of their own, something like the old-fashioned English Alexandrine, or the πολιτικοὶ στίχοι of the degenerate periods of Greek literature. He compares it to the verses quoted by Lord Byron from the " Lamentable History of Miss Bailey " :—

"A captain bold, of Halifax, who lived in country quarters.

The popular poetry of no other Slavonic race exhibits this metre.

The loss of culture which Servia was obliged to suffer when passing under the yoke of the Turk was in some measure compensated by the outburst, in the succeeding century, of a vigorous national life among the Dalmatians, especially in the little republic of Ragusa (called by the Slavonians Dubrovnik), which reached a high pitch of civilisation. During the fifteenth, sixteenth, and seventeenth centuries this city, now in a state of decay, was a kind of Slavonic Athens. The influence of Italian literature then culminating, was further strengthened by crowds of learned Greeks, Chalkokondylas, Laskaris, and others, who found refuge within its walls when Constantinople was taken by the Turks.

The city of Ragusa (to use its Italian name, which is more familiar to us) was founded by fugitives from

Epidamnus in the middle of the third century A.D. It is said to have been called from the rock Lausa, close by which it is situated.[1] Although surrounded by powerful neighbours, it managed for a long time to preserve its independence, and had extensive commercial relations, not only with the interior of the Balkan peninsula, but with Italy, Sicily, Spain, Greece, Alexandria, and the East. Its relations with Venice were very close, and a dialect of Italian was spoken within its walls as well as Slavonic. It is thus that we find Italian and Slavonic forms of the names of the leading Ragusan families. Gradually the Venetians became masters of the whole Dalmatian coast, with the exception of Ragusa. The little republic did not lose its independence till the year 1808, when it was taken by the French and annexed to the newly-founded Illyrian kingdom. But this creation was not destined to last long; by the Congress of Vienna in 1814, Ragusa and the Dalmatian coast were handed over to the Austrian empire.

It does not come within the scope of my little book to give a complete account of Dalmatian poetry. Lyrics generally and the lyric drama seem to have been its staple productions. Hannibal Lucic (1480–1525) was a very popular poet in his day, author of love-songs, a drama, and translations, published first by his son, Anthony, at Venice, in 1556, and reprinted by the indefatigable Dr. Gaj, who occupied himself

[1] Thus: Lausa, Rausa, Rachusa, Ragusa. See Pipin and Spasovich, 168.

with editing the Dalmatian classics at Agram in 1847. Very celebrated in its time was the "Jegjupka" or "Gipsy" of Andrew Cubranovic (1500–1559). We are told of the poet that he was originally a silver-smith, but deserted this craft and betook himself to that of the Muses. "The Gipsy" is said to have been evoked in this wise. The author was, on one occasion, following a young lady, the object of his affections, and urging his addresses, when she turned round and said scornfully, in Italian, to her attendant, in the hearing of the poet, "Che vuole da me questo zingaro?" (What does that gipsy want with me?) The despised lover took up the word of reproach, and wrote a poem in which he introduced a gipsy prophesying their various fortunes to a company of ladies, and concluding with an expostulation to the hard-hearted nymph for her obduracy. Schafarik speaks of this piece with great enthusiasm, and calls it "a truly splendid flower in the garden of the Illyrian Muses."

The chief of the Ragusan poets was Ivan Gundulic (sometimes called by his Italian name of Gondola). The "Osman" on which his fame rests is an epic in twelve books, and celebrates the victory of the Poles under Chodkiewicz over the Turks and Tatars in 1621 at Choczim. Gundulic died in the year 1638, aged fifty, having discharged several important public offices in the state. "His death," says Schafarik, "was not too early for his fame, but too early for literature and the glory and prosperity of his country." After the earthquake of 1667 Ragusa never recovered its former prosperity. The influence of the Renaissance and of Italian literature upon the Dalmatian authors is very conspicuous, as is shown in the abundance of translations from the Greek, Latin, and Italian classics. Professor Armin Pavic has written an excellent history of the Ragusan drama, which tells us how active it was.

I shall include in this chapter a few remarks on the scanty literature of the Slovenes. We find them frequently styled Wends, and their language Wendish, —an inconvenient term, as it causes some confusion with the tongue of the Lusatian Wends, who belong to the western branch of the great Slavonic family, and are included partly in Prussia, partly in Saxony. Their literature will form the subject of a future chapter. The Slovenish language is spoken in Carinthia, Carniola, and a portion of Styria, where it begins just south of Klagenfurth. It is also the vernacular of some parts of Hungary. These provinces have accompanied the various fortunes of the Austrian empire. The importance of Slovenish literature is indeed slight, but their language (for it can assert higher claims than those of a dialect) has acquired a great interest from the views of Kopitar, Miklosich, and others, who regard their country as the cradle of the old Slavonic, now used only as the ecclesiastical language.[1] It was here, according to some traditions, that Cyril and Methodius principally laboured.

I have already alluded to the efforts of Ljudevit

---

[1] See the further discussion of this subject in the first chapter.

Gaj to construct a regular South Slavonic language,
and to weld the Servian, Croatian, and Slovenish into
one harmonious whole. Great difficulties, however,
stand in the way. If a mere literary language is
created, it will become unintelligible to the humbler
classes, and this will greatly assist the insidious
efforts at Germanisation which are constantly going
on under the influence of the Government. If the
people are to remain Slavs, they must be educated
in their native language. Slovenish stands in nearly
the same relation to Servian and Croatian as Slovak
to Bohemian—it has preserved many older forms.
Slovenish has kept the dual not only in pronouns and
substantives, but even in verbs; and many other
peculiarities could be specified approaching far closer
to the antique type. A fair idea may be formed of
the area over which this language is spoken if we
consider it as extending to Klagenfurt in the north,
Fiume (Slavonic, Reka) in the south, Agram and
Varasdin on the east, and the Adriatic on the west.
A good grammar of it was published by Kopitar at
Laibach in 1808, which contains an introduction with
a classification of the Slavonic languages. This was an
invaluable work for the time ; nothing so good on
Slavonic philology appeared till the " Institutiones
Linguæ Slavicæ Dialecti Veteris " of Dobrovsky, in
1822. An excellent grammar of Slovenish, by Schuman,
a pupil of Miklosich, has recently been published at
Laibach. The orthography of the language has been
very much improved, and it is to be hoped that some
of the Germanisms which now disfigure it will be

expelled. A very elaborate "Deutsch-Slovenisches Wörterbuch" was published at Laibach in 1860, in two stout octavo volumes. The expenses of its production were defrayed by a sum of money left by Bishop Wolf. I am told by a Slovenish friend that the Slovenish-German part is in course of preparation, and may be expected before long. Although so little cultivated, this Slavonic language is one of the most interesting on account of the curious forms it exhibits.

In the old Slovenish language are the celebrated Frisingian manuscripts, so called because discovered at Frising, in Bavaria, in 1807; they are now preserved in the museum at Munich. They have been assigned to the ninth or tenth centuries; and, if this date is correct (and there does not seem any reason to dispute it), this must be the oldest piece of Slavonic writing in existence. These fragments have been edited by Köppen, Kopitar, and Miklosich. Their contents are of a religious character. Schafarik is inclined to take a later date than some other Slavists, and assigns them to the tenth century. We must remember that Christianity was taught among the Slovenes very early : even in the seventh century Italian missionaries from Aquila, and German from Salzburg having visited them. Their history as an independent people was soon brought to a close. After having formed a portion of the great Slavonic empire of the half-mythical Samo, who ruled from 627 to 662, they fell under the yoke of the Bavarians, and subsequently became

subject to the Franks. Since this time they have
formed a portion of the German, and subsequently
the Austrian, empire, and duchies have been carved
out of their territories. Considering the great persecutions which they endured for so many centuries,
it is indeed marvellous that their language has been
so well preserved. The celebrated Baron Herberstein,
whose work, " De Rebus Muscoviticis," furnishes
such an interesting account of Russia in the sixteenth
century, was a Slovene by birth, having been born at
Vipach, in Styria. He has told us how his Slavonic
origin was a frequent cause of reproach to him among
his schoolfellows.

Professor Jagic, in an article in the *Archiv für
Slavische Philologie*, I. 450, explains the Latin letters
in which the Frisingian fragments are found as follows.
He supposes that some German preacher of the
Latin rite, struck with the great success which the
Slavonic missions had had among the Slovenes,
adopted part of their ritual, with some slight modifications. The language is at best of a very mixed
character, and seems to complicate rather than explain
the difficulty of the origin of the Palæoslavonic.
The whole question of the lives and working of Cyril
and Methodius is involved in difficulties. It has
never been clearly made out at what time and where
the version of the parts of Scripture which they translated was executed. Some have thought that the
Slavonic apostles carried their version with them
from Thessalonica into Moravia ; others that it was
made when they were among the western Slavs, and

Professor Miklosich thinks that the Slovenes extended over a much wider extent of territory than at present. Political and religious feelings have been imported into this question, which, as Pîpin truly observes, has almost become an Austrian-Catholic dispute against a Russian-Orthodox.

The Slovenes are poorer in ballads than most of their Slavonic brethren, so that here we have no fine collection of national poetry to fall back upon dating from a remote past. A vigorous impulse was given to their language and literature by the labours of Primus Truber, born in 1508 near Laibach, still the great centre of Slovenish culture. He was an inde‐ fatigable Protestant preacher, the intimate friend of Melanchthon, one of those noble-hearted workers whom we frequently find in the early history of a language. Persecution was soon active against him and the detestable Ferdinand I. (almost as hateful as the second of his name, who deluged Bohemia with blood) issued orders for his arrest—a proceeding which would probably have been followed by his summary execution. Truber, however, fled to the court of Christopher, Duke of Wurtemberg, who pro-tected him. Here a printing-press was set up under the patronage of Ungnad, Baron von Sonneg, and other Protestants, which was busily employed several years. The Glagolitic types, with which most of the books were printed, became, curiously enough, at a later period, the property of the College de Propa-gandâ Fide, at Rome. The productions of this press are regarded as great bibliographical curiosities. The

Gospel of St. Matthew was published in Slovenish in 1555, and, two years later, the whole New Testament. A copy of this rare work is preserved in the Bodleian Library. Although the sphere of his labours was necessarily limited, we find in Truber as genuine a worker as Luther or Calvin. Considering that his efforts were to evangelise his people, shall we not say of him " magna voluisse magnum "? Piety, love of country, learning, energy, all were there ; only the vulgar element of success was wanting, and his poor Slovenes were too few to spread his fame. Let us direct attention, be it but for a moment, to this neglected apostle of an obscure country, and piously clear the weeds from his grave. He died in 1586, having seen a good old age ; but his labours were destined to be brought to nothing by the odious policy of Ferdinand II., whose misdeeds are fully recorded in history.[1]

A good co-operator with Truber was Juri Dalmatin, the year of whose birth is unknown. He studied at Tübingen, and appears to have been a learned man, as he talks of having translated the Scriptures from the "springs" of the original languages. In 1583 he went to Wittenberg to superintend the publication of his Bible, which duly appeared the following year. This Bible is justly called by Schafarik "the master-piece of the old Protestant literature of the Wends." It is now a great bibliographical rarity, but remains a

---

[1] Kopitar does not hold the worthy father quite guiltless of having foisted Germanisms upon the language, especially an *article*, which no Slavonic language ought properly to have.

monument of the piety and learning of the man who accomplished so grand a labour. The latter days of this worthy preacher seem to have been greatly troubled, on account of the persecutions previously mentioned. We hear accounts from Valvasor, in his well-known "Honour of the Duchy of Carniola" (*Ehre des Herzogthums Krain*),[1] of his being protected and concealed by Baron von Augsberg in a crypt under a stable in his castle. It is a great pity that so little has been written in a form accessible to Western readers on the labours and sufferings of the chief workers of the Reformation in these provinces. It is clear enough in the history of the world that not merely heroism of the individual is necessary, but there must be some grand show-place for him in which he may display his heroism, if he is to get recognition. How many readers have heard even the names of these obscure apostles?

As Truber was to the Slovenes, so was Michael Bucic (between 1564–1574) to the Croatians. He made use of the so-called Provincial Croatian dialect, which the most approximates to the Slovenish.[2] Thus, in Croatia, as in Carinthia, the cultivation of the national language was greatly fostered by Protes-

---

[1] This work, although written in German, is regarded with great pride by the Slovenes. It appeared in 1689 in folio at Laibach. The author impoverished himself by publishing it, owing, among other causes, to the expensive plates.

[2] Classed as Croato-Slovenish in the list of dialects in the first chapter.

tantism. Bucic published several books in Croatian, but the details of his life are meagre. He was ultimately driven from his native country, but his fate is not known. Literature in the province of Croatia did not have a very great development. The cause of this may be traced to its union with Hungary. It was thus politically separated from Dalmatia, and from Servia it was divided both politically and religiously. Latin became the language of the Church and of culture, as in Hungary. Many of the nobles, however, showed a patriotic spirit, and did what they could to foster their native tongue. Thus we are told that Count George Zrinski, who died in 1603, had a printing-press on his estate.

In the South-Slavonic provinces, as in Bohemia, Protestantism was flourishing very vigorously till stamped out by Ferdinand II. The sanguinary means by which this was accomplished are to be read of in some of the darkest of those pages upon which the history of the House of Habsburg is recorded,—at best but a dreary catalogue of civil and religious persecutions. It is gratifying to think that the attempt to force all these peoples into a most unwilling homogeneity has resulted in a complete failure, never more conspicuous than at the present time. In the year 1584, the first Slovenish grammar was printed at Wittenberg by Bohoric, a schoolmaster of Laibach and pupil of Melanchthon. In 1592, the first Slovenish dictionary was published by Hieronymus Megiser, under the following title: "Dictionarium quatuor linguarum, videlicet Germanicæ, Latinæ, Illuricæ, quæ vulgo Slavonica appellatur, et Italicæ sive Hetruscæ auctore Hieronymo Megisero. Gratz, 1592." After the Protestant movement had been annihilated by Ferdinand II., a complete torpor fell upon the unhappy country, as in the case of Bohemia. This gloom lasted during almost the whole of the eighteenth century. But a revival took place at the beginning of the present, and the Slovenes can now show a fair array of authors. Two literary societies have been founded, which busy themselves with the publication of a journal and useful books. The great centre of this activity is Laibach.

CHAPTER VII.

THE WESTERN BRANCH.—EARLY LITERATURE OF POLAND.

In treating of early Polish literature, I shall fix for my period that which extends from the earliest times till the year 1606, which marks the arrival of the Jesuits in the country under the influence of Sigismund III., and here we shall find in reality that the Polish literature, however much it has been developed in modern times, in the early period is one of the scantiest.

The language is still spoken by about ten millions of people, and probably, after all, the Pole has more to dread from the German than from his brother Slavonians. Polish is being faster eliminated from the Grand Duchy of Posen than from Galicia and Russian Poland. It is not recognised as an official language in the former country any more than in the territories appropriated by the "Moskals," but the Germans alone have been guilty of the insolence and bad taste of changing the names of many Polish towns and villages, which had become historical, into such monstrosities as Bismarcksdorf, Weissenburg, and Sedan. A recent writer in the Bohemian Journal has noticed the gradual receding of the Polish language from Lithuania, where, we must remember, it was rather superinduced as the idiom of the upper classes and culture, and was never on the lips of the people properly so called. The Lithuanian language, which must always possess a great fascination for the student of comparative philology, has not risen above the dignity of the tongue of peasants. Before this country was attached to Poland, the White Russian was the official language, and in this the laws of the land were promulgated.

We cannot promise our readers the same feast of popular poetry among the Poles as they will find in other Slavonic countries. Legendary lays in the style of the Russian bîlini are wholly wanting, but they undoubtedly existed in the earlier times. Just as Macaulay detected and restored to something like its original shape a lyric fragment in the chronicle of the Monk of St. Gall, so a curious reader may find, from the poetical colouring of the page, many a lay imbedded in the prosaic writings of Gallus, Kadlubek, and Dlugosz. Wiszniewski, in his "History of Polish Literature," has collected several of these allusions, and Gallus, the old Latin chronicler of the twelfth century, gives a long translation of a poem written on Boleslas (or, in Polish, Boleslaw) the Brave, which I will not inflict upon my readers, however interesting it might prove to the antiquarian. Some old Polish songs of the sixteenth century are printed in Wojcicki's "Library of Ancient Writers," but the work most complete in its plan is that of Oskar Kolberg, the publication of which was commenced at Warsaw in 1857. This

bids fair to be an exhaustive collection of Polish
songs, proverbs, and traditions, and is well worth
the attention of those who busy themselves about
folk-lore.   Before dismissing this subject of popular
literature, allusion may be made to the works of
Oleska, and Zegota Paul on Galician poetry : there
are also the " Songs of the Polish People of Upper
Silesia," edited by Julius Roger, Breslau, 1863 ; a
collection of national tales and proverbs of Galicia,
published by Baracz ; and the "Aberglauben aus
Masuren," by Töppen, will be found interesting.[1]

A great deal of the early literature written in Poland
is in the Latin language.   The use of Latin seems to
have soon begun among this people, probably introduced by the foreign ecclesiastics with whom the
country was flooded.   The earliest specimen of the
Polish language is the so-called Psalter of Queen
Margaret, discovered in 1826, at the convent of St.
Florian, near Linz, in Austria, which dates from the
middle of the fourteenth century.   It was edited by
Dunin-Borkowski, at Vienna, in 1834.   It has since
formed the subject of a valuable monograph by
Professor Nehring.   According to an article by
Leciejewski in a recent number of the " Archiv," in
its present form it is but a copy of a much older
text.   Connected with this period is the ancient
Polish hymn or war-song (for it was a mixture of
both), attributed to St. Adalbert of Prague, a great

---

[1] I regret that, after careful search, I have not been able to
find any specimens of Polish popular poetry which would
possess attractions for the general reader in a translation.

apostle among the Slavs. This is the *Piesn Boga Rodzica*, an address to the Virgin Mary, which is said to have been always sung by the Poles when advancing to battle. It will be found prefixed to the " Historical Songs " of Niemcewicz, and has been translated after a fashion by Bowring ("Specimens of the Polish Poets," p. 12). Rakowiecki is inclined to think that this production dates from a period not earlier than the fourteenth century, but the whole history of the celebrated song has been fully handled by Nehring in the "Archiv für Slavische Philologie " (vol. i., p. 73). The oldest known text of it is in a manuscript of 1408, preserved in the Biblioteka Jagiellonska at Cracow. Janko von Melstin, the Castellan of Cracow, left a sum of money to the church of All Saints at that city, to provide for the singing of this song on certain occasions. In the deed of gift it is entitled, *Salutaris illa et plena cœlestibus mysteriis cantilena Boga Rodzicza Dziewicza.*

In a manuscript of 1456 we have another copy of the song, with the addition of six verses. The first printed form of it appears in 1506 in Laski's " collection of Polish Laws." The legend, which assigns its composition to St. Adalbert, was gradually springing up, " Prima omnium devotissima et tanquam vates regni Poloniæ cancio seu canticum Boga Rodzicza manibus et oraculo St. Adalberti scripta." This poem always enjoyed great popularity among the Poles. As a proof, we might quote the entry in the account-book of Sigismund I., preserved among the national archives of Warsaw,—*Rustico qui cantabat Boga Rodzicza coram domino principe, ad mandatum S. M. dedi* 3 *grossos.* The old historian Dlugosz had long before called it *patrium carmen.* The result of Professor Nehring's investigations is that the song was probably modelled upon Bohemian hymns, and he cites some from which particular expressions have been taken. I have thought it allowable to discuss at some length the origin of this remarkable poem, which has exercised such a talismanic influence upon the Poles, and concerning which there is no account in the English language which can be relied upon. This poem was translated into Latin Sapphics by the Polish poet of the Renaissance, Sarbiewski, of whom I shall shortly speak more at length. A great many Church songs were composed by a certain John Lodzia, who was bishop of Posen from 1335 to 1346, one to the Virgin Mary,—"Salve, salutis Janua," another beginning, "Lux clarescit in vitâ," &c. These productions appear to have enjoyed great popularity in Poland for a long time. Unfortunately, they are in Latin, and cannot have reached the people. It is this exotic culture, so prevalent throughout Poland at all stages, which almost justifies the severe remark of M. Courrière that they have always been the least Slavonic of the Slavonic peoples. Of Lodzia we are told by the old chroniclers that he was greatly addicted to the Muses, but led a life much too jovial for an ecclesiastic.[1] And here I may find

---

[1] Röpell, "Geschichte Polens," ii. 561.

a convenient place for mentioning the fragments of Polish manuscripts which careful antiquaries have succeeded in discovering, hidden as they were in public or private libraries, sometimes even fastened in the binding of a book, as several precious Bohemian pages have been found. Two fragments of this kind were published by Dr. Celichowski in 1875; the same scholar also printed at Posen the Latin-Polish vocabulary appended to the "Jus Magdeburgicum" dating from the fourteenth century. This "Jus Magdeburgicum" was the code of laws by which the German artisans in the large towns were governed, for we must not forget that the trade of Poland was chiefly in the hands of foreigners.[1]

Macieiowski has printed a version of the 50th Psalm, which he assigns to the end of the thirteenth century. The "Psalter of Queen Margaret," as it has been called, belongs undoubtedly to the second half of the fourteenth century. It has been named from Margaret, the first wife of King Louis of Hungary. This princess died in 1349. The book has been supposed to belong to her, from the letter M. inscribed upon it, and the arms of Anjou. Röpell, however, rather leans to the opinion that it belonged to Mary, the daughter of Louis.

The so-called Bible of Queen Sophia, or Bible of

---

[1] This probably explains the language of Boorde: "Theyr rayment and apparel is made after the High Doche fashion, with two wrynckles and a plyght: *theyr speech is corrupt Doche.*" See Boorde's "Introduction of Knowledge," p. 169. Reprint by Mr. Furnivall, for the Early English Text Society.

Szaroszpatak, has been edited by Malecki. Mention
of this remarkable book was made in the description
of a tour by Count Teleky; this attracted the attention of Dobrovsky, the eminent Slavist, who brought
it to the notice of Bandtkie, author of a "History of
Polish Literature"; scholars, however, did not occupy
themselves with it till it was again brought forward in
the second edition of Dobrovsky's "Slavin" edited by
Hanka. The Bible is imperfect, and only contains
the early books, *e.g.*, the Pentateuch, Joshua, Ruth,
and Kings.[1] It is said to have been written for Sophia,
the fourth wife of Jagiello about the year 1455, but
the tradition is perhaps not very well founded. Besides
the Psalter previously mentioned, the memoirs of a
Janissary, about which I shall speak at greater length
shortly, and the chronicle of Chwalczewski, it forms
the most valuable memorial of the Polish language
as it existed before the sixteenth century. A few
other remains may be mentioned, the Prayer-book
of Waclaw (*Modlitwy Waclawa*), edited by Alexander
Prezdziecki, the fragment of a sermon on marriage
(*Ulamek starozytnego kazania o malzenstwie*) printed
by Gloger, a letter of St. Bernard by Kluczycki; to
these may be added notices of some Polish glosses
and verses in three Latin manuscripts by Szujski
also of a manuscript of Polish sermons by Ketrynski.
Altogether it may be said that the number of known

---

[1] There are, however, portions of Judith, Tobit, and Daniel
To judge by the facsimile appended to Malecki's elaborate
edition, the codex must be a very handsome one. He traces
the first mention of it to the year 1604.

Polish manuscripts written before the sixteenth century, although small, has been greatly augmented by
discoveries during the last few years.

The early writers in Latin deserve a brief mention.
One of the first was Martin Gallus, supposed by some
from his name to have been a Frenchman.   This,
however, has been disputed by Lelewel, who considers
that it was merely a translation of some such name as
" Kura " into Latin.   Röpell remarks with truth that
all we know with certainty about him is that he lived
at the court of Boleslaw III., surnamed the Wry-
mouthed, whose praises he sings.   There seems to be
considerable reason to believe that he was a foreigner ;
but even his Christian name, Martin, is more or less of
a conjecture.   He lived between 1110 and 1135, and
has left us a chronicle written in Latin in a style
unusually crabbed ; Mickiewicz, however, in his
lectures praises his descriptive powers.   This work
is of great value as containing the earliest forms
of the many quaint legends with which Polish
history is so thickly garnished.   To this must be
added the chronicles written by Matthew Cholewa
and Vincent Kadlubek or Kadlubko (perhaps a
corrupt version of the German Gottlieb), two bishops
of Cracow, and that of Bogufal, bishop of Posen ;
all made use of Latin, just as was customary with our
own mediæval chroniclers.   Kadlubek died on the
8th of March, 1223.   About 400 years later (viz. in
1633) his bones were brought to Sandomir and he
was canonised.   The style of this work is somewhat
inflated, but the great popularity which it enjoyed

for a long time in Poland is shown by the many manuscripts of it still existing. The chronicle of Bogufal, which is written in a very dry, annalistic manner, extends to the year 1250. Other chroniclers followed, such as Dzierswa and Janko von Czarnkowo, but the teaching was always ecclesiastical and the idiom Latin. In England the influence of a healthy spirit of nationality succeeded in shaking off the pedantries of monkish compilers on the one hand, and the spurious French of the school of " Stratford atte Bow " on the other ; but the use of the classic tongues was firmly engrafted in the Polish people by the multitude of foreign ecclesiastics who inundated the country. No Robert Grossetête, as in England, appealed against them, no statutes of provisors or præmunire limited their numbers and authority. All compositions written in a language foreign to their author are at best sickly exotics ; and we may safely say that had Gibbon carried out his intention of writing his great work in French, he himself would have been as much a loser as the English language in being deprived of so noble a monument.

The unfortunate tendency of the Poles to copy other people, even at the period of their greatest prosperity, when, if ever, a national spirit asserts itself, is seen in the number of foreign words introduced into the language, terms of trade from the German, of fashion from the French, and of science from the Latin. One of the quaintest pages of the historian De Thou, is that in which he describes the entry of the Polish embassy into Paris to offer the crown to Henri de Valois. The inquisitive courtiers of the capital were as much astonished at the elegant French and Latin of the strangers as they were at the peculiar costumes, their closely-cropped heads, and the quivers of arrows at their backs. The Polish Jesuits employed a vicious style in their numerous sermons, orations, and works of devotion, and, turning the language from its natural channels, tried to force its constructions into analogies with the classical idioms. The encouragement of this hybridism continued from the time of Sobieski till the extinction of the monarchy, the kings of the house of Saxony, ending with the coarse and illiterate Augustus III., being absolutely ignorant of the language themselves and in no way encouraging it. The cultivation of Polish was never more active than when the country had been dismembered; the exiles, who probably now found their native tongue to be their greatest bond of union, busied themselves in developing it, and the works of Lelewel, Niemcewicz, Mickiewicz, Slowacki, and Krasinski were produced.

With the reign of Casimir III. (1333–1370), called the Great, begins the period of national prosperity in Poland. In this reign were passed the Statutes of Wislica, a complete code of Polish laws. These were promulgated in Latin, but a translation into Russian was published for the benefit of the King's other subjects. In 1386 Lithuania was joined to Poland by the marriage of its Prince Jagiello with Hedwig (Jadwiga), the Polish heiress. The Queen was mainly instru-

mental in creating the University of Cracow, but it
was not actually founded till 1400, when she was no
longer living.   In the year 1474 the first printing-
press was set up at Cracow, which continued to be
the capital of the kingdom till it was removed to
Warsaw by Sigismund III.   The press at which this
first book was printed was that of Günter Zainer, who
was probably, to judge by his name, a German.   The
writings in Polish during this period, as previously
stated, are exceedingly meagre.   A few hymns (the
doctrines of Wickliffe and Protestantism were gaining
ground among them as among their brother Cechs)
and some statutes are all that have come down.   In
a law of Casimir IV., in 1442, we have some curious
old forms, showing how much nearer the Polish
language of that time was to the Palæo-Slavonic.
Writers in Latin abounded at this time ; of these
the most celebrated was Jan Dlugosz (Latinised into
Longinus, and we must remember that every man
turned his name into Latin then), bishop of Lemberg
(Pol. Lwow), now capital of the Austrian province of
Galicia.   His history is very valuable for its matter,
and is by no means wanting in beauties of style.   He
is the great authority for the reigns of the three first
Jagiellos.   Unfortunately, it is in Latin, for Polish
authors despaired of composing history in their native
tongue, and at that time the same opinion appears to
have been prevalent in England.

Dlugosz was a scholar of great learning, a talented
diplomatist, and a citizen of sturdy and unstained
character.   For the compilation of his history he

accumulated a vast stock of materials, both from
Polish and foreign sources ; in the latter part of his
life he learned Russian, so as to be able to read the
Chronicle of Nestor.[1]

At this time the Poles were not without some
legendary poetry, but it has, unfortunately, disappeared, leaving only the titles and commencement
of the verses, as is the case with the songs in the
" Complaint of Scotland."[2]   In 1828 was printed at
Warsaw, in the " Collection of Polish Authors " (*Zbior
Pisarzow Polskich*), a manuscript supposed to have
been written about 1500, entitled "Memoirs of a
Polish Janissary" (*Pamietniki Janczara Polaka*), to
which allusion has been made previously.   The story
is interesting, and contains some important historical
details, which have been cited by Mickiewicz in his
lectures. It has been shown, by the Bohemian scholar
Jirecek, that the writer was a Serb, Michael Konstantinovich, of Ostrovitza.   His " Chronicle,". which
describes the defeat of Wladyslaw III. at Varna, and
Jan Albrecht in Bukovina, was probably written by
him in Poland, and in the Polish language, from
which it was translated into Cech.   Michael was
born in 1430, and taken prisoner by the Turks in
1455.   He served among the Janissaries ten years,
while Mehmed II. was sultan, and then escaped to
Hungary.

About this time (1473) Poland produced her one

[1] Pīpin and Spasovich, ii. 468.
[2] See " The Complaynt of Scotlande," 1549, edited by
Dr. Murray for the Early English Text Society.

man of genius, universally known, Copernicus, a native
of Thorn, whom Germany has in vain attempted to
appropriate. It seems probable that the family of
Copernicus had originally emigrated from Bohemia,
as would appear from the name (Kuprnik).

The period from 1548 to 1606 is considered to be
the golden or classical age of Polish literature. The
country seemed to have a great future before it, and
to bid fair to become the dominant power in Eastern
Europe. Under the first Sigismund Poland was the
land of religious toleration, and many sectaries found
refuge in the country, including the Socini. Lelius
Socinus had visited Poland in 1552 ; Faustus arrived
in 1579 and settled at Cracow, whence, after a sojourn
of four years, he transferred his residence to Pawli-
·kowice, a village in its vicinity, belonging to Christopher Morsztyn, whose daughter Elizabeth he soon
after married. He endured persecution from the
Romanists, and on one occasion his library and
manuscripts were destroyed by a mob. He afterwards
removed to Luklawice, also near Cracow, and remained
there till his death in 1607. Socinus did not compose
a catechism of his religious belief, although he
intended to do so. Some of his followers collected
and arranged the doctrines either established or
approved of by him, and they published their
catechism at Rakow in Polish in 1605.

Protestant doctrines were professed by many of
the most noble families in Poland, and there were
many presses devoted to their propagation. According
to Krasinski, Skarga, the eminent preacher, of whom

more anon, complains that more than two thousand
Romanist churches were converted into Protestant
ones. As in Bohemia so in Poland, the Jesuits were
most active in getting possession of and burning all
documents connected with the spread of Protestantism. It is impossible to travel in either of these two
countries or in the Slovenish and Croatian provinces
of Austria without coming upon their traces. In no
part of Europe, not even in Spain or Italy, was their
work more complete and efficacious.

In the diet of 1552, deputies were chosen to
be sent to the Council of Trent. These were
Drohojowski and Uchanski, two Polish bishops,
both of whom were well known to lean to
Protestant views. In fact the Pope had written
to the king of Poland in 1556, about Uchanski,
describing him as "maxime hæresis infamiâ la-
borantem." Modrzewski was appointed secretary,
and the views he propounded as to the demands
which the deputies should make from the Holy See
are very extensive. They are given at length by
Krasinski,[1] and show plainly what religious men in
Poland thought. At the diet of Piotrkow in 1555
the chamber of nuncios, or house of commons, represented to the king the necessity of convoking a
national synod, composed of all religious parties.
The king was to preside, and the Church was to be
reformed by adopting the Holy Scriptures as the

[1] See "History of the Reformation in Poland," by Count
Valerian Krasinski, i., 219.

only basis of its reconstitution. Representatives of all the religious sects of Poland were to be admitted on equal terms with the Roman ecclesiastics, and the most eminent Reformers of Europe, such as Calvin, Beza, and Melanchthon, were to be invited. The eyes of the Reformers were, however, especially turned to the well-known John Laski, or à Lasco as he is sometimes called in a Latinised form of his name, a man well known in our own country.

Gradually, however, as before mentioned, the Jesuits brought about a complete change. The national elementary schools, chiefly in the hands of the Protestants and Calvinists, are said to have amounted in the sixteenth century to 1,500, with 30,000 pupils. They disappeared without a trace. The Socinian school at Rakow was closed in 1638, by the orders of the diet, and finally all Socinians were expelled from the Republic by a law of the year 1658.

Thus this state of things was soon to pass away under the great Jesuit reaction. The country reached the height of its prosperity in the reign of Sigismund II. (Augustus), 1548–1572. After this it began to decline, the fierce political factions hastening its end, and, worst of all, the *liberum veto*, viz., the power which a single nuntius had of stopping the proceedings of the diet. This occurred for the first time in 1652, when Sicinski, the deputy for Upita, uttered the words, "*Niepozwalam*," I forbid.[1]

---

[1] Szujski, one of the last historians of Poland, justly remarks upon this privilege, that it soon led to a *liberum conspiro*.

This was in the reign of John Casimir. "Ruptures of this kind," says Lelewel, the Polish historian, "now became more and more frequent. The queen, Louisa Maria, knew how to profit by them, and, unfortunately, exercised a great influence over the king." Legnich, in his "Jus Publicum Regni Poloni" (1742), enumerates thirteen occasions on which this pernicious custom had broken up the diet. It was not put a stop to till just before the final partition of Poland. In 1561 a translation of the whole Bible was published at Cracow. Previous to this there had been a version of the New Testament by Seklucyan printed at Königsberg, originally a Polish town, in 1551. The Bible of 1561 forms a handsome folio with many curious woodcuts, and is now a book of great rarity. The Jesuit Wujek made another translation in 1599. The first Protestant Bible was published in the year 1563 at Brzesc, and another translation in 1632 at Danzig. The latter has been in use ever since. Education spread more and more, but it was confined to the clergy and nobility, the peasantry everywhere remained in the grossest ignorance. The development of the native language was still depressed by the influence of Latin, which was extensively employed, both in historical compositions and poetry. The reputation of Casimir Sarbiewski (or, in the Latinised form, Sarbievius) has been spread through Europe. His lines are frequently quoted by persons who have little or no idea of the nationality of their author. But of all writers in Latin it is probable that Martin Kromer (1512–1589) has gained the greatest reputation. His

o

book, "De Origine et Rebus Gestis Polonorum,
Libri XXX." (the Latinity of which might almost be
compared to that of Livy or Tacitus), gives a complete view of Polish history from the earliest times to
the end of the reign of Sigismund I. It is need-
less to say that, in a work written at such a time,
a thoroughly critical spirit can hardly be expected,
and accordingly all the untrustworthy, but still very
amusing, legends of early Polish history are related
with the same minuteness and picturesqueness with
which Livy describes the death of Servius Tullius or
the warlike achievements of Coriolanus.

The earliest Polish poet is Rej of Naglowic. His
father, of a very old family, had settled in Galicia,
or Red Russia, where our author was born, about
1507. Like many men who have become celebrated afterwards, he passed his youth in idle-
ness, and began his studies late. He wrote many
works of various merit, and, as this was a great
period of religious dispute throughout Europe, soon
distinguished himself as a defender of the doctrines of Calvinism, to which he was attached. He
translated the Psalms, wrote commentaries on the
Gospels (*Postylla Polska*), a catechism and an Explanation of the Apocalypse. In 1560 appeared his
"Picture of the Life of an Honourable Man" (*Wize-
runek Wlasny Zywota Czlowieka Poczciwego*), a long
rambling poem, full of quaintness, something like
the "Steel Glass" and other productions of our own
Elizabethian authors. His best work was written
in his old age, viz., "Zwierciadlo albo Zywot Pocz-

ciwego Czlowieka" (The Mirror, or Life of an Honourable Man), published in 1567. The critics agree in praising this poem as being full of good sense and deep reflection conveyed in a lively and dignified style.[1] Rej died in 1569. The influence of the Renaissance was now strongly felt in Poland, and had its representative in Jan Kochanowski, called the Prince of Polish Poets, born in 1530. The Kochanowskis were a poetical family. Andrew, the brother of John, translated the Æneid; his cousin, Nicholas, wrote some miscellaneous poetry; his nephew, Peter (1566–1620), translated the "Jerusalem Delivered" of Tasso. The life of John Kochanowski was uneventful. His culture was foreign, chiefly acquired in Italy and at the University of Padua. He also lived several years in Paris. He returned to Poland in 1557, and some time afterwards married and settled on his paternal estate, Czarnolas. The latter part of his life was rendered melancholy by the death of his favourite daughter, Ursula. The poet himself died in the year 1584.

In the writings of Kochanowski we see the influence of the literatures of Rome and Greece, of Petrarch and of Ronsard, the acquaintance of the latter of whom the poet made in France. The Polish writer attempted many styles of composition. In epic poetry he wrote "The Game of Chess," an imitation of Vida ; "The Standard or Investiture of Prussia " (*Praporzec albo hold pruski*)—a fine description of the fealty given by Albert of Brandenburg

---

[1] Pipin and Spasovich, ii. 484.

to Sigismund Augustus, in which the history of
Poland is represented in a series of pictures ; "The
Expedition to Moscow of the Hetman Christopher
Radziwill" (1581), &c. He was the author of the
first drama, "The Sending of the Greek Ambassadors" (*Odprawa Poslow Greckich*), which was acted
at the marriage of Jan Zamoyski and Katherine
Radziwill, on the 12th January, 1578. Before this
time mysteries and sacred dramas had been frequent
in Poland. At first they were played in churches,
but, as in the twelfth century, Pope Innocent III.
severely blamed the clergy for this breach of clerical
decorum, they were transferred to churchyards and
schoolrooms. Religious plays of this kind, according to M. Spasovich, are still occasionally acted in
Poland on Saints' days.

But to return to Kochanowski. The subject of his
drama is taken from Homer ; the ambassadors are
Ulysses and Menelaus, who come to Paris to demand
surrender of Helen. This piece of the Polish poet
has earned the very warmest commendations of the
critics. Besides these works, Kochanowski published,
in 1578, an excellent translation of the Psalms, still
in general use ; at this time, in England, we could
only solace ourselves with the doggerel of Sternhold
and Hopkins. He wrote also odes, elegies, epigrams,
and idyls. In a satire addressed to Sigismund
Augustus, he lashes his countrymen for their mania
for imitating foreigners and passion for luxury—
two faults which accompanied the Polish nation to
the close of their history. In the year 1580, on the

death of his beloved daughter Ursula, whom he
called the Slavonic Sappho, and to whom he hoped
to hand on his lyre, he composed his " Treny "
(Lamentations), so justly praised by Mickiewicz in
his " Lectures on Slavonic Literature." These verses
alone would show Kochanowski to have been a true
poet.

Besides these he gave his countrymen versions of
portions. of Homer, Horace, and Cicero, and of the
so-called Anacreontic odes which enjoyed such a
popularity for many centuries, and passed for genuine
productions of the Teian bard. Besides Polish
poems, he was author of some elegies and epistles in
Latin, one of which is amusing as satirising the
French and Henri de Valois. Most readers have
read how the cruel poltroon fled from Cracow,.
pursued by the nobles of his court with cries of
" *Serenissima Majestas, cur fugis ?* " and never
slackened rein till he saw himself safe beyond
the frontier. Kochanowski has a sarcastic epistle,
addressed " Gallo Crocitanti," from which I take the
following lines :—

> Et tamen hanc poteras mecum requiescere noctem,
> Nec dubiis vitam committere, Galle, tenebris.
> State, viri : quæ causa fugæ ? non Trinacris hæc est
> Ora, nec infames funesto vespere terræ
> Sarmatia est quam, Galle, fugis, fidissima tellus
> Hospitibus.

Kochanowski still keeps his. popularity among his
countrymen, and many of his best lines have passed
into proverbs. One of them is quoted in a letter   •

which the uxorious Sobieski wrote to his wife, the fair Frenchwoman who may be said to have almost changed the destinies of Europe, giving her an account of the glorious battle in which the Turks were driven from Vienna.[1]

Kochanowski was convinced that he would be immortal, and, in an imitation of Horace, prophesied that he would be read by the Russian, the Tatar, the German, the Spaniard, and even the remote Englishman.[2] Some of this prediction has not yet been verified, and I fear that to most of my countrymeñ the very name of Kochanowski is unknown. Perhaps this little book may do something to remove the total ignorance.

The priest, Stanislaus Grochowski (1554–1612) need not detain us long. He is chiefly a writer of fulsome panegyrics ; among the rest he has verses on the False Demetrius and his wife, Marina Mniszek. For his satire, "The Women's Circle" (*Babie Kolo*), he seems to have got into a good deal of trouble with the bishops of his time.

In the person of Szymonowicz, whose name has

---

[1] It is well known that Sobieski had belonged to the party in the interests of France, and was consequently opposed to that of Austria. Louis XIV. had, however, treated slightingly the Polish Queen, who, as mentioned above, was of French extraction, and so great was her influence over her husband, that Sobieski was induced to assist the Austrians against the Turks.

[2] Slavonic authors have not always been noted for a modest opinion of themselves. The lines of Derzhávin, in which he prophesies his coming glories, will occur to all students of Russian literature.

been Latinised into Simonides (1554–1624), a writer
of pastorals has appeared. These productions are
very much praised by Mickiewicz in his lectures.
He considers Szymonowicz the second best writer of
bucolic poetry after Theocritus. According to this
critic he greatly surpasses Virgil, who had no dramatic
talent, which Szymonowicz has, and is also a better
painter of nature. He is certainly free from the
strange jumbles of the Latin poet, who is always
mixing up the mountain scenery of Arcadia with the
flat plains of Mantua. The most celebrated of his
poems are " The Pair of Lovers " and " The Reapers."
But Szymonowicz was something more than a poet ;
he was a philanthropist. He everywhere appears as
the advocate of the unhappy serfs, and puts into their
mouths many lamentations about their hard fate.
This was not done with a view to any democratic
propaganda, because it was impossible that artificial
productions of this nature could circulate among the
illiterate peasantry; but with the object of telling
some very disagreeable truths to their masters which
might lead to the amelioration of their condition.[1]
The next poet of importance who ornaments Polish
literature is Klonowicz, or, as his name was Latinised,
Acernus (1545–1602).[2] His works may be classed
under two heads: 1st, Descriptive, including his poems,
" Flis," in Polish, and " Roxolania," in Latin ; and
2nd, Didactic, such as " Worek Judaszow," or " The
Bag of Judas," and "Victoria Deorum ;" the former

---

[1] Pïpin, ii., 499.
[2] The word *klon* signifies maple (Lat. *acer*).

in Polish, the latter in Latin. " Flis" is a name given to the boatmen of the Vistula, and under this title the poet represents himself as sailing from Warsaw to Danzig. Hence he takes occasion to describe the scenery on the banks, and to give many directions about shipbuilding. In the " Roxolania" we have a picture of Galicia, or Red Russia, his native country. " The Bag of Judas" is a strange poem, rightly styled by M. Spasovich as little more than a legal treatise in verse. The false school of didactic poetry seems to have early taken as strong hold of the Poles as it did of the French in the eighteenth century. The " Victoria Deorum " is a long Latin poem on moral philosophy. The title is taken from a portion of the work which describes the battle between Jupiter and the giants. The poem has an undercurrent of politics, like the double allegory in the " Faërie Queene." The Titans are the Polish magnates and szlachta ; Jupiter is the king. I will just mention in passing Orzechowski, a priest, who wrote a strange work, entitled " Quincunx," a strong assertion of the authority of the Church.

Rhetoric and pulpit eloquence, as may easily be imagined, were greatly fostered by the Jesuits, who now began to swarm into Poland. Among the most successful cultivators of these forms of literature was Peter Skarga, the court-preacher of Sigismund III., who earned the appellation of the Polish Chrysostom. Skarga has left a host of sermons and religious works behind him, among which may be mentioned " Lives of the Saints," " Discourses for Sundays and Saints'

Days," " Discourses on the Seven Sacraments," &c. For a glowing eulogy of him we must turn to the " Lectures on Slavonic Literature," by Mickiewicz, previously mentioned. He expressly praises his sermons preached before the Diet: on account of his freedom of speech, Skarga is said to have been many times in danger of his life. He everywhere, however, appears as the uncompromising advocate of the order of the Jesuits, which he joined in 1568. He had much to do with the stamping out of Calvinism in Poland, and the Greek Church in Lithuania. It is a pity that in some respects the Poles did not listen to his fiery eloquence. In the third of his sermons before the Diet (*Kazanie Sejmowe*) he foretells only too clearly the downfall of his country, in consequence of the perpetual feuds among the nobles, as was prophesied nearly a century later by John Casimir, the king, when he abdicated. Skarga is considered by Polish critics to have raised the prose style of the language to its highest pitch of excellence ; some, however, object to the many Latinisms which he introduced. The writing of history in Latin was still actively pursued ; in addition to Kromer, previously mentioned, we have Wapowski and Guagnini (an Italian, in the Polish form Gwagnin). The first historical work compiled in Polish was the " Kronika Polska," reprinted at Warsaw in 1823. This was a very considerable production for those times ; and England, we must remember, could not at that time boast of a national historian, unless we wish to see one in Holinshed, Hall, or Grafton. A very curious work is the "Coats of Arms of the Polish Knighthood" (*Herby rycerstwa polskiego*), Cracow, 1584. Here the armorial bearings of Noah, Alexander the Great, and Darius are given among others.

In 1582, Stryjkowski published his chronicle at Königsberg (*Krolewiec*). It is a book quite *sui generis*, containing a great quantity of valuable information about Lithuania and the eastern parts of Poland. The author not only learned the Russian and Lithuanian languages, but traversed all the most remarkable portions of the countries described in search of antiquities. His work is full of information, but is put together without much skill.

With this work I close my account of early Polish literature, bringing it down to the year 1606, called by critics the commencement of the influence of the Jesuits.

CHAPTER VIII.

THE EARLY LITERATURE OF BOHEMIA.[1]

THE present century has witnessed what must certainly be considered a remarkable phenomenon—the
resuscitation of the language and literature of Bohemia.
Speaking roughly, from 1620 to 1820 there was no
such thing as a Bohemian nationality. At the close
of the eighteenth century, Dobrovsky had looked
upon the total extinction of the Cech language as
proximate. Pelzel, in 1798, compared the condition
of Bohemian with that of the Lusatian-Wendish, or
Sorbish, at Leipzig, in the fourteenth century, which
was occasionally heard from peasants in the market-
place, but was rapidly receding. In German, Pelzel
wrote his history; and in the same language nearly
all Drobrovsky's works are composed.

The French Revolution, which stirred so many
nationalities, was certainly not without its influence
upon the Bohemians. The labours of Dobrovsky,
a patriot as well as scholar, created a band of en-
thusiastic students, who applied themselves to the

---

[1] In this chapter I have occasionally called the Cech language
Bohemian. It is right that the reader should know clearly the
relation in which these appellations stand to each other. The
name Cech is that used by the natives; the word Bohemia
(Boii-heim) carries with it the name of the Celtic tribe which
originally occupied the country. See page 33.

history and antiquities of their country. Up to that time Bohemian early literature had been neglected, and many valuable memorials had been allowed to perish. There was now to be a close search all over the country to gather these neglected relics, and some startling results, as I shall show, followed.

The earliest period of Bohemian civilisation had witnessed two influences,[1]—first, Latin-German; and, secondly, Greek-Slavonic. The use of the Latin alphabet may have been introduced even in heathen times from the connexion of the country with Germany, and would be increased by the baptism of the Moravian prince, Moimir. Rostislav, a prince of Moravia, invited the celebrated missionary, Methodius, into his territory, who was afterwards appointed by the Pope Archbishop of Moravia, and there baptised the Cechish prince, Borivoi, and his wife, Liudmila, now included among the saints of the country. The legend of Saint Wenceslaus, pre-served in Russian memorials, tells how Liudmila herself wrote books, and caused her grandson, Wen-ceslaus, to study Slavonic works. According to tradition, even in the latter part of the eleventh century there existed a Slavonic school (*famosum studium Sclavonicæ linguæ*) in the Vysehrad, and there St. Procopius, the Abbot of the Sazavski Monastery, studied. To this Procopius tradition assigned the Cyrillic part of the Gospels of Rheims, mentioned in a previous chapter. Among the fragments of Palæoslavonic given by Professor Jagic

---

[1] P. and S., ii., 803.

in his interesting "Specimina Linguæ Palæoslovenicæ," St. Petersburg, 1882, is one from a Pannonian-Moravian "Service-book" (*Slouzhebnik*) of the Roman Catholic Church, which was discovered at Kiev. The language of this production shows many Bohemian influences, and exhibits such an early form of the Old Slavonic language that the Professor does not hesitate to assign it to the tenth century (p. 33). These fragments would thus follow next in order in point of antiquity to the Frisingian mentioned in a preceding chapter.

But things changed after the death of Methodius; the Pope condemned the Slavonic liturgy, and the Sazavski Monastery was given to Latin monks. From this time the Latin ritual prevailed, but many remains of the old church were to be found scattered among the people, upon which, no doubt in a great measure, Hus built his reforms. Even in the fourteenth century there were "schismatics and infidels" (according to the expression of the papal bull of 1346) who would not use the Latin ritual, and for these Charles IV. founded the Slavonic monastery of Emmaus, where monks, invited from Bosnia, Dalmatia, and Croatia, performed the service in the Slavonic language. A solitary relique of this orthodox period of the Bohemian Church, according to many critics, is the hymn, *Hospodine pomiluj ny* ("Lord have mercy upon us"). This ancient piece is printed in the "Vybor z Literature Ceske" (vol. i., p. 27),[1]

---

[1] A valuable work published by the Bohemian Literary Society. It gives extracts from the leading authors with biographical and critical notes. Two volumes have appeared.

both in its most ancient form and in the modified one in which it is still sung in the churches.

We now come to more slippery and uncertain ground. In 1817 was discovered the fragment called *Libusin Soud* ("the Judgment of Libusa"), which was sent to the newly-founded Bohemian Museum anonymously, but the sender was afterwards ascertained to have been Kovar, the steward (*Rentmeister*) of Count Colloredo. From the time of its appearance, the genuineness of this poem was stoutly contested. The curious reader will find a full discussion of the subject in Jirecek's "Genuineness of the Königinhof Manuscript" (*Die Echtheit der Königinhofer Handschrift*). It must be confessed that the question is surrounded with difficulties, and the argument insisted upon by the brothers Jirecek, that, at the time when these productions came to light, there was no one sufficiently acquainted with the old Bohemian language to fabricate them, seems to be partially met by the fact that two poems for a long time deceived experts, which have since been ascertained to be spurious—the Love-song of King Wenceslaus, and the Song on the Vysehrad.[1]   Both of these were unfortunately included in the valuable "Selections from Bohemian Literature" previously mentioned, of which two volumes have already appeared. Their existence shows that a forger was busy somewhere. These questions seem as little

---

[1] It is but fair to state, however, that these two pieces contain many clumsy expressions not found in those poems which are claimed to be genuine.

likely to be settled now as they ever were, and Professor Sembera, of Vienna, has recently thrown down the gauntlet again, asserting that "The Judgment of Libusa" was fabricated by Linda, a Bohemian poet of third-rate merit, whose works are now almost forgotten, and Hanka, the custodian of the museum library, and discoverer of the manuscripts of Königinhof. Dobrovsky did not hesitate to brand this poem as a forgery.

The story of the Princess Libusa will be found in the old chronicler, Cosmas of Prague, who is full of wonderful legends, probably belonging to the common stock of the Aryan mythologies. It reappears subsequently in the so-called chronicle of Dalimil, of which I shall have occasion to speak at some length, and forms an amusing chapter in the history of Wenceslaus Hajek. However mythical this lady may be, the Bohemians have accepted her as their tutelary Athena, as we are reminded by her statue erected in the Museum Buildings at Prague. The poem represents how Libusa, the daughter of Krok, was a princess and judge among her people, like the Veleda of Tacitus; but, when called on one occasion to settle a question of inheritance between two rival claimants, one of them, Chrudos, refuses to abide by her decision. He says that the land is but illgoverned which is ruled by a woman, and Libusa, disgusted at her want of influence over her savage subjects, recommends them to choose a man capable of wielding a sword. The difficulty was solved, as all readers of Bohemian history know, by her marriage with the good peasant, Premysl, from whom sprang the old line of Bohemian princes. According to Cosmas, the buskins of the worthy countryman were to be seen in his time suspended in the citadel of Prague.[1] The manuscript of the Judgment of Libusa will be found in the National Library at Prague. Sembera quotes the opinions of some palæographers who dispute its authenticity; the linguistic forms are perplexing; he asserts that the concoctor considered that, the nearer he got to the ecclesiastical Slavonic, the older he would make his poem appear. We shall presently see how these same ideas actuated the forger of the modern glosses in the " Mater Verborum." Want of space prevents us from doing anything like justice to this intricate question, but a cloud seems to hang over many of the earlier specimens of Bohemian literature. The piece has been assigned to the ninth, or even the eighth century, by those who vindicate its authenticity.

I now turn to the celebrated Königinhof Manuscript. The following are the circumstances of its discovery :—In 1817, Hanka, then a very young man, and engaged in editing selections from Old Bohemian literature, paid a visit to a friend at Königinhof (Kralove Dvur), a village in the north-eastern corner of Bohemia. Here he was introduced to the vicar of the place, named Borc,[2] who casually men-

---

[1] Tollit secum suos cothurnos ex omni parte subere consutos, quos fecit servari in posterum et servantur Wissegrad in camera ducis usque hodie. See Schafarik, " Slawische Alterthümer," ii., 422.   [2] Pronounce Borts.

tioned that some old weapons, including arrows, were·
still preserved in a room in the church.   On search-
ing these stores several manuscripts were found, and,
among others of less value, the collection of historical
and lyrical pieces which has since become so famous.
Concerning its genuineness there has been a storm of·
controversy, in which the works published on both·
sides would themselves form a literature.   The assail-
ants urge the sentimental tone of many of the pieces,
more resembling the style of poetry of the beginning
of this century ; the anachronisms (*e.g.*, mention of
drums and tournaments), and the incorrect linguistic
forms.   Persons from the Slavonic mythology are introduced in great abundance, such as Tras and Morena,
and make us think of the additions to the " Mater
Verborum."   Lumir, the bard, who, with his voice
and song, could move the Vysehrad, reminds us of
Boian, the nightingale of ancient days, in the Russian " Story of the Expedition of Igor," mentioned
in a previous chapter.   A very stout defence, however, is made in M. Jirecek's book.   It is but fair
to say, that some of the arguments which apply
to the " Judgment of Libusa " do not affect this·
collection.   We are told that many words, which·
Hanka himself could not explain, or explained·
wrongly, have been made clear by the discovery of
subsequent manuscripts, especially the " Legend of
St. Catherine," preserved in Sweden, whither many
Bohemian treasures were taken during the Thirty
Years' War.   In the Vybor the date of the Königinhof
Poems is fixed at the thirteenth century ; but, in a

recent article by M. Gebauer ("Archiv für Slavische Philologie," vol. ii., p. 155), it is shown that part of the poem of "Jaroslav" is copied from an old Bohemian translation of Marco Polo, executed about 1320, and thus the composition of these pieces is, to say the least, shifted a full century later—for the view of M. Jirecek that the translator of Marco Polo copied from the Königinhof Manuscript will hardly recommend itself to our readers. The contents of this collection are partly epic and partly lyric; it consists of twelve parchment leaves. The epic pieces are spirited, and many of the shorter poems very elegant.

To enable the reader to judge for himself, I have selected a few lyrics, which I shall present in a prose version; the colouring may perhaps be lost, but accuracy will be preserved :—

THE ROSE.

O thou rose, thou red rose,
Why hast thou bloomed so early,
Why, having bloomed, art thou frost-stricken?
Why, frost-stricken, dost thou fade?
Why, having faded, dost thou fall?
I sat during the night—I sat long,
I sat till cock-crowing ;
No longer could I keep awake ;
All the pine-torch was burnt out.
I slept : it appeared to me in my dream
How from me, poor girl,
From the finger of my right hand
The golden ring fell :
The precious stone was lost :
I never found the stone—
I never met my love.

The following is also touchingly worded :—

THE LARK.

A maid was weeding hemp
In her master's garden,
A lark asks her
Why she is so sad?

How can I be glad,
Little lark?
They have taken away my love
To a stone tower.

O that I had a pen,
I would have written a letter,—
Thou, dear little lark,
Wouldst have flown with it.

I have no pen, no paper,
Or I would have written a letter.[1]
Thou, dear little lark,
Wouldst have flown with it.

I have no pen, no paper,
Or I would have written a letter.
Salute my love, then, with a song,
And tell him that I die of grief.

---

[1] This poem has been a great stumbling-block to the critics.
How could a country girl in the thirteenth century talk of writing a letter? To this, those who vindicate its authenticity, reply that similar expressions are found in Servian and Malo-Russian poetry in the mouths of rustic maidens. We cannot expect to find consistency in popular poetry, as may easily be seen in the Bulgarian lay on page 138.

THE FORSAKEN.

Ah ! ye woods, ye gloomy woods,
  Woods of Miletin,
Why are ye green
In winter as well as summer ?
I should be glad, did I not weep,
Were not my heart troubled ;
But tell me, good people,
Who would not weep thus?
Where is my father, my dear father ?
Buried in the earth.
Where is my mother, my good mother ?
The grass grows over her.
I have no brothers, no sisters—
And they have taken away my love.

The tone of this poem reminds us of Burns's lyric, " The Lovely Lass of Inverness," but the lay of the Scotchman is more direct and impulsive.

THE CUCKOO.

In a broad field an oak stands ;
On the oak a cuckoo
Utters her note, and laments
That it is not always spring.
How could, then, the corn ripen in the field
If it were always spring ?

How could the apple ripen in the garden
If it were always summer ?
Or how could the corn freeze in the heap
If it were always autumn?
How sad it would be for a maiden
If she were always alone !

An English version of these poems, including the " Judgment of Libusa," was published by the Rev.

A. H. Wratislaw, at Cambridge, in 1852. To this the reader must be referred who wishes to become more acquainted with the subject. The translations are in rhyme, and scrupulously accurate. The same, unfortunately, cannot be said of those of Sir John Bowring, which contain many ludicrous errors, owing to his imperfect acquaintance with the Bohemian language. In fact, with but few exceptions, up to the present time Slavonic literature has been either en-tirely ignored in this country, or presented in a tra-vestied and garbled form. Hence the majority of Englishmen have a fixed idea that nothing of the kind exists. Perhaps some of the extracts cited in this little book may do something to disabuse them of such prejudices and erroneous opinions. I have devoted considerable space to the discussion of this Königinhof Manuscript on account of the great interest the subject has aroused among foreign critics. The manuscripts containing these poems are freely shown to visitors at Prague. Moreover, the Kralodvorsky Rukopis has been photographed, and the various readings described most minutely in a pam-phlet by the present librarian, M. Vrtatko. Every-thing appears to have been done by the authorities to avoid mystification. Unfortunately, the subject has never been debated in a temperate manner. The great *animus* shown by the Germans is only too apparent in their attacks.

Whatever may be the case as regards the genuine-ness of this collection, that the hand of the forger, led by a narrow spirit of false patriotism, was being employed, is clear from the additions which have been made to the " Mater Verborum " in the library of the Museum at Prague.   This valuable codex, which is on parchment, and of the thirteenth century, is a Latin vocabulary compiled by Solomon, Bishop of Constance, in Switzerland, who died in 920.

To this some Bohemian monk had added important glosses.   The manuscript was presented to the Museum, soon after its foundation, by Count Joseph Kolovrat-Krakovsky, but since its reception there a number of glosses have been added by a later hand. The illuminations have also been tampered with, and to two of the figures the names Vaceřad and Miroslav have been added.   All these additions to the original were adopted by Palacky and Schafařik in their " Oldest Monuments of the Bohemian Language " (*Die ältesten Denkmäler der böhmischen Sprache*), and have in this way found their entrance into many works on Bohemia.   Some of the critics have pointed unmistakably to Hanka as the forger.   If for no other reason, it would be suspicious that among the glosses we find many forms which in his imperfect knowledge of the structure of the Bohemian language he had supposed to exist, but which subsequent philological investigations have shown to be impossibilities.   And thus I gladly leave this uncertain ground for one which is more certain, and feel how difficult it is for a foreigner to enter into such minute points of criticism.

One of the first results of the acquaintance of the Cechs with Latin literature was the development of religious poetry and the legend. We thus have a great many versified lives of the saints, which need not be cited here at length. Among these is the legend of St. Procopius, previously alluded to, and the legend of St. Catherine, which is considered the best of these productions. The manuscript of the latter poem has been brought back from Sweden, whither it had been removed during the Thirty Years' War, and is now preserved at Brünn in Moravia.

A work of some importance is the so-called chronicle of Dalimil. It belongs to the fourteenth century. This production, reminding one of our own Robert of Gloucester or the Bruce of Barbour, is a tedious and somewhat colourless production; it is written in octosyllabics, and extends from the creation of the world—your old chronicler never began later—till the year 1314. The literatures of most European countries have productions of the same kind, destitute of poetical merit, but interesting to the philologist and antiquarian. From the notice, prefixed to the selections in the " Vybor," we gather that the author was a Bohemian knight; but nothing is known of any person named Dalimil. The work is inspired by a frantic hatred of the Germans, as just at this time the princes of the House of Luxemburg (which gave to the Bohemians, among others, John, the blind king, slain at Crecy, their best sovereign, Charles IV., and his drunken and notorious son, Wenceslaus), were introducing everywhere German habits and the German language. The chronicle is, of course, uncritical, and full of the picturesque stories

·told by Cosmas,[1] and forming an integral part of Bohemian history till the end of the eighteenth century.   The once popular work of Wenceslaus Hajek teems with these legends.   In 1762, Gelasius Dobner published a Latin translation of Hajek with critical notes, a work which, as F. Prochazka said, " mentiendi finem fecit " in Bohemian history.

The stories about Krok and his three wise daughters, and the fruitless attempt of the prophetess, Libusa, to enforce her decisions, have been already told ; Libusa, or Lubusa, as she is called, thus replies, according to the chronicle :—

I will now tell you frankly
Although you have ill-treated me,
And have so despised me,
He would be a depraved man
Who would do evil to the commune for his own advantage.
The commune is the protection of all ;
He who attacks it wants sense.
If you lose the commune, do not count upon a place of refuge.
Without the commune there will be a continual quarrel.
It would have been better for you to have acquiesced in my
          decisions
Than to have a man for ruler.
The hand of a maiden strikes lightly,
But there is great pain in the blow of a man.
You will first understand me
When you see your ruler on a throne of iron.
If a stranger shall rule over you,
Your language shall not last long,

---

[1] The old Bohemian chronicler, who occupies the same place among the Cechs as Nestor among the Russians and Gallus among the Poles.   He died in 1125.

It is melancholy to be obliged to live among strangers,
But when a man is sad he can comfort himself among his own
    people.

Afterwards Lubusa says :—

> I know well
> Who ought to be your master.
> Follow where my horse leads.

And then, being a prophetess, she guides them to
the abode of the peasant, Premysl.   Here we find
the primitive ploughman of the Aryan legend, the
Mikoula Selianinovich of the Russians, and Piast
of the Poles.   Of the former, from whom the first
royal family of the Poles is reported to have sprung,
we have the following account in Kromer, " De
Origine et Rebus Gestis Polonorum, 1568."[1]   " Erat
Crusviciæ oppidanus, Piastus nomine, Cossisconis
filius, statura infra mediocrem, crassis atque robustis
artubus, mediam ætatem supergressus, agello modico
colendo et mellificio vitam sustentans, homo simplex
et justus et beneficus in egenos atque hospitalis, pro
modo facultatum suarum."   But to proceed to
Premysl :—

> The lords follow the horse,
> And come to the river Bielina,
> The horse follows the course of the river,
> And arrives at some fallow land,
> Where a tall man is working,
> Premysl's horse bounds forward to this man,
> And stops, careering before him.

---

[1] Vide *supra*, page 193.

The countryman chides the strangers for inter-
rupting his labours; he prophesies that he shall
rule over them with a rod of iron because they would
not obey the maiden. Out of his spade, which had
been stuck in the earth, grew five branches, and
out of the branches nuts. Libusa is married to this
worthy, and the city of Prague is afterwards founded.
The prophetess herself gives orders for its erection,
and its name is to be taken from the word *prah*,
signifying door-sill.[1]

> There, where I show you,
> On the Moldau below Petun,
> A carpenter is making a door-sill with his son ;
> On account of this sill, call the place Praha.

Here and there we have some curious stories illustrating the animosities between the Germans and
Bohemians; the latter seem to have had a presenti-
ment that they were to be overwhelmed by the
stronger nationality. In one part we are told of
a prince who ordered the noses of all the Germans
in the country to be cut off, and sent them home in
this plight. He also gave a *hrivna* (a piece of gold)
to any man who brought him a hundred German
noses. In the early chronicles of our own country
we find similar curious stories illustrating the feeling
existing between the English and Welsh.

The English reader may well be surprised at the

---

[1] This derivation, like many others of the same kind, is a
whimsical one. Tomek ("Dejepis Prahy," vol. i., p. 4) more
properly connects it with *praziti*, to burn wood, to clear a part
of a forest.

literary activity of this little country at so early a
period—the period, let us remember, of our own
Wickliffe, Chaucer, and Gower. But the fate of the
two lands was to be widely different : England to
advance in constitutional development, and con-
tinually to extend her territory; Bohemia to lose
her civil and religious liberty, and to have all her
political aspirations crushed. The influence of German romanticism was now to be very great among
the Cechs. Together with tournaments and other
knightly institutions, the minne-singers also appeared
at the German courts, among whom King Wenceslaus I. was, according to tradition, included.
To this period belongs the Alexandreis, a translation from the German or Latin. There is little
distinctly Bohemian about the poem. Tales of
Troy, Alexander the Great, Arthur and his Round
Table, and Charlemagne and his Peers, formed the
great subjects of literature throughout Europe at
the period. More curious matter can be found in
the "Satires on the Trades" (*Satyry o remeslnicich*),
and a poem on the Ten Commandments. Some of
these pieces show a good deal of humour, and remind us of Dunbar and Lindsay. They are anonymous; but we meet with a man whom we can
definitely fix upon as an author in Smil of Pardubic,
surnamed Flaska, a leading Bohemian of his day.
But little is known of his life; he was killed in a
skirmish in the year 1403, three years after our own
Chaucer died. His chief work is the "New Council,"
one of the innumerable beast-epics so much in vogue

in the Middle Ages. Others are, however, assigned to him, of which the most original and amusing is the "Dialogue between the Groom and Scholar" (*Podkoni a Zak*), a quaint piece of mediæval humour, which gives us a picture of Bohemian social life.

A valuable legal document belongs to this period, the "Book of the old Lord of Rosenberg." It is the earliest specimen of Bohemian prose, and extremely curious as illustrating legal customs among the Cechs. Rosenberg was Royal Chamberlain from 1318 to 1346, and died the following year. Another legal work of importance is the "Exposition of the Law of the Land of Bohemia" (*Vyklad na právo zeme Ceske*), by Andrew of Dubá, Chief Justice of Bohemia from 1343 to 1394. For those interested in Slavonic legislation, the best work is by Macieiowski, previously mentioned.

Large portions of the Bible were translated into Bohemian during the thirteenth and fourteenth centuries. The version was completed at the beginning of the fifteenth century. Wickliffe says of Anne of Luxemburg, the first wife of Richard II., "Nobilis regina Angliæ soror Cæsaris habet evangelium in lingua triplici exaratum scilicet in lingua bohemica, teutonica et latina."[1] There are two early versions of the Psalter, the Clementine at the end of the thirteenth or beginning of the fourteenth century, and the Wittenberg at the beginning of the fourteenth also. It is to be regretted that such doubts have been thrown upon the fragments of the early version of the Gospel

---

[1] Pauli, "Geschichte von England," iv., 705.

of St. John. This manuscript is said to have been found by Hanka in the binding of a book entitled "Disciplina et Doctrina Gymnasii Gorlicensis," 1595, but Sembera refuses to believe that it is genuine. He is wrong, however, in supposing that such a book does not exist, for it may be seen in the Library of the Bohemian Museum. The Bohemians have not allowed Sembera to make his attacks with impunity, and, in the year 1881, what seems a satisfactory defence of these fragments by Dr. John Gebauer was published by the curators of the Bohemian Museum. Since the death of the iconoclastic veteran, which occurred more than a year ago, a posthumous work by him has appeared, attacking the Kralodvorsky Rukopis. The great animosity with which these literary disputes are carried on can only be explained by the political hatred existing between the Cech and the German : the latter is very eager to stamp out all signs of Slavonic nationality in the territories which he has appropriated. Unfortunately, as in the case of Sembera, many of the foes of Bohemia are of her own household.

Another early chronicle deserving of mention is that by Pulkava, a priest. It extends from the earliest times to the year 1330. Pulkava died in 1380. His work is in prose, and was originally written in Latin, but afterwards translated by the author into Cech. I now come to the curious prose-poem called "The Weaver" (*Tkadlecek*), after the name of its author, who lived in the first half of the fourteenth century. In this production he celebrated the fair Adlicka, one

of the beauties of the Bohemian Court.   The piece
is full of the usual conceits of the age; thus we are
told   that   "that   super-excellent,   widely-renowned
queen of highest race, who is named Honour, sent
her mantle, embroidered with various imperishable
flowers, to her by her highest confidant, whose name
is Circumspection."   We might here be almost reading
a Bohemian translation of Skelton's "Garlande of
Laurell."   The piece is somewhat monotonous, but
the style is easy and elegant.   Whether it is original
or only an adaptation is a matter of controversy.   It
very much resembles a production called "Der
Ackermann aus Böhmen," of which four manuscripts
have been preserved.   Dobrovsky considered the
Bohemian to be the original; according to an interesting article by Gebauer ("Archiv für Slav. Phil.,"
iii., 201), they are probably both adaptations of a
piece which is now lost.

As a specimen of this curious production, which is
not without a certain dignity and pathos, I add the
conclusion of the address of Misfortune to the
Weaver :[1]   "How much more fortunate, then, dost
thou desire to be, that I may honour thee more than
the Emperor Julius, or the King Alexander, or the
excellent, truly excellent Emperor Charles, at this
time King of Bohemia ?   Who, powerful as they

---

[1] I have made use of the version of Mr. Wratislaw so as to
call attention to his work, "The Native Literature of Bohemia
in the Fourteenth Century," which will enable the reader to
form a correct idea of the great intellectual activity of the
little country at so early a period.

were, could not at times escape my power and my contrariety. Prithee inquire how many of my misadventures have happened to those only whom thou knowest, and of whom thou hast heard in thine own days, whether of higher or lower rank ; and neither thou nor any one else will be able to express in writing or words how many times this has happened to them. And, passing over all other misadventures, write down only those which those kings who have been in the land of Hungary have had from me ; there will be no end to them. Ah ! if thou wilt, as thou canst, recollect thine own adversities only in thine own mind ; how many of them hast thou also had from me? For it would have been more proper to cry out against me about them, or to argue with me about that which once threatened thy life, thy property, thy honour, and all the good that thou hadst, and it would have been convenient to speak of that rather than of that damsel of thine. Therefore, Weaver, hold thy peace, speak no more with me of thy darling. Take me not for so weak a power, think not that I am thine equal. . . . . Know that I rule thee and every man mightily by my power. Thou seest thyself that I pass by nothing ; I let nothing pass me without an answer from me. I do as the sun, that shines to the whole world, and is light in itself; to young and old, to Pagan and Jew, to Christian and Greek, to good and bad, to poor and rich alike. Even so there is none of these that has not at some time experienced my assaults. Endure them likewise, Weaver, according to custom."

No one can deny that there is something dignified and pathetic in these lines, and they form a very interesting specimen of early Bohemian literature.[1]

Passing by a number of mediæval legends and tales, common to the literature of other European nations, and of which Bohemian versions exist, such as the story of "Flore et Blancheflore," there were also others that had to do with native subjects, as the two chronicles of "Stilfrid and Bruncvik," supposed by some to have been originally written in verse.   By these productions we see that the Bohemians and Western Slavs generally were under the influence of Latin culture, and we have found the Eastern Slavs under that of Byzantine Greek.   The two lines are pretty clearly marked out.

But the great glory of Bohemian literature in the fourteenth century is Thomas of Stitny, a voluminous writer, chiefly on religious subjects.   The notices of his life and works I shall take from the introduction to the selection in the "Vybor" (vol. i., p. 635).   The biography of Stitny is, at best, but scanty.   He was born of a noble family, probably about 1330, and was certainly alive at the close of the same century.   He appears to have been a well-educated man, to have studied at the University of Prague, then newly founded, and also to have been acquainted with the German and Latin languages.   His chief works are

---

[1] Some of the expressions remind one of the old Russian poem, entitled "Grief and Misfortune" (*Gore i Zlostchastie*).

a treatise on "General Christian Matters," in six books, which was edited in 1852, and the "Books of Christian Instruction," reprinted, with an introduction, by Vrtatko, the present librarian of the Museum, in 1873. The style of Stitny is easy and flowing, and we can see from his writings that Bohemian prose was developed at a time when our own was in but a rudimentary condition.   In some respects I might compare him with Reginald Pecocke, who, however, flourished a century later than Stitny.   The man seems to have been very much before his age in using his native language as a vehicle for religious and philosophical treatises.   He says in one of his works : " Why should I, being a Cech, be afraid to write to my countrymen in Cech ?   I will write in Cech, because I am a Cech, and Almighty God loves Cech as much as He does Latin."   The writings of Stitny amount in number to twenty-six ; of these many still remain in manuscript, but at this we must not be surprised, when we remember that only quite recently a society has been formed in England to edit the unpublished works of Wickliffe.   The philosophy of Stitny has formed the subject of a book by Hanus, published in 1852.

The next work of importance is a Bohemian version of "The History of the Trojan War," composed by Guido of Colonna, from Dictys Cretensis and Dares Phrygius, which, to judge from the number of manuscripts in existence, would appear to have been a favourite work among the Bohemian knights. It was one of the first books printed in the Cech

Q

language, and issued from the press in 1468, at Pilsen.

I now come to the great name of Hus,[1] a man who has covered his country with glory, and earned a splendid reputation as one of the precursors of Luther. It would be idle to recapitulate the facts of his life; they belong to universal history, and are well known to all readers. I shall here only deal with the literary side of his character. During the latter part of the fourteenth and the beginning of the fifteenth century, the University of Prague was at the height of its splendour, and the doctrines of Wickliffe soon spread among the professors and students. Owing to the connexion between England and Bohemia in the time of Richard II. many Cech students came to the University of Oxford, among others a monk named Hieronymus, better known as Jerome of Prague. In the same way an Englishman, named Payne, going to Prague, spread abroad the teaching of Wickliffe. This man was for some time principal of St. Edmund Hall, Oxford, 1410–1415. He soon enjoyed a great reputation among the Hussites, and was sent as a delegate to the Council of Basle. Cochlœus, in his " Historia Hussitarum," thus speaks of him :—
" Petrus Payne ingeniosus magister Oxoniensis, qui articulos Wiclephi ex libris ejus punctatim et seriatim

---

[1] For a full and fresh account of Hus, based upon original documents, see the third volume of Professor Tomek's " History of the City of Prague," p. 433. I have retained the Bohemian spelling of the name, which, in the original language, signifies " goose."

deduxit et suis opusculis pestiferis imposuit, arte infe-
riores sed veneno pervicaciores ; quæ Wicleph obscure
posuit iste explanavit." Payne is supposed to have
died at Prague in 1455.[1]

Hus was born in 1369, took the degree of M.A. in
1396, and was made rector of the University in 1402.
The Papal schism at this time raging, and only to be
terminated by the Council of Constance, caused the
doctrines of Wickliffe to be more widely spread, and
Hus became one of their great propagators. His
Bohemian writings were collected and edited by
Erben in 1865–68; they are of a miscellaneous
character, and for the most part controversial. The
" Vybor," vol. ii., contains selections from his Postils,
and from a work entitled, " The Daughter; or, the
Knowledge of the Right Way to Salvation " (*Dcerka ;
aneb o poznani cesty prave k spaseni*). The great
Reformer did almost as much for his native tongue
as Luther for German. He corrected the translation
of the Bible, re-arranged the Bohemian alphabet, and
fixed the orthography. Nine letters written by Hus
while in prison have been preserved. Of these, three
are printed in the second volume of the " Vybor " ;
there is also an account of the death of Hus by Peter
Mladenowic, who acted as notary to one of the noble-
men who accompanied him to the Council of Constance, and was an eye-witness of the proceedings
from the beginning. Hus, as is well known, was
burnt in 1415, and his disciple, Jerome, the year
following.

[1] Krasinski, "Reformation in Poland," i., 72.

I must pass over here the Hussite Wars. Nor can
I pretend to give anything like a complete list of the
many writers of political and religious pamphlets.
Several heroes of the time were as vigorous with the
pen as with the sword. There is a lack, however, of
original work, as in so much of our own literature at
the period. Bohemia, during the Middle Ages, saw
an Occleve and a Hawes, but certainly never boasted
a Chaucer. Translations of the travels of Marco
Polo and our Sir John Mandeville enjoyed great
popularity. Peter Chelcicky deserves a passing
notice as a popular writer. He was one of the leaders
of the United Brethren, and, like our own Bunyan,
of humble origin, being a cobbler by trade ; hence
his nickname, Kopyta, or the shoe-last. His works
were all written between 1430 and 1456. The two
most celebrated are his " Postils " and the " Net of
Truth " (*Sit viry*). The opinions of this man are,
indeed, very striking if, we consider the age in which
they were uttered. He is as outspoken against war as
a Quaker, and looks upon the artificial distinctions
of society with the most democratic contempt.

In 1488 the whole Bible was printed in Bohemia
for the first time. The first regular printing-press at
Prague had been set up the preceding year. Bohemian Bibles were also printed at Nuremberg and
Venice. At the latter place the Calixtines had a very
handsome edition committed to the press in the year
1506. Under George Poděbrad, a native, who had
been elected king, the national language and literature were still further developed. Poděbrad had

already been regent, and enjoyed much influence among his countrymen; and the Bohemians were so moved by the eloquence of the Calixtine priest, John Rokycana, who urged the Diet not to appoint a German prince, but a man of their own nation, that he was unanimously elected by the states. The Emperor Frederick was at first opposed to the appointment, but was ultimately compelled to assent; and, at a conference in 1459, invested George with the insignia of royalty. Distasteful as this election had been at first to the Germans, it was still more offensive to the Pope, who disliked the Calixtine opinions of Poděbrad; and when that monarch afterwards offered to lead an army against the Turks, the Papal legate was instructed to say that it was far more advantageous for Christian potentates to turn their arms against the heretic king than against the infidels. In the year 1464, Poděbrad sent an embassy to the French king, Louis XI., to attempt a settlement of the religious difficulties then agitating the Christian world; but the mission was a failure. The Bohemians were too deeply tinged with heresy for the most Catholic king to care for closer dealings with them. An account of this embassy was kept by one of the attachés, named Jaroslav, and the manuscript was preserved in the archives of the town of Budweiss. In 1827 it was discovered there by Palacky, the celebrated historian, who printed it in the "Journal" of the Bohemian Museum in 1827. On this occasion it appeared with several gaps, as the censorship was strict in Austria, and publications in the Bohemian language were viewed with particular disfavour. At a later period, when these rules had been relaxed, and it seemed possible to print the manuscript in its entirety, the document had disappeared, spirited away probably by some over-officious ecclesiastic, who thought its contents injurious to the interests of the Roman Catholic Church.[1]

Passing over a few chroniclers, such as Vavrinec z Brezové (born, 1370, and died, according to Jungmann, in 1455), who wrote in Latin a valuable "Historia de bello Hussitico," of which there is an early Cech translation, and Bartosek z Drahynic, we come to the period of the Renaissance. One of the most interesting writers of this time was Jan Hasisteinsky z Lobkovic, whose satire, "Lament of St. Wenceslaus over the Morals of the Cechs," was written in Latin. He was also a remarkable traveller, having visited Jerusalem, Arabia, Egypt, Asia Minor, Greece, Sicily, and other places. The Cechs were always fond of making pilgrimages to the Holy Land; and in Martin Kabatnik, a member of the United Brethren, we have one of these travellers. He was a citizen of Leutomischel, and himself unable to read and write. His work was accordingly taken down from his dictation by Adam Bakkalar (the Bachelor?), a notary of the same town. Kabatnik commenced his journey in March, 1491, and returned in November, 1492. The manuscript of this interesting voyage is preserved at Prague. It has been printed many times,

---

[1] See the Introduction to the "Diary of an Embassy," translated by A. H. Wratislaw, 1871.

first in 1518, and forms one of the curious memorials of the Old-Bohemian press.

Valuable works on law were written by Ctibor and Viktorin. The latter also translated some of the writings of St. John Chrysostom and St. Cyprian. In his introduction to the former, he makes a good defence of writing in the Bohemian language. Jan Ceska translated portions of Cicero and Velensky, Seneca. Gregory Hruby z Jelené (called Gelenius, in the fashion of Latinising names which was then so very prevalent) published versions of Chrysostom, St. Basil, Cicero, Petrarch, Erasmus, and others; and his son, Sigismund, at the invitation of the great Dutch scholar, went to Basle and worked at new editions of the Greek and Latin classics. Besides these labours, he published, at Basle, in 1536, his "Lexicon Symphonum," which may be styled an early attempt at comparative philology, for in it he strives to show the connexion between Greek, Latin, German, and Slavonic. Space ought to be found here for a few words on the writings of Dubravius, bishop of Olmutz, although unfortunately he used the Latin and not the Bohemian language. He was born about 1489 and died in 1553. His curious book on fish-ponds and fish (*Libellus de piscinis et piscium, qui in eis aluntur, naturâ.* 1547.) is partly known to Englishmen by the citations in Izaak Walton, with whom the bishop was a great authority on these points. The work, however, which especially entitles him to mention is his elaborate history of Bohemia, in thirty-three books, from the earliest days

to the coronation of Ferdinand I. at Prague in 1527
—the termination of Bohemian independence.   It is
the same period at which Palacky brings his monumental history to a close.   The work of Dubravius
with those of Cosmas and many others will be found
in the " Rerum Bohemicarum Antiqui Scriptores,"
Hanover, 1602.

When we consider the learned men produced by
Bohemia at this period, we cannot wonder that they
are proud of it, and call it their golden age.   But a
great disaster was now to fall upon the Bohemian
people and the Bohemian language.   At this time
its history as a separate nation begins to wane.
Although the scope of this little work is not historical, a short digression may perhaps be pardoned.
In the year 1471 the illustrious Poděbrad died.   In
1526, in the reign of Louis, king of Hungary and
Bohemia, the sanguinary battle of Mohacs was fought,
on which occasion the Cechs and their allies were
defeated.   The king was killed while attempting to
escape from the battle.   Louis was the last male of
his family, and accordingly Ferdinand I. of Germany
claimed both the vacant crowns,—Hungary, by virtue
of a family compact, for this was a period of European
history, we must remember, when a nation was frequently treated as an entailed estate, and Bohemia, in
right of his wife, Anne, sister of the deceased monarch.
These pretensions were, however, quite new to the
Magyar and Cech, among whom the monarchs had
up to this time been elective.   In Bohemia he was
only opposed by Albert, duke of Bavaria, and was,

accordingly, accepted as king on the 22nd October, 1526. On the 4th February, 1527, he and his wife were crowned in the cathedral of Prague. The new monarch soon found himself in opposition to his subjects; he had stipulated at his coronation to govern according to the laws of the much-beloved Charles IV. In Bohemia the power of the sovereign was extremely limited, since, without the consent of the Diet, he could not impose taxes, raise troops, make war or peace, coin money, or pass and abrogate laws. But there were not only political, but religious difficulties to be surmounted by Ferdinand; in no European country did these rage so much as in Bohemia; the Cechs had already led the van in liberty of opinion, and the doctrines of Luther rekindled the torch which had been for some time smouldering. Ferdinand proceeded very gradually in his work of disintegration; he tried to weaken the independence of the city of Prague by separating the magistrates of the old and new town, and declaring that all attempts to reunite them were high treason, an ancient and ill-defined accusation in Bohemia as in England.

For some time, the states showed a vigorous resistance, but afterwards yielded; and when Ferdinand came to Prague in 1547 four of the ringleaders in the opposition were executed.[1]

[1] For a complete and interesting account of these struggles, see " Resistance of the Bohemian States to Ferdinand I.," by K. Tieftrunk (in Cech). I must here acknowledge my obligations to the "History of Bohemian Literature," by the same author.

In spite of their grievous political struggles, this seems to have been a period of great intellectual activity among the Bohemians, and many works were published in the Cech language, upon which German had as yet made no serious encroachments. In the year 1533 appeared the first grammar, by Benes Optat. Verse writers abounded at the time, but no poet of eminence. Jungmann, in his "History of Bohemian Literature," a monument of erudition, gives us long lists of compositions of this kind, but they can only be interesting to the antiquarian and the philologist.

A man of note, however, was Veleslavin, 1545–1599, an indefatigable worker in literature, being, like our own Caxton, both printer and author. Balbinus the Jesuit, a Bohemian patriot of the seventeenth century, who did much for his country at a period of great degradation, has well said : "Quidquid doctum et eruditum Rudolpho II. imperante in Bohemiâ lucem adspexit, Weleslawinum vel autorem vel interpretem vel ad extremum typographum habuit." Valuable works on natural history were produced at this time, such as herbals, among which may be mentioned a translation from the Latin of Andrew Matthiolus by Thaddeus Hajek. This Matthiolus, or Matthioli (by birth an Italian) was the physician of the Arch- duke Ferdinand. A copy of the "Herbal" is shown among the treasures of the Museum at Prague : it is illustrated with excellent woodcuts. Many good works on law appeared; and there are huge masses of sermons which I shall not disinter. Simon Lomnicky

(born in 1560) has left a great deal of poetry; he
was the laureate of the Emperor Rudolph II., who
did so much to make Prague a literary and artistic
centre.   He also saluted the unfortunate "Winter
King" and his wife, the Princess Elizabeth of England, with a "carmen triumphale."   The poet was
severely wounded at the battle of the White Mountain,
and spent the rest of his life in poverty, but the
stories of his sufferings have probably been greatly
exaggerated.   Lomnicky is at best but a poor writer:
Jirecek says, with truth, that his compositions are but
little better than rhymed prose.[1]   His comic pieces
and satires have merit; his didactic poem, "Instruction to a Young Nobleman," has some good sound
sense in it, but the metre is heavy.   To this period
belongs the Bohemian historian, perhaps more
correctly *chronicler*, Hajek.   But little is known of
his life, except what may be gathered from his
writings.   He appears to have been a Roman Catholic
priest, and to have died in the year 1553.   This
chronicle is a very interesting production, but, of
course, cannot be expected to show much critical
power: these were not the days of criticism.   He
incorporates the old legends of Cosmas and
Dalimil, just as Kromer, the Polish historian, tells
the . stories of Popiel and other traditions, but
happily for his country, Hajek uses the Cech
language.   The work was very popular, and was
soon translated into German.   Interesting also is the
journey of Christopher Harant into the Holy Land.

[1] "Anthology," vol. iii., p. 275.

A new edition was published by the Bohemian Literary Society, in 1854. The unfortunate author was one of those decapitated on the memorable June 19, 1621, on the subjugation of the country after the terrible battle of the White Mountain. Harant set out on his journey at the end of April, 1598, with some companions, all dressed as friars of the order of St. Francis. The description of Jerusalem and the holy places is very full, but the book is too much swollen by historical and geographical digressions. The amount of learning contained in it is great, and gives one a favourable idea of a Bohemian nobleman of the time. Interesting also is the book of Wenceslaus Vratislav, of Mitrovic (1576–1635), describing his captivity during three years in a dungeon at Constantinople. The letters of Karl ze Zerotin, a Bohemian nobleman of this period, have been recently edited by Vincent Brandl. This eminent man belonged to the sect of the Moravians, and was for some time in the service of Henri IV. of France, concerning whom he has left some interesting details. He was with this monarch at the siege of Rouen,[1] which was raised on the 20th of April, 1592. From some unexplained cause, we find that Zerotin left the king's service. He remained faithful to Ferdinand II. during his struggles with his rebellious subjects, but for all that was subsequently compelled to leave his country on account of his refusal

---

[1] See the interesting article of M. Léger in "Nouvelles Études Slaves," "Quelques Documents Tchèques relatifs à Henri IV.," p. 247.

to quit the communion of the Bohemian Brothers.
He accordingly retired to Breslau, in Silesia, where
he died in 1636.

After the battle of the White Mountain (*Bila Hora*),
in 1620, when the forces of the newly-elected King
Frederick were defeated, the Bohemian nationality
fell. The whole country was to be Germanised, and
books in the Cech language were hunted up in all
quarters and burned. The Jesuits were very active
in these labours; one especially, Andrew Konias,
probably the greatest book-burner whom the world
has ever seen, boasted that he had been instrumental
in destroying 60,000 volumes. Bohemia, after these
tragic events, sank into a deep lethargy. Her nationality was annihilated. Carlyle has graphically told
us that Germany came out of the Thirty Years' War
brayed as in a mortar, but Bohemia suffered even
more than her enemies. She also had the misfortune
of seeing many of her most precious Slavonic manuscripts carried off.

With the year 1620 terminates the golden age of
Bohemian literature. With the exception of a few
names worthy of honourable mention, it was not to
be resuscitated till the second decade of the present
century.

And here a few words may be said about the
Slovaks, a people living in the north-western corner
of Hungary. Their language is interesting to philologists as exhibiting an earlier form of Cech, which
latter they used for a long time for such literary works
as they put forth. They continued to employ it till

the close of the eighteenth century, when Bernolak published the first Slovakish grammar at Presburg, in 1790.[1] The attempt to form a new literary language was, perhaps, on some grounds to be deplored. The Slovakish has to struggle between Magyar, German, and Bohemian influences. The Magyar is anxious to depress the Slav, and to spread his own language throughout the so-called kingdom of Hungary. He has, in a great measure, succeeded; the Slovakish nobility are now almost entirely Magyarised, to take Kossuth alone as an instance. For a short time a Literary Society existed among the Slovaks for the publication of good books and a journal. This was suppressed by the Magyars, who do all they can to heap contempt upon the Slovaks. A favourite saying among them is *Tot nem ember* "the Slovak is not a man." But let us hear the account of M. Reclus, who may be considered an unprejudiced observer: "Les Slovaques sont aussi bien doués physiquements que leurs pères de la Vallée de l'Elbe; en général, grands, robustes, bien faits, agréables de figure, ils ont la tête moins forte que celle des Tchèques, mais leur front est large et découvert, bien encadré d'une chevelure abondante." Lastly, the Bohemian resents the attempts at separation by the Slovak, and considers him to be weakening the Slavonic cause by his division. It seems most probable that in the long run the German language will be the gainer by the struggles between these nationalities. Some years ago

[1] The latest Grammar is by Victorin, the last edition of which was published in 1865. There is also a Dictionary by Loos.

a work was published by the Cech Literary Society
(*Matice Ceska*), entreating the Slovaks to abandon
their attempt, and citing a formidable list of authorities
against them.   The wars between the Magyars and
Slovaks, which ended in the complete subjugation
of the latter, cannot be described here.   There is no
early Slovak literature, with the exception of a few
songs of trifling importance.

CHAPTER IX.

THE WENDS IN SAXONY AND PRUSSIA.

THE little Slavonic island, as it were, in a German sea, which is situated partly in the Prussian and partly in the Saxon territories, has attracted scarce any attention in the rest of Europe. The German affects to treat the Wend of Lusatia with somewhat of the contempt assumed by the Englishman for the Celt, and hopes for his speedy amalgamation with the Teutonic race. It must be noted that these Slavs never call themselves Wends, but Lusatians, Serbs, or Sorbs.

They are the remnants of the powerful tribes which once occupied nearly the whole of North Germany. According to Budilovich, previously cited, who has published a valuable map, clearly showing the spread of this little Slavonic people, they number 96,000 Upper Lusatians, and 40,000 Lower, giving a total of 136,000. Pfuhl, however, the author of the best Wendish dictionary, makes the numbers much higher, amounting even to 200,000.

As the object of my little work is not historical, it will be impossible to trace the early fortunes of these tribes, who have successively passed under the dominion of the Poles, forming part of the kingdom of

Boleslas II. and the Cechs.   In the early part of the
seventeenth century most of the Lusatians had become annexed to the Electorate of Saxony, with the
exception of the small part about Kotbus, which had
belonged to Brandenburg since 1445.

But in 1815, after the resettlement of Europe, con-
sequent upon the fall of Napoleon, a great part went
to Prussia, and, according to the statistics of Budilovich, all the Lower Lusatians, amounting to
40,000, belong to Prussia, and of the Upper Lusatians, 44,000, so that the greatest portion of this
people are under her direct sway ; but a closer union
between all the Sorbs has been created since the war,
in which Saxony was made an integral part of the
German confederacy.

In an interesting article, contributed in the year
1856[1] to the Bohemian Magazine, by Michael Hornik,
or Hornig, we have an account of such authors as
have made use of the Sorbish language.   The details
are, at best, but scanty, and I have extended the scope
of this chapter somewhat later than the other ones
for this very reason.   Treating of the Upper Lusatian
first, Hornik divides the period of its development
into three ; but it is with the two first of these only
that we shall have to do.

(1) 1512–1704.
(2) 1704–1837.
(3) 1837–1856.

The first printed book in the Sorbish language was

---

[1] " Part I.," p. 67.

the little Catechism of Luther,[1] which was published in 1597 by the Pastor Worjech, or Warichius, as he was sometimes called, according to the fashion of Latinising names. This, however, was not the first time that any Sorbish words had been in print, for we find the names of plants in that language given in the work of Franke, published in 1594, called "Hortus Lusatiæ."

In the year 1627 a translation of the "Penitential Psalms" was published by the Pastor Martin, and in the year 1659, a Bible history for Roman Catholics. In the year 1706 Michael Brancel, or Frencel (as he was called by the Germans), published a translation of the New Testament into Sorbish. When Peter the Great passed through Saxony on his travels, Brancel presented some of his labours to the tzar, with an address. In 1689, Zacharias Bierling published a grammar of the language, which he quaintly entitled, "Didascalia, seu Orthographia Vandalica," in which he adopted an orthography more nearly resembling German, contrary to the Jesuit Ticinus, who, following a very just analogy, had adopted the Cech and Polish as a model, using the following sensible remarks :—"Accedit, quod nostra soror sit Bohemicæ, utpote ex eadem matre Slavicâ originem trahens, et proinde congruum est, ut iisdem characteribus utatur."

In the years 1693–96 a dictionary of the language was published by Abraham Frencel, son of the above-

---

[1] The same book, the translation of which forms so inte-esting a memorial of the Old-Prussian language.

mentioned author. Frencel, following the usual
vagaries of the authors of his time, as such writers as
Minshew among ourselves, derives Sorbish from
Hebrew. Many of his works still remain in manuscript. He had faith in his native language, for he
prophesied a great future for it, and that he would
have many followers in his attempt to trace its grammatical laws, "quos linguæ sorabicæ dulcedo ac
necessitas mecum in sui amorem atque studium
rapiet." Towards the close of the same century
(in 1696) a Roman Catholic version of the Gospels
and a hymn-book (*kancional*) were compiled. During
the Thirty Years' War the country of the Sorbs was
very much devastated, and the people suffered
severely; and the same horrors occurred in the
Seven Years' War in the next century. The Brothers
Martin and Jiri (George) Simon, founded a Sorbish
seminary in Prague in 1704; the first was a Carme-
lite chaplain there; the second a priest at Bautzen.
Many authors of religious works appeared about this
time, but their productions cannot interest the general
reader, and it would be useless to make a mere catalogue of names. For the Roman Catholics, Swotlik
translated the Bible from the Vulgate. His version,
unfortunately, is still confined to manuscript. Another
one, however, was printed in the year 1728. In
1806, Möhn translated some extracts from Klop-
stock's "Messiah" in the metre of the original.
Attempts were also made at the same time to publish
some periodicals in Sorbish, with but little success,
however.

R 2

With the year 1837 a new and important period of Sorbish literature begins, but it cannot be discussed in these pages, as I profess to deal only with the earlier times.

I shall now take a short glance at the condition of the Lower Sorbish, which has always been much less developed than the Upper. The first book printed in it was by Albin Möller, in 1574, consisting of a hymn-book and catechism. We can see that the torch was kindled by the Reformation, as in the case of other Slavonic languages. Chojnan, a pastor in Lubin, during the period 1642–1664, wrote the first grammar, which has remained in manuscript; in the latter half of the same century Körner also compiled a dictionary, which likewise has remained unpublished. At the commencement of the eighteenth century, Bohumil (Gottlieb) Fabricius published his translation of the New Testament (first edition, 1709). King Frederick I. of Prussia encouraged the labours of Fabricius, but his successor, Frederick William (1714–1740), was no friend to the Sorbs, and endeavoured in every way to amalgamate them with his German subjects. At the end of the eighteenth century Frico published a translation of the Old Testament.

At the present time we find almost the same struggles going on between the Germans and the Sorbs as between the English and the Welsh. Everything which ridicule and other agencies can bring about has been done : the language has been driven from the schools, and German pastors, where possible,

have been forced upon the congregations. We are
told that one poor woman, upon the death of whose
husband a funeral-sermon was preached, remarked
that all she could understand of the discourse was
that her deceased partner was named Hans. The
Germans, as Hornik tells us, are indefatigable in their
eagerness to uproot the Wendish language, consoling
themselves, sometimes, with the idea that the schools
will destroy it, and sometimes, the railways. It is
just the same talk which we constantly hear from
the English Philistines, whose object is to stamp
out the Welsh language. In spite of all these efforts
at Germanisation, the Sorbs still maintain their
nationality, though Herr Andree, in his " Wendische
Wanderstudien" (Stuttgart, 1874), would have us think
otherwise. In this case, however, the wish is probably
father to the thought. According to Hornik, it is
the great object of the German officials to make the
Wendish-speaking population appear as few as possible
in all Government reports.

At the present time they appear to be a cheerful,
well-conducted people, devoted to agriculture. They
are all Protestants, with the exception of 12,000
Roman Catholics. In the year 1854, about 400
Sorbs, for the most part from Prussia, emigrated to
Texas under the leadership of their pastor, Kilian.
Here they settled in Bastrop County, and have
preserved their native language till the present day
by means of their schools and their two churches,
where the service is conducted in the Wendish
language.

In later times[1] the Sorbs have occasionally distinguished themselves and made some political figure.
Meantime their Casopis, or journal, appears twice a
year at Bautzen, and contains many excellent articles
written both by Upper and Lower Wends, dealing
with Wendish philology and their early and modern
history. Before leaving this interesting little people,
we must not forget the large collection of their
popular songs published by Haupt and Schmaler
in 1842–3. Attention may also be called to
" Wendische Sagen, Märchen und abergläubische
Gebräuche, gesammelt und nacherzählt von Edm.
Veckenstedt, 1880." These are the great days of
folk-songs and folk-tales, and nationalism in literature.
Even so obscure a people as the Lusatian Wends
may be found to yield a treasure to those who are
curious in these matters.

[1] See Hornik's Essay in " Slavianski Slovnik," p. 94.

CHAPTER X.

THE POLABES.

BESIDES the Lusatian Wends, of whom such scanty fragments now exist, there were two other great Slavonic families which once occupied the northern coast of Germany. They have been classified by Schafarik, in his "Slavische Alterthümer," as follows:—

1. The Lutitzer, or Weleten, who inhabited the country between the Oder, the Baltic, and the Elbe, called in Slavonic Labe, whence the name Polabe, or people living on the Elbe; these again were divided into many subordinate tribes, which need not be recapitulated here. The traces of some of these peoples may be found in the local nomenclature,—all the north part of Germany being studded with towns and villages which carry with them unmistakable proofs of their Slavonic origin.

2. The Bodritzer, also sub-divided into many tribes, dwelling westward of the Lutitzer in the present Mecklenburg and Holstein.

Of the Slavonic languages spoken in the north of Germany the Lusatian Wendish and Kashubish (a dialect of Polish, and therefore included under that language) are alone living. Polabish is the only one of those which are extinct which has bequeathed any memorials to us, and these memo rials are but scanty. It is considered by Schleicher, owing to the possession of nasals and other peculiarities, to have more affinity to Polish than Cech. During the first five-and-twenty years of last century, this Slavonic language gave its expiring gasp in the eastern corner of the former kingdom of Hanover, and especially in the circuit of Lüchow, which, even up to the present time, is called Wendland—Wends being the name by which the Slavs were of old time called by the Germans, and the term is still applied to the Sorbs and the Slovenes. The language of the latter, being sometimes styled Wendish, causes an unnecessary confusion with the Lusatians, whereas the Slovenes belong to the eastern and the Lusatians to the western branch of the great Slavonic family.

Between the years 1691 and 1786 certain vocabularies and dialogues in this language were taken down, and it is upon these that Schleicher has based his grammar.[1] The following are some of the chief memorials of this interesting language :—

---

[1] See "Laut- und Formenlehre der polabischen Sprache, von August Schleicher," St. Petersburg, 1871. This was a posthumous work, edited by Leskien. There is also a work by the Russian Slavist, Hilferding, "Pametniki nariechia Zalabskikh Drevlian i Glinian," St. Petersburg, 1856. Schleicher appends a vocabulary, in which he corrects the orthography of the Polabish words. Of the highest value are the collections published by Dr. Pfuhl, in the Journal of the Lusatian Society, mentioned in the previous chapter. Here the vocabularies and other fragments are printed *verbatim*; and, without wishing to undervalue the importance of the glossary of Schleicher, it seems preferable to have the words in such orthography as

1. A German-Wendish Dictionary, compiled at the end of the seventeenth century by Christopher Henning, by birth a Lusatian, who spent the last forty years of his life as a clergyman in the little town of Wustrow (Slavonic, Ostrov), near Lüchow. The pastor was inducted in 1679, and died in the year 1719, aged seventy. His first collection was accidentally burnt in the year 1691; but he went to work again with a brave heart and finished a second in 1705. Most of his words were taken down from the lips of a peasant, named John Janisch. In the time of Henning, the young people were already ignorant of the language, and the old people gave their information about it reluctantly from fear of being laughed at. Divine Service is said to have been held in Wendish at Wustrow even so late as the year 1751. Of the materials accumulated by Henning two MSS. remain, the first of which is preserved in the library of the Upper Lusatian Learned Society ("Oberlausitsche Gesellschaft der Wissenschaften") at Görlitz, and the other at Hanover. Of one of these a copy was made, which was long preserved in the family of the Von Platows, and printed by Count Potocki in his "Voyage dans quelques Parties de la Basse-Saxe pour la Recherche des Antiquités Slavs ou Vendes," Hamburg, 1795. This work teems with mistakes and is now valueless; it belongs to the category of such publications as Masch's

suggested itself to the person who heard them and took them down. I have used Dr. Pfuhl's collections throughout this chapter.

" Idols of the Obotrites" (*Die gottesdienstlichen Alterthümer der Obotriten*).[1]   In these productions and many similar ones before the time of Dobrovsky we get a great deal of Slavonic enthusiasm, but little science or criticism.   An Englishman is forcibly reminded of the vagaries of such Celtomaniacs as Dr. Pughe.

2. The Lord's Prayer.   Of this two versions have been preserved : one is appended by Henning to his Dictionary, and there is another version preserved in the year 1691 by the pastor, Mithof, who was a friend of Leibnitz.

3. A Comic Song, being a kind of catch, to be sung by three persons, preserved by Henning, and printed in the collection of Lusatian songs published by Haupt and Schmaler at Bautzen, previously alluded to.

4. A little French-Slavonic vocabulary compiled in the year 1698 by Johann Friedrich Pfeffinger, and included by Eccard in his " Historia Studii Etymo-logici Linguæ Germanicæ," Hanover, 1721.   Said by Hilferding to be full of errors.

5. Slavonic Words and Dialogues collected by a certain farmer, named Johann Parum-Schultz, at Süthen, in the country, formerly occupied by the Slavonic tribe of the Drevianians.   This indefatigable man appears to have occupied himself many years with a kind of chronicle of the chief events of his parish.   Amidst a great deal of miscellaneous and

[1] Vide *supra*, p. 9.

trivial information, he has recorded much that is valuable, especially when he treats of ancient customs prevalent in his neighbourhood, or once existing, of which an account had been given him by elderly persons. On page 131 of his manuscript, the compiler remarks that in this year (1724 or 1725) he wishes to say something about the Wendish language. Some of the old people spoke half Wendish, half German. His sister, about five years younger, understood something of the Wendish language, but his brother, eight years younger, nothing at all. He (the compiler) was a man of forty-seven years of age. When he and about three other persons in his village were gone, no one would know properly how a dog was called in Wendish. This precious manuscript is still in the possession of his descendants in Süthen, his native village. Unfortunately, eleven leaves have been torn out by an unscrupulous person to whom it was lent.

6. A collection of 300 words, printed in 1744 in the "Hamburgische Vermischte Bibliothek" of no especial value.

7. The Lord's Prayer and a Protestant *Beichtformel*, or Form of Confession, taken down about the middle of last century by the burgomaster Müller at Lüchow, from the dictation of his grandmother, Emmerentia Weling. In the same way, the late Edwin Norris told us that he could repeat the Lord's Prayer and Creed, which he had learned from the dictation of an aged Cornishman who had retained it in his memory long after the language had ceased to be spoken. This *Beichtformel* has been printed

in a very careless manner in Potocki's work, previously alluded to.

8. One hundred and one Slavonic or Wendish words, with German translation, taken down by a certain Hintz, at Lüchow.

I have thought myself warranted in giving at some length the sources of our information about Polabish, because the works in which these vocabularies have been reprinted, are in languages which it is not very much the fashion to study in this country, and therefore the account may be new to some of my readers. The parallel between Cornish and Wendish is curious; both died out in the eighteenth century, and have left but few memorials. As many of these vocabularies were taken down by men but ill acquainted with any Slavonic language, from the mouths of people who in their turn were imperfectly acquainted with German, we can easily imagine that many mistakes have arisen. Sometimes matters were even more complicated; because the only German which the Polabish peasant understood, besides his native Slavonic, was Platt-Deutsch. Some amusing examples are given by Schleicher in his Grammar (pp. 12, 13), of which the two following may suffice. Thus Pfeffinger, in his little French-Slavonic Vocabulary, which I have marked No. 4 in my list of documents, has the following: "De l'Acier, Stohl, ou Eycratina." Here the peasant has misunderstood him, and has given him the past participle of the verb "to steal," "oukradenii, gestohlener."

Henning has entered among his words, *greusvai*,

Bär, ursus, and the mistake must have arisen in the following way :—the Platt-Deutsch equivalent of the German *Birne* is *Bere,* and this led the Slav to give the Slavonic word for pear.

These, with a few other less important vocabularies, are the last remaining fragments of the language of the Polabish Slavs, who have been either extirpated by the Germans or mixed up with them, leaving only memorials in the bullet-shaped Slavonic skull, the provincialisms of here and there an obscure village, and some names of places.

The subject of the Germanisation of the Baltic Slavs has been thoroughly handled by Perwolf, in his work published at St. Petersburg in 1876. The Teutonic hand has lain heavily upon the unfortunate Slavs from the time of Charles the Great to that of the Prussian kings almost within our own time. In the fourteenth century, we are told that the Hochmeister of the Teutonic order, Siegfried von Feuchtwangen, used to say that he never enjoyed a meal unless he had previously hanged a couple of Prussian,[1] Pomeranian, or Polish peasants.

In conclusion, I have thought it worth while to add a few words on Slavonic proverbs. Of these there are rich collections, as might be expected among peoples who have so much oral literature.

[1] By this word is meant, not the German Prussians, as we are accustomed to use the word, but the original Prussians ; a people cognate with the Lithuanians and Letts, whose language became extinct in the sixteenth century, and has left only a few vocabularies, and a translation of Luther's catechism. Vide *supra* p. 11.

On the Russian proverbs good works have been published by Snegîrev and Dahl, and of the Malo-Russian by Dragomanov (*Malorousskia Narodnia Predania i Razskazi*). An excellent work is that published by the poet Celakovsky at Prague, in 1852, in Cech, "The Wisdom of the Slavonic People in Proverbs" (*Mudroslovi Slovanského Narodu v Prislovich*). They help us to form an idea of the modes of life and habits of thought of these races. Let us take as examples the following Russian ones :—

Poverty is companion of stupidity.

White hands love the labour of others.

The ears do not grow higher than the forehead.

In a good head are a hundred hands.

Liberty is better to a bird than a golden cage.

To speak truth is to lose a friend.

The grave sets the crooked man straight, and a stick the obstinate man.

Measure ten times, but only cut once.

Dear but precious, cheap but spoilt.

We do not plough or sow for fools, they grow of themselves.

If you make yourself a sheep, there are plenty of wolves ready.

Ivan plays on the pipe, but Mary is dying of hunger.

Play for the cat, tears for the mouse.

As the priest, so is the parish.

A flattering speech is more powerful than a stick.

You cannot drain a river with a spoon.

Better to live in poverty than with riches in slavery.

The tongue is little, but it commands the whole body.

The following are from the Polish :—
Bread on a journey is never a heavy burden.
Plenty of talk and the wolf gets among the sheep.
When you've no goods, the king can take nothing.
Where God builds a church, the Devil builds a chapel.[1]
A fool gives, a wise man takes.
One fool makes many.
There must be great hunger when one wolf eats another.
One raven does not pick out the eyes of another.
Ignorance causes astonishment.
He who gave teeth will give bread for the mouth.
He who does not wish to give has plenty of ways of excusing himself.
To him who rises early God is bounteous.
He who doesn't know how to pray ought to go to sea.
The favour of a lord rides on a piebald horse (*i.e.,* is full of variety).
The silence of a fool makes him pass for a wise man.
You can't shut the door with your head.
Thanks pay no taxes.
The rabbit has more than one entrance to its hole.
Drunkenness is voluntary madness.

[1] *Cf.* the well-known lines of Defoe.

APPENDIX.

———◆◆———

I HAVE relegated to this part of my book a few points of more minute detail, which may be interesting to the specialist.

Page 4.—The monograph by Miklosich is entitled, " Die Slavischen Elemente im Neugriechischen." Colonel Leake had long before remarked: "In many instances the ancient name has received a Sclavonian termination in *ista, itza, itzi, ava,* or *ova ;* in others the name is entirely Sclavonian, and often the same as that of places in the most distant parts of Russia, or other countries where dialects of Illyric are spoken."

Page 8.—This curious craze about the Slavs is still turning up, but cannot now be considered worthy of any serious attention. It will be observed that the *t* in the word Wiltshire is derived from the word *tun,* and the form is Wilsætas ; we never find Wiltsætas.

Page 15.—The word *ploug* is connected by Schleicher with the root *plou, navigare* (See " Die Formenlehre der kirchenslawischen Sprache," p. 161) ; also in the same work the remarks on the foreign words in Palæoslavonic (p. 141), where Schleicher holds the Slavonic *khleb,* bread, to be derived from the Gothic *plaibs.*

Page 34.—As regards the word Antes, the other name applied by Jordanes to the Slavs, they appear never to have used it themselves, and Schafarik connects it with a Gothic root.

Page 35.—A proof that the words *slava* and *slovo* are from the same root is afforded by the Little-Russian language, in which *slava* means *discourse*. See Piskounov, "Dictionary of the Oukraine Language" ("Slovnitza Oukrainskoi Movi"), Odessa, 1873.

Page 62.—The use of the word *pogan*, pl. *poganî*, among the Slavs led the Emperor Constantine Porphyrogenitus into a strange mistake when he wrote: "καὶ γὰρ παγανοὶ κατὰ τὴν τῶν Σκλάβων γλῶσσαν ἀβάπτιστοι ἑρμηνεύονται." See Mr. Freeman's interesting paper, "Some Points in the Later History of the Greek Language" (*Journal of Hellenic Studies*, vol. iii., part 2). He justly remarks: "Constantine's knowledge of Latin must have been but small." His mistake certainly proves that the word must have become thoroughly Slavonised.

Page 91.—The reproaches which Ivan addresses to these monks would make us believe that they were in the habit of leading very jovial lives, and fully supporting the traditional views of the monastic character.

Page 92.—It was edited by Bodianski in 1848. Krizhanich was very bold in his views; he even went so far as to hope to create a common Slavonic language, which should be intelligible to all members of the family, whether Russians or Poles, Serbs or Cechs.

Page 113.—A version of the New Testament into Malo-Russian was published at Vienna in 1871 by Koulish and Pouloui.

Page 188.—A very interesting account of the foundation of the University of Cracow is given by Caro in the second volume of the "Geschichte Polens." A Jew was provided for the scholars from whom they might borrow, when in need, at the rate of 19 per cent. (ii. 337).

S

Page 190.—According to another account, the family of the astronomer came from a place near Frankenstein, in Silesia, formerly called Koppirneck, now Köppernick.

Page 205.—Besides the hymn, "Hospodine pomiluj," there is also another of great antiquity addressed to St. Wenceslaus, beginning, "Svaty Václave, vevodo ceské zeme" (Holy Wenceslaus, lord of the Bohemian land). See Tieftrunk, "History of Bohemian Literature," p. 24.

Page 206.—The whole history of the discovery of the Bohemian manuscripts will be found described in "Die Cecho-Slaven, von Vlach und Helfert," Vienna, 1883.

As early as the years 1803 and 1804 fragments of writing had been noticed in the crypt of the church at Königinhof by a certain Franz Stovicek, but the discovery was allowed to go by without any further attention.

The difficulty about drums being mentioned in the Königinhof manuscript has been fully met by its defenders. They are mentioned by Leo the Deacon, in the tenth century, who tells us that the Byzantine emperor, John Zimisces, in his journey from the Balkan to the Danube, ordered the drums to be beaten (τὰ τύμπανα παταγεῖν).

INDEX.

ALBERT the Bear, 35
Alexis, 85, 96
Ammianus Marcellinus, 39
Andree, 245
Anne of Bohemia, 220
Antonovich, 107
Asparukh, 32
Augustus III., 187

BALBINUS, 234
Bandtkie, 184
Baracz, 180
Barbour, 215
Barsov, 69
Bastrop County, 245
Bautzen, 243
Bayazet, 150
Berlić, 145
Bernolak, 237
Bezsonov, 59, 69, 112, 136
Bezzenberger, 11
Bielowski, 77
Bierling, 242
Bodenstedt, 111
Bogisic, 123
Bogomile, 122
Bogorov or Bogoev, 125
Bogufal, 185
Bohoric, 176
Boleslaw III., 185
Boorde, 183

Borivoi, 204
Boris of Bulgaria, 123
Boris Godunov, 94
Bosnia, 37
Boudilovich, 240
Bouslaev 70, 79
Bowring, 152, 213
Brandl, 236
Brankovich, 154
Brezové, V. z, 230
Brückner, 95
Bucic, 175
Budini, 37
Burns, 212

CASIMIR III., 187
Casimir IV., 188
Casimir John, 201
Catherine II., 109
Celakovsky, 254
Celichowski, 183
Cenova, 10
Chalkokondylas, 166
Charles the Great, 35
Charles IV., 205, 215
Chelcicky, 228
Cholakov, 128
Cholewa, 185
Chozdko, 110
Chwalczewski, 184
Clarke, E., 112

Clement, 119
Cochlœus, 226
Collins, 82
Copernicus, 190
Cosmas, 208
Constantine Porphyrogenitus, 3, 33
Courrière, 79, 182
Courtenay, Baudoin de, 9
Ctibor, 231
Cubranovic, 168
Cybulski, 23

DAHL, 254
Dalimil, 215, 235
Dalmatin, 174
Danichich, 148
Daniel, the Igoumen, 75
Daszkiewicz, 103
Dechanski, 148
Defoe, 255
Derembourg, 122
Derzhávin, 198
Diocleus, Presbyter, 146
Dlugosz, 71, 182, 188
Dobner, 216
Dobrovsky, 20, 34, 203, 222
Dometian, 147
Donalitius, 10
Doushan, 148
Dozon, 125, 126, 134, 135, 140, 141
Dragomanov, 102, 107, 111, 254
Drinov, 31
Drouzhinin, 116
Dubravius, 231
Dunbar, 219
Dunin-Borkowski, 180

ECCARD, 250
Eliade, John, 24

FEDOROV, Ivan, 86
Ferdinand I., 173, 232
Ferdinand II., 174, 176
Feuchtwangen, S. von, 253
Finlay, 124
Fiol, S., 86, 106
Fiume, 170
Fletcher, Giles, 86
Franke, 242
Frederick William I., 244
Frencel, M., 242
Frencel, A., 242
Furnivall, F. J., 183

GAJ, 146, 167
Gall, St., Monk of, 179
Gallus, 71, 179, 185
Gebauer, 210, 221, 222
Gedeonov, 27
Geitler, 13
Gibbon, 124
Gloucester, Robert of, 215
Gorazd, 120
Grebenko, 111
Gregoras, Nicephorus, 151
Grigorovich, 115
Grochowski, 198
Grossetête, 186
Gundulic, 168
Günter, Zainer, 188
Gwagnin, 201
Gyda, 78

HAJEK, 207, 216, 235
Hanka, 208
Harant, 235, 236
Hartknoch, 11
Haupt, 246
Hedwig, 187
Henning, 249
Henri de Valois, 197
Henry the Lion, 35

Henri IV., 236
Herberstein, 12, 85, 172
Herodotus, 37
Herzegovina, 37
Heylyn, 82
Hilferding, 9, 69
Hill, T. F., 118
Hornik, 241, 245
Horsey, 87
Hus, 226, 227

ILARION, 70
Ilovaïski, 27, 31, 74
Ivan the Terrible, 74, 87

JACOB, Theresa von, 152
Jagic, 8, 13, 115, 122, 128, 172, 204
Jagiello, 11, 187
James, R., 51
Janisch, 249
Jelené, Greg. z, 231
Jerome of Prague, 226
Jirecek, 22, 85, 206
John of Bohemia, 215
John the Exarch, 119
Jordanes, 30, 34
Jungmann, 234

KABATNIK, 230
Kacic-Miosic, 150, 151
Kadlubek, 71, 185
Karamzin, 28, 40, 84
Khmelnitzki, 102
Khrabr, 37, 121
Kiev, 71
Kirievski, 69
Klonowicz, 199
Kochanowski, 195, seq.
Kolberg, 179
Kollar, 23, 97
Kolovrat-Krakovsky, 214
Konias, 237

Konstantinovich, 189
Kopitar, 20, 23, 171
Köppen, 171
Korobeinikov, 77
Kosóvo, 150
Kotoshikhin, 92
Koubasov, 91
Koubrat, 32
Koulish, 110
Kourbski, 90
Kouripeshich, 152
Kouyaha, 28
Kovar, 206
Krasinski, Z., 187
Krasinski, Val., 191
Krizhanich, 97
Kromer, 193, 217
Kroum, 124
Kurschat, 10
Kvitka, 111

LAIBACH, 177
Laski, 192
Lazarus of Servia, 155
Leciejewski, 180
Léger, L., 65, 122
Legnich, 193
Leibnitz, 250
Lelewel, 185, 187, 193
Lermontov, 69
Leskien, 12, 17, 248
Linda, 207
Lindsay, 219
Lodzia, 182
Lomnicky, 235
Longfellow, 153
Loos, 238
Louis XI., 229
Louis, King of Hungary, 232
Lucic, 167

MACIEIOWSKI, 149
Mackenzie and Irby, 158

Maksimovich, 106
Markovich, 111
Masch, 249
Matthiolus, 234
Maurice, 43
Maximus, 17
Megiser, 177
Melanchthon, 173
Metlinski, 106
Methodius, 205
Mickiewicz, 185, 187, 201
Miklosich, 13, 17, 66, 165
Miladinovtzi, 125, 132, 137
    144
Militza, 155, 158
Milman, 124
Milutinovich, 163
Mithof, 250
Miyatovich, Madame, 150, 153
Mohacs, 232
Möhn, 243
Möller, 244
Müller, 251
Murad, 125

NALIVAÏKO, 104
Napoleon, 241
Nehring, 25, 180
Nesselmann, 11
Nestor, 71
Neuri, 37
Nicon, 98, 117
Niemeewicz, 181, 187
Nikítin, A., 75
Norris, 251
Novakovich, 149

OCHRIDA, 120
Olearius, 96
Oleg, 72
Oleska, 180
Optat, 234

Orzechowski, 200
Ostromir, 73, 115
Oustrialov, 29
Oxford, 88

PALACKY, 214, 229, 232
Panagiouritche, 130
Parum-Schultz, 250
Pavic, 169
Payne, 226
Pecocke, 225
Pelzel, 203
Peter the Great, 57, 118
Petranovich, 164
Pfeffinger, 250
Pfuhl, 248
Pliny, 39
Poděbrad, 228, 232
Podkova, 103
Pogodine, 74
Polo, Marco, 210
Popov, Nil, 113
Potocki, 249
Pougachev, 139
Poushkin, 46, 69, 72
Prochazka, 216
Procopius, St., 204
Ptolemy, 36
Pughe, 250
Pulkava, 221

RAICH, 31, 149
Rakow, 190
Rakowiecki, 181
Ralston, W. R., 65, 69, 136
Rambaud, 48, 49, 55
Rawlinson, 38
Rayachevich, 165
Razin, Stenka, 59, 139
Reclus, 238
Rej, 194
Rhys, J.,

Ribnikov, 69
Ristich, 165
Roger, 180
Röpell, 183, 185
Rosen, 128
Rosenberg, 220
Roudchenko, 110

SABBAS, St., 147
Sakcinski, Kuk., 147
Samo, 171
Samokvasov, 43
Sarbiewski, 182, 193
Sathas, 3
Schafarik, 3, 17, 18, 30, 31,
   63, 149, 214, 247
Scherzl, 14
Schleicher, 10, 248, 252
Schlözer, Kurd de, 41
Seklucyan, 193
Sembera, 207
Sheïn, 112
Shousherin, 98
Sicinski, 192
Sigismund I., 181
Sigismund II., 192
Sigismund III., 178, 188
Simeon of Bulgaria, 119
Simeon, St., 147
Simon, M. and J., 243
Skarga, 190, 201
Skelton, 222
Skourlatovich, 56
Slowacki, 187
Smil Flaska, 219
Sneglrev, 254
Sobieski, 187, 198
Socini, 190
Solomon, Bishop of Constance,
   214
Sprogis, 11
Sreznevski, 47
Stasov, 47

Stephanovich, V., 143
Stitny, 224
Stoyanov, 127
Strossmayer, 127
Stryjkowski, 202
Swotlik, 243
Sylvester, 88
Sylvestre de Sacy, 118
Szymonowicz, 199

TAMM, 64
Theophanes, 44
Thomsen, 26, 63
Thou, de, 186
Tieftrunk, 233
Töppen, 180
Truber, 173
Tübingen, 21
Tzamblak, 148
Tzankov, 7
Tzertelev, 106

VALVASOR, 175
Veckenstedt, 246
Veleslavin, 234
Verkovich, 127
Viktorin, 231, 238
Vladimir Monomakh, 77
Vodnik, 158
Vratislav, of Mitrovic, 13, 236
Vostokov, 16
Vrtatko, 213

WAPOWSKI, 201
Wenceslaus, 215, 219
Wickliffe, 219, 220
Wiltaburg, 3
Wojcicki, 179
Wolf, 171
Worjech, 242

Wratislaw, A. H., 213, 222, 230
Wujek, 193

Yermak, 51, 53
Yesipov, 17

Zabielin, 27, 42
Zerotin, 236
Zherebtzov, 119
Zhukovski, 46
Zolkiewski, 104
Zrinski, 176

THE END

WYMAN AND SONS, PRINTERS, GREAT QUEEN STREET, LONDON, W.C.